MW00960265

FORGOTTEN SEASON

A LOGAN FAMILY WESTERN - BOOK 4

DONALD L ROBERTSON

COPYRIGHT

Forgotten Season

Copyright © 2019 Donald L. Robertson
CM Publishing

Books@DonaldLRobertson.com

❀ Created with Vellum

PROLOGUE

The black horse dashed through the scattered timber. His rider leaned forward, hugging the animal's neck; an occasional round whipped past him. When the 530-grain lead Minié balls struck the trees around him, it sounded like they were being slapped with hammers. Too often, the rounds whizzed by much too close, but that was to be expected. These Southern boys were no slouches when it came to shooting. The big man, his mouth close to his horse's ear, said, "Come on, Blacky. Not much farther to go and we'll be out of here."

The man was dressed in Union blue. His yellow first sergeant stripes glistened in the morning light. He had accomplished his mission and was returning to his unit. On the way to deliver the message, he had detoured around the battlefield as much as possible. Now he was closing in on the roar of battle. It was not unlike him. He had never shirked responsibility and always stepped up when a volunteer was needed.

When he reached the edge of the timber, he could see the Confederate line, slightly past him, advancing. A short distance from the gray line, a pocket of Union soldiers were about to be overrun.

He turned Blacky directly toward the pocket of men. No sooner had he broken out of the tree line than a yell went up from the advancing rebels, accompanied by heavier fire. He spurred his mount and, guiding it with his knees, pulled his Henry from its scabbard. He had gotten the lever-action .44 from a salesman who visited the front. The Army provided few.

A Reb jumped up and Blacky hit him, knocking the man beneath the racing horse's feet. His scream was cut short and they were past. The sergeant had time to fire only one shot, striking one of the attackers, before he was yanking Blacky to a stop and leaping off.

He worked the lever as he hit the ground, ejecting the spent casing and ramming in a live cartridge. The Rebs were almost on top of them. Praying that he wouldn't see his brother over his sights, and knowing as fast as he was firing, he wouldn't be able to stop if he did, he continued his fire. Men were dropping in front of him like puppets with their strings cut, but puppets didn't bleed and scream.

He felt something pluck at his left shirtsleeve, feeling like a bee sting. The Henry was empty. He dropped the weapon to the ground and grabbed a big Remington .44 from one of the saddle holsters and fired until it was empty. Men were stacking up almost at his feet. He drew the other Remington just as a Reb came from the other side of Blacky, dashing under the black's neck. The Reb carried a Pattern 1853 Enfield with a seventeen-inch bayonet on the end of the barrel.

The sergeant raised his revolver and fired, striking the Reb in the face, even as he knew he hadn't been quick enough. He felt the sickening pressure as the long bayonet went all the way through his right side. Yanking his mind away from his injury, he fired again and again until he had a moment to reach down, grasp the rifle, and pull the bayonet out of his body. He threw the rifle to the ground and continued firing.

He felt a hard blow to his left leg, but Blacky was standing next to him, shielding him, so he leaned against his horse. Only then was he able to feel the big animal's shudders as the heavy Minié balls, meant for him, plowed into Blacky. But the black horse kept to his feet, giving the sergeant a solid side to lean on. Of a sudden, he realized there were more men in blue around him and firing. The line had broken. The Southern boys were starting to break. *The war's got to be over soon,* he thought, sick of the death. Firing was letting up throughout the line. He took a deep breath and turned toward his dying horse. Something slammed into his head. He grasped at the saddle horn. The world started rushing away as though he were looking at it through the wrong end of a spyglass. *I'm sorry, Ma.* Then, nothing.

1

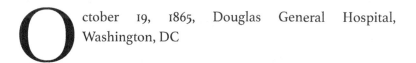

Octber 19, 1865, Douglas General Hospital, Washington, DC

Sister Deborah Coleman paused to wipe the sweat from her forehead. Sad and frustrated, she removed an embroidered handkerchief from her upper left pocket and dabbed the wet beads that had formed on her nose and hairline. Finished, she unceremoniously stuffed the soggy handkerchief back into its pocket.

Going back to her duties, her thoughts returned to what was on everyone's minds. In just a little over one month, the hospital would be closing, and the patients would be scattered throughout the system. It wasn't good, especially for the long-term ill and those being treated by the specialists.

As she walked through the ward, she stopped to check each patient. First, their pulse. After determining there was a heartbeat, she felt their forehead for a fever. It was hard to tell. Though all of the windows were open as wide as possible, attempting to combat the unseasonably high October temperatures in Washington, DC, was almost impossible. Hence, all patients' bodies were hot.

A stray, soft brown curl escaped from under her cap when she turned to check the next patient. Impatiently, she pushed it back, irritated at the natural curls that seemed to have minds of their own, and examined the big man. He had been in a coma since they brought him in the afternoon of April tenth.

All of his visible wounds had healed without infection, and, thank the Lord, that was a major miracle. He had been shot in the left arm and the left leg, breaking the femur. He would forever walk with a slight limp. On top of that, he had been bayoneted in the right side, a type of wound that usually guaranteed infection followed by death. Finally, the wound that had stopped him was the bullet to the head. Fortunately, it had not penetrated his brain, but had gouged a three-inch-long trench in the right side of his skull before continuing on its way. She often marveled that the big man had not died of secondary infection, nor of increased cranial pressure from the blow to his head, but here he lay, his chest rising and falling in a regular rhythm.

She thought of the work that had been put into Hank, even though he might never realize it. Every day his body had been exercised. Either she or an orderly spent at least an hour working the muscles in his arms and both legs, after the break in the left leg healed. That had been by order of Dr. James, and it had paid off. Though he had lost some of his muscle tone, he had retained quite a bit.

There was a bowl and pitcher of water next to his bed, a clean cloth placed alongside. Deborah picked up the cloth, poured some water on it, wrung it out over the bowl, and, holding the wet cloth at one end, swung it around and around in the air, allowing evaporation to cool it. After cooling the cloth, she softly wiped it across his forehead. There was no response. She continued with the cloth until she had completely wiped his face and neck. Then she rinsed and wrung as much of the water out as possible, folded the cloth, and laid it back over the side of the basin while she stood looking down on Henry.

He had strong features. *He's quite handsome,* she thought, *in a rugged sort of way.* When the doctor had first examined him, and then regularly over the past six months, she had seen his eyes. They were a striking light blue, *almost like looking into a cloudless sky.* Even though he was unconscious, when the doctor held his lids open, his eyes seemed to gaze right through her. Henry, that was what they called him, unfortunately they had yet to identify him, was a big man. At six feet two inches, the doctor had measured him, it was difficult keeping his feet under the covers.

Deborah brushed his light brown hair back from his forehead. His hair was damp from the cool rag and sweat. She placed the back of her small white hand on his forehead and waited for a moment. No fever. Her eyes followed his frame down the bed, where his feet were, again sticking out from under the sheet. The beds were too short for men of his height.

She had been assigned to this patient by Dr. Louis James, the cranial specialist. Henry was very lucky to have Dr. James interested in him. In fact, that was why he had been admitted to the Douglas Hospital.

Dr. James had sent David, the orderly, to the battlefront to find men just like this. Men who had multiple wounds, including a head injury. David had brought Henry back from that awful fight. It had been a long journey. To this day, it surprised her that Henry had survived the ride in the wagon, but fortunately, he had.

When he arrived, it was obvious the rigors of war had been telling on him, even before he was shot. Henry weighed only 175 pounds. A man with his frame and those extraordinarily wide shoulders could easily have weighed 200 pounds carrying no fat, but all of the men who came in were malnourished, many suffering from scurvy or *the fever,* or worse.

What Henry had done was heroic. David came back with a

story that brought both chills and excitement. Within a month of his admission, President Johnson had shown up to award him the Medal of Honor. He was unconscious then and remained unconscious now. Her gaze drifted past his chest, his arms, such strong arms, now growing thinner and weaker with no use, his slim waist, long legs, and finally back to his face.

With a start, Deborah realized Henry's eyes were open and focused on her. She turned to the nearest orderly and in an urgent voice said, "Get Dr. James, now!" She called after the departing orderly, "Tell him it's Henry."

The orderly whipped around and raced out of the ward. At the mention of Henry, many of the patients had risen and were looking toward his bed. Moments later, Dr. James, his hair flying, came running into the ward, straight to Henry's bedside.

He arrived to hear Henry utter his first word in six months, a hoarse whisper. "Water."

Deborah quickly poured a glass half full, lifted Henry's head, and held the glass to his lips. Henry sipped a little and held it in his mouth, obviously savoring the wetness. Then he tried to drink what was left in the glass, but Deborah said softly, "Slowly, just a little at first."

Henry took two more sips.

Dr. James stepped to his side and said, "Good morning. I am Dr. Louis James. How do you feel?"

The man looked around the room, then back at Dr. James. "Where am I?"

"You are in the Douglas Hospital in Washington, DC. You have been very sick. Now, how do you feel?"

Henry looked at Deborah and in a soft Southern drawl said, "You're mighty pretty."

Deborah blushed. She had heard this before and not only from her patients, but somehow this statement was different. She patted his shoulder. "Thank you. But you're the important one here. Please answer the doctor's question."

Henry turned back to the doctor, coughed, cleared his throat, and said, "What did you ask?"

Dr. James smiled and said, "How do you feel?"

The man thought for a moment. "A little foggy, tired. How long have I been here?"

The doctor looked at Sister Deborah, then back at Henry. "You've been here for six months. Do you remember anything?"

Henry seemed to concentrate; then a frown covered his face. "I don't remember anything. What's going on?"

The doctor glanced at Deborah then back to Henry. "You have suffered a major head wound. It may take a while for you to regain your memory, or it may never return."

"I've got to get out of here." The big man yanked the sheet back, tossed his long legs over the side of the bed, and stood, immediately collapsing to the floor. He grasped at Deborah as he was going down, and she piled on top of him.

"Oh," she said, quickly extricating herself, rising and attending to her patient. "You will go nowhere until you are stronger, but just to ask, where would you have gone?"

Two orderlies grasped Henry by the upper arms and lifted him back to the bed. Dr. James stretched the man's legs out, and Sister Deborah spread the sheet over him. The doctor looked around for a chair, and an orderly hurriedly placed one near the head of Henry's bed.

"What's wrong with my legs? Why can't I stand?" Henry looked around the ward. "What am I doing in a military hospital?"

Dr. James took a seat. "I'll explain why you're here. But first, I want you to relax and let me check you over. What you've just done is very trying on the human body."

The doctor took his time examining Henry. When he had finished, he sat back in the chair. "You are in the Army and have been wounded in numerous places. You have been unconscious for six months, and the war is over."

Dr. James watched Henry closely.

"The war?"

"You have no recollection of the war?" Sister Deborah asked.

Henry looked at her and then back at Dr. James before he answered, "None."

The doctor nodded. "I suspected this might happen, if you ever woke up. You are suffering from amnesia. It was probably caused by the bullet that hit you in the head. It didn't penetrate, but hit with sufficient force to do damage to your memory. How much, I cannot say. Your memory may return in a day or two, or possibly never."

Henry looked from Dr. James to Sister Deborah, then at the orderlies and patients watching. "I've been unconscious . . . for six months?"

"Yes," Dr. James replied. After that long, it is a miracle you have awakened. Are you hungry?"

Henry thought for a moment. "I *am* hungry. I reckon if I'm going to get my strength back, I'd best be eating."

"Good," the doctor said. "You're becoming more cognizant." At Henry's questioning look, the doctor said, "Aware, more aware. That's a very good sign. Since you don't remember anything, then I'm sure you don't know you are a hero."

"Hero? Me? How?"

"If you will look on the table next to your bed, you will see a medal. That is a very special medal. It is given to only a few people. It is the Medal of Honor. It was presented to you by none other than President Johnson. Do you remember President Johnson?"

Henry shook his head, confused and agitated. He rose in the bed on his forearms. "No, I don't remember President Johnson, I don't remember the war, and I danged sure don't remember this hero tomfoolery!"

Dr. James turned to Deborah. "Get him something to eat, and

try to keep him calm. By all means, do not let him go back to sleep. I want him awake for a while. I'll be back later."

Deborah had already sent an orderly for food. She sat in the chair Dr. James had vacated.

"Please, Henry, try to relax. I know this is a shock, but your memory will most likely return."

Henry took a deep breath and relaxed back onto the bed. He stared up at the ceiling. "If I've been out for six months, how do you know my name?"

"It's not your real name. At least, I don't think it is. The three men who accompanied you here said they just gave you that name because of what you did."

"What I did?"

The food arrived, and Deborah and the orderly helped Henry sit up. With two pillows between his back and the wall, he was able to sit enough so the food tray could be placed on his lap. He looked at it for a moment. It was a tray on which sat a bowl of pasty oatmeal and a tiny pitcher of milk.

"Is this all?" Henry asked.

"For now. Let's see how your stomach handles the oatmeal. We've managed to get some food and water down you while you were unconscious, but I fear it was insufficient for the demands of your large frame. It has mostly been this oatmeal and milk. We could give you nothing that required chewing."

"Thanks, I think."

Henry poured the milk on the oatmeal, mixed it with the spoon, and tasted it. To no one in particular, he said, "Not bad." He then looked up at Sister Deborah. "Now about my name."

"Yes," Sister Deborah said, "your name is Henry Remington, and the story goes that you saved over a dozen men from certain death at the hands of the Rebels."

"Aye, Nurse. 'Tis the truth you be tellin', for 'tis no story, though it tells wilder than the most adventuresome tale."

Sister Deborah spun around to see a large man, his chest

bulging the buttons on his tunic, standing in the doorway of the ward. She smiled and said, "Sergeant MacGregor, it is nice to see you. Will you look at who is up and eating?"

"Aye," the sergeant said, striding to Henry's bedside. "It is a blessing for sure. I'm glad to see you eating. Though I doubt that gruel can rightly be called food. 'Tis a shame Wade and Darcy are not here. Is it a nice nap you've had, laddie?"

Henry looked over the big man, but had no memory of him. "You're a big one, aren't you? How do I know you?"

The sergeant looked from Henry to Deborah. "He's not rememberin'?"

The nurse answered, "He is not, Sergeant MacGregor. He is suffering from amnesia, probably caused by the bullet wound to his head."

The sergeant nodded and looked back at Henry. "'Tis a wonder you're still with us. Never have I seen anyone bleed so much as did come from your body. Why, you was shot in your leg and arm, and then a Johnny Reb got close enough to shove one of those pigstickers on the end of his rifle clean through you. You shot him, pulled it out, and went on killing Rebs.

"You kept the killin' up until relief reached us. 'Tis a sight I'll not be wanting these innocent eyes to see again, I'll tell you. Just as relief arrived, some hooligan of a sniper got the range and popped you in the head. We all figured you was dead for sure."

Deborah watched Henry to see if there was any spark of memory or recognition at the story—nothing.

Henry shook his head. "I don't remember anything, but what you've said still doesn't explain how I got this name Henry."

"Well, lad, since we didn't know your name, we decided to come up with one. You showed up on your black horse with a Remington on your hip and two hanging in holsters on your saddle. In your hands you had a fully loaded Henry rifle. Since we couldn't find any identification on you, Darcey Wade and me, we decided to call you Henry Remington."

Henry couldn't help smiling. "Well, I guess it stuck."

"Aye, it did. We took you back to the field station, and they asked us your name. That's what we told 'em—First Sergeant Henry Remington." MacGregor puffed up and stood tall with his thumbs behind his red suspenders. "'Tis a fine name, I'm sayin'. I'm thinkin' even your blessed mother, may she be well, would like the name. By the by, First Sergeant Remington, we have all your belongings. Everything excepting your horse. He was a splendid animal, but he died in the hail of gunfire that took you down. Sorry, lad."

"I'm sorry he's dead," Henry said, "but honestly, I have no memory of him. Nothing is coming through."

"Too bad, it is, but I'm thinking you'll be getting back your thoughts." MacGregor tossed a wink to Henry and turned to the nurse. "How long is it, would you think, before this fine fella is ready to take his leave of this place?"

Deborah looked askance at the man. "Sergeant, do you understand that Henry just returned to consciousness? He will have to regain his strength, and anyway, it is not up to me. It is up to Dr. James. We will be closing the hospital in a month. He may be able to leave by then, but he may not. It is possible the Army will want him transferred. Now, he is looking tired, and you should be leaving. Feel free to come back tomorrow."

Henry rose on his elbows. "Mac, I like the name you gave me, but call me Hank. Henry sounds too highfalutin' for me."

The sergeant nodded to Henry. "Aye, I'll do that, and tomorrow, I'll be bringing the crew, laddie. Maybe you'll be remembering them. Best I leave now before Sister Deborah has me thrown out like the worst bum from a tavern."

She couldn't help smiling. "Thank you, Sergeant MacGregor. First Sergeant Remington needs his rest. Have a good day."

"Ma'am," the sergeant said. He touched his forehead with a knuckle and strode from the ward, whistling a Scottish jig as he left.

Deborah turned back to Hank. "See, I told you that you were a hero. You saved those men's lives. Now, would you like some rest?"

"No, ma'am, I'd like something substantial to eat, and to stretch my legs. I'm feeling some better already."

"Oh, good," she said, standing up, tossing the sheet back, and reaching for his legs.

"Ma'am," Hank said in a sharp tone, "I can do it."

She stopped and straightened, watching. Hank slowly moved his legs to the side of the bed, allowing them to drop, his feet resting on the floor. She knelt and, lifting one foot at a time, placed slippers on his feet. Once standing, she moved quickly to his side and held out her arm for him to grasp. He used her arm to pull himself up, and lurched to his feet, swaying from side to side. Once balanced, to her consternation, he released her arm and eased a foot forward, then the other. Gradually, he made it across the ward, turning for the opposite end of the room.

"Do you feel like walking that great a distance, Sergeant?"

"Well, ma'am, I don't feel terrific, but I ain't gonna lay in that bed. I've been there too long."

With his statement he started for the door. Once during his walk, he stumbled and grabbed the end of a bed. A gasp rose from the other wounded, who were following his progress with astonishment and hope. Holding to the bed, he regained his balance and continued, reaching her to a resounding ovation from his fellow patients and nurses.

He made three round trips before allowing himself to rest. Though he was tired, he could sit and stand without assistance. He sat on the edge of the bed, reached for the sheet, and slid his legs under it.

"You're doing quite well. Did the movement help you remember anything?"

He shook his head. "No. My head is still as blank as an empty sheet of paper. I'll be glad when it starts coming back."

Deborah watched him sympathetically. "Yes, I'm sure you will, but I'm also sure it will happen. If not now, later. And, while you're waiting, you're making new memories. Don't forget that."

"I'll make a point of remembering that, Nurse," he said, a wry grin on his face.

Her cheeks rosy, mostly with embarrassment at her familiarity with her patient, she clapped her hands together in finality before retreating from the room and her feelings. "Now, I do have other patients to attend to. Get some rest and I'll see you get some solid food soon."

"Sister Deborah, before you leave, can I ask you a question?"

"Certainly, you may."

"Most folks seem to call you sister instead of nurse. Is there a reason for that?"

"Sergeant Remington, I have no idea when or where it began, but nurses are called sisters. It's just a replacement for nurse."

"Thank you."

She whirled about and headed away from Henry's bed. "Eat your food when it gets here so you can build up your strength."

2

The lamps were dark on the ward. Hank lay stretched out, his feet—sticking past the bed, the sheets and blankets—were cold. The temperatures of November had cooled suddenly, especially at night, returning to the miserable damp cold expected during this time of year. A month had passed, and his mind was still blank. It was like living in a mist, with all of the truth obscured beyond the fog—there but hidden.

Frustration rode him like a demon, but Deborah's presence always brightened his day. Since he needed exercise, she had gotten permission to take him on walks. They usually walked over to the park and mostly talked about her life. She had grown up in Syracuse, New York. Her father was a doctor; her mother utilized every minute of her day by taking care of her high-spirited children and working at the Syracuse House of Refuge, an orphanage. Her mother labored diligently, trying to improve the plight of homeless children. It was obvious Deborah loved and respected her mother and father. Her face always took on a soft glow when she spoke of them. Spending time with Deborah was the brightest spot in Hank's day.

One of the other ways he had found to push frustration and

boredom away was to work. After completing his first conscious week, he had started helping around the hospital. First, easy menial chores, then, as his strength improved, he moved on to the heavier duties required of the maintenance men. After a short time, he found he needed more activity and started looking for work. There was little to be had. MacGregor had warned him of that.

Ahh, MacGregor, he thought. *A man of great humor, but also great temper.* After Hank had been awake for two weeks, MacGregor had suggested he go to the paymaster and get the process started in order to get paid. He was still in the Army, and they owed him months of back pay. Fortunately, MacGregor, whom everyone called Mac, had the foresight to remind him to bring his citation and medal. He also obtained a statement from Dr. James showing his admittance date and in what battle he was wounded.

The four of them—Mac, Wade Dillon, Darcy Smith, and himself, all resplendent in uniform—marched down to the paymaster's office and were promptly told to wait by a pompous corporal who stared at them through thick glasses.

After taking their seats, Hank began to examine the building. It was a large hall, about two-thirds filled with desks; the other third was crowded with soldiers, sailors, and Marines. Most were here to receive their last paycheck before finding their way back home. The two groups were separated by a counter that ran the full width of the building.

At each end and in the middle of this long counter, half doors had been built to allow entrance into the inner sanctum. Above the counter was an endless array of steel bars, ostensibly to keep the rabble from attacking the sacred members of the holy payroll department.

Most of the clerks were bent over their desks, scribbling on sheets of paper. Once they were finished with one sheet, they would lay it in a specific pile and pick up another from a different pile. They worked continuously, moving papers from one stack to another, hardly ever looking up. Other men were scattered behind the counter, seemingly bored, but talking to those who were on the opposite side of the bars.

They had waited for about an hour when Sergeant Liam MacGregor lost his temper. Hank was relaxing, waiting his turn and watching people. He noticed the sergeant rise and move to the clerk who had directed them to have a seat. They had been talking for several minutes when a blast of abuse issued from the fine sergeant's mouth, all of it directed at the scrawny clerk.

Immediately, a captain looked up from his desk at the rear of the crowded hall, rose, and marched to the rescue of his shaking clerk. Hank immediately stood and moved to join Mac. As he was nearing the counter, he heard the word *hero* stated emphatically by the sergeant. Almost at the same time, the captain noticed him coming to the counter and turned to address him. Normally, Hank did not wear his medal, but at the insistence of MacGregor, he had attached the Medal of Honor to his blouse. The captain's eyes fell on the medal. He came to attention and saluted Hank. Puzzled, he returned the salute.

"Captain, I'm sorry for the disturbance. My friend Sergeant MacGregor can be rather intimidating. We'll be glad to wait our turn."

"First Sergeant . . . Remington is it?"

"Yes, sir."

"Let me thank you for your service and apologize for my clerk's inconsiderate response to you." The captain turned to the clerk. "Do you see that medal on the first sergeant's chest? Memorize it! That is the Medal of Honor. It is the highest award given by your country. When you see one, you will come to attention and salute. You will then find a solution for whatever problem the man might have."

Turning to Hank again, the captain said, "Corporal Penwick

will be glad to help you. It was nice meeting you." Finished, the captain turned and strode back to his desk.

"How can I help you, First Sergeant Remington?" Corporal Penwick said. Now contrite, the corporal seemed to sincerely want to help.

Hank said he had not been paid since April, explaining he had been in the hospital unconscious for all of that time.

"Aye, laddie," MacGregor said to the clerk, now mollified and back to his jovial self. "He saved us for sure." Several other men had gathered around to see the medal and hear what Mac had to say. "Those Rebs had us cut off. It would've been the end of us had not this fine first sergeant"—here Mac put his hand on an embarrassed Hank's shoulder—"rode through the midst of them. He had a Henry in his hands and started firing. He was dropping Rebs with every shot. When the rifle was empty, he drew those big Remingtons and kept shooting."

By now a crowd had gathered on both sides of the counter, everyone leaning in, listening intently.

"There was dead piled up all around him. Our cavalry was finally breaking through. See those two boys over there?" He pointed to Wade Dillon and Darcy Smith. "They was fighting there, too. Henry here gets hit in his arm, but slowing down, he isn't. Next, a Minié ball finds his leg and broke it, but now he's leaning against his devoted black steed, who I'm saddened to say was killed in the hail of lead.

"All of a sudden it is—" he stops and looks around the hall, every person intent on the story "—that a Reb breaks through to him and runs one of those long pigstickers right through his gizzard. Now I'm asking you, does he go down?" Before anyone could answer, MacGregor says, "No, sir! He does not. He shoots that Reb what poked him, pulls his last Remington out of the holster, and continues to fire. By this time the Rebs are stopped and our cavalry has broken through. Henry here drops his Remington to his side and looks around. And that's when it happened. Out of nowhere, sniper most likely, a ball comes sailing in and slams him in the head. Now he's bleeding from everywhere, but that last one sent a spray of blood over everyone near, and Henry collapsed."

At this point Mac reached up and put his thick arm around Hank's wide shoulders. "But the good Lord was watching over him. After six months of being in a coma, here he is alive and well."

Applause and cheers echoed throughout the hall, from in front of and behind the counter. Hank, his face red as an apple, raised a hand to wave to everyone, and then leaned over to MacGregor and said, "Mac, you ever do that again and I'm going to kick your butt all the way back to Scotland."

MacGregor looked at him with feigned indignation and said, "I was just trying to help you get paid, laddie."

Hank turned back to the clerk, who had stopped filling out paperwork and was looking up at him.

"Sergeant Remington, we can't find your records, but the captain said to expedite your pay from the date you entered the hospital. So, if you will sign this receipt, I'll pay you right now."

Hank took the pen the man handed to him and scrawled "Henry Remington" on the space reserved for signature. The clerk took the paper and stepped back to the cashier, who looked at the amount and then counted out $185. The clerk came back to the window and, in turn, counted the money out for Hank.

Wade clapped Hank on the shoulder and said, "Let's go have a drink."

Without hesitation, Hank replied, "No, I don't drink."

Everyone stopped. "How do you know you don't drink?" Wade asked.

Hank, now puzzled himself, looked around at the bustling city. "I don't know how I know; I just know. Come on, we need to talk."

"Where is it you're headed, bucko?" MacGregor asked.

"Back to the hospital. I feel like I'm remembering something, and I want to talk to Dr. James or Deborah."

The three men fell in step as they headed back to the Douglas General Hospital, Hank in the lead, with Mac alongside, and Wade and Darcy following. Hank's mind was whirling. *Where did the idea that I don't drink come from? Is there more? Is my memory coming back?*

The men reached the hospital and Hank led the way to the doctor's office. He knocked and, without waiting, opened the door and stepped inside. Dr. James looked up from a report he had been examining. "Hello, Henry. How can I help you?"

Hank quickly explained what had happened. "Is there a chance I'm getting my memory back, Doc?"

The doctor nodded. "It is certainly possible. Has anything else happened? A memory of a face or incident?"

Hank thought for a moment, his mind suppressing any further memories. "No, nothing."

"Sorry," the doctor said, "these transient thoughts or actions surface occasionally without the mind opening to release more. Don't get me wrong, it could mean the beginning of a full return of your memory. However, you'll have to wait and see."

"Thanks, Doc, any idea how much longer you want me to stay here?"

"I was considering your situation when you knocked. I really don't think there is much more we can do for you. Your recovery is close to a miracle. You have only a slight limp from your leg injury, and all of the other injuries have completely healed. This is Wednesday; let's keep you a couple more days. I'll run a few tests to check your motor skills and, assuming they are acceptable, we'll turn you loose on Friday. You'll be discharged just before we start moving. How does that sound?"

Hank's face broke into a wide grin. "That'll be fine with me, Doc."

"I have one more thing for you, Henry. I should probably wait until Friday, but I'm not much of a military man myself. When you read it, you'll notice they indicated John Doe, now known as Henry Remington. I'm sorry, but if you ever remember your real name, you'll need to contact the War Department. Otherwise, under your real name, you could be listed as either deceased or missing in action. The last could become desertion if you are recognized before you remember your name, so keep this with you." He opened his desk drawer, pulled out an envelope, and handed it to Hank.

Hank took it, opened the envelope, and extracted a single sheet of paper. He looked it over and slid it back into the envelope. "Thanks, Doc. Friday it is." He turned and led the three men out of the doctor's office, through the waiting room, and out of the hospital. "Where can a man get a decent meal around here?"

"Well, dang it, Hank," Darcy said, "what was in the envelope?"

Hank grinned again. "My discharge, boys. Effective Friday, I am no longer in the Army."

The three men pounded Hank on the back. "Let's eat," MacGregor said. "I'm thinking a thick, juicy slice of prime beef will suit your tasters supremely well, and 'tis the right place I know. Follow me."

The men sat around the table, silent, as they devoured their meals. This was the first time Hank had tasted steak as far back as he could remember, which was about a month. It was delicious. The only dampener on the party was the price of the steak. If he had decided on pork or chicken or fish, his meal would've been no more than four bits. But when he ordered steak, the price jumped to two dollars and fifty cents. He couldn't believe the difference.

When the men finished eating and sat around talking, Hank said, "Why do you suppose a steak is so much more expensive?"

Wade spoke first in his slow Texas drawl. "Supply and demand, ole son. The war et up all the beef, and now the North is hurtin'. They's just flat out of cows."

"Yessiree," Darcy said, "whilst we been waitin' for a discharge, we been watching the price of beef keep on goin' up."

"Aye, 'tis a sad thing. I feel for these people. I'm imagining it'll take years for 'em to grow enough of them cows to satisfy their need."

The waiter brought a big piece of cherry pie to each man and set a small pitcher of thick cream on the table. All four of them poured the cream over the pie and went to work making it disappear.

After savoring each bite, Hank leaned back and rubbed his stomach.

"I have to say, hospital food doesn't hold a candle to this place, but if I eat here too often, it'll take all three of you to get me into a saddle."

The other three men nodded, satisfied smiles on their faces. Wade leaned toward Hank. "I've been telling these yahoos we have the solution to the meat problem."

Darcy spoke up. "Yep. Wade's been talking about this since we noticed the price of steak going up in the restaurants."

Wade leaned across the table. "I'm tellin' you, it ain't just steak. Darcy and I've been stopping by the meat markets. All beef prices are climbin' sky-high. We've got a big opportunity. All we have to do is take advantage of it."

The waiter reappeared. "Anything else, gentlemen?"

Hank looked around the table. The men were shaking their heads. "We're fine, how much do I owe you?" The other men started to object, and Hank held up his hand. "You boys have stuck by me for quite a while. Consider this a down payment on what I owe you."

"You're owing us nothing, laddie," MacGregor piped up. "We're owing you our lives, but I'm thanking you for my meal."

Wade and Darcy nodded as Hank paid the waiter. Once the man had left the table, Hank turned toward Wade. "Tell me about this opportunity."

"Cattle," Wade said. "Thousands of cattle. They're roamin' free on the range in Texas. Darcy and me are from a little place in South Texas called Refugio. West of there, cattle are as plentiful on the open range as mosquitoes on the coast. They're wild as old bears and twice as mean, but they can be herded."

"Whatcha planning there, laddie, to run them wild cows all the way back to Washington?"

"Heck no, Mac. Back in the fifties, there was cows pushed out to Californy and the gold fields. I was just a young tyke then, but I remember my pa talkin' about it. I've been hearin' about these railroads out to Kansas and Missouri. All we've got to do is round up and brand them wild critters and head 'em north. We find a railroad, sell them cows, and go back for more. Why, we'll be richer than that feller Vanderbilt."

Hank laughed, enjoying Wade's enthusiasm, his interest piqued. "How many people have done this so far?"

Wade shook his head. "Ain't no one I know of, but that don't mean it won't work. I guarantee you it's gonna happen, if not this year, the next or the next, but it'll happen!" With his last statement Wade brought his fist down on the table so hard the remaining dishes jumped. Several people looked his way, frowned, then turned back to their conversation.

Hank thought about it for a moment, then shook his head. "Sorry, boys, I've got to find out who I am. I can't go traipsing around Texas looking for cows. I need to head for Kentucky or Tennessee. I've been told that's what my accent sounds like. Maybe I can find someone who knows me there."

"Aye, 'tis important to know your name." MacGregor's eyes twinkled. "I'm thinkin' a nurse by the name of Deborah Barrett Coleman might be interested in knowing your real name."

Hank eyed MacGregor for a moment. "She's a nice lady. With all of those doctors around, I doubt she has much interest in me."

"I've seen you two talking. I'm telling you, and you can believe this as if it came from your own sweet mother's lips, I ain't seen her look at any doctor the way she looks at you."

Darcy grinned. "He's right, Hank. Sister Deborah looks at you like she's got plans for you."

Hank shook his head. "You two are pulling my leg." Hank looked out the windows of the restaurant. "Looks like it's starting to snow."

"Don't forget what I'm tellin' you, Hank," Wade said. "With all them cows, there's money just for the takin'. That is, if you're of a mind to do a little work."

Hank slid his chair back, wiped his mouth with his napkin, and stood. "I need to get back to the hospital and get started packing. Although, there sure ain't much to pack." His three companions rose. All of the men were still in uniform and made a handsome group as they weaved their way through the tables to the restaurant door.

MacGregor, following Hank, leaned forward and spoke softly so only the first sergeant could hear. "Don't you be breaking that lassie's heart, now. She has her cap set for you."

3

F riday morning dawned cold and windy, but no rain. Hank had finished his noon meal, the last at the hospital. Everyone was in a rush to get the patients and supplies moved.

He returned to his ward and packed his small bag of belongings. Mac and the boys had kept the remainder of his gear when he was brought in. Now he sat on the edge of his bed, deep in thought. How could he figure out who he really was? He had been told his accent sounded like he was from either Tennessee or Kentucky, maybe Georgia. How could he search those states? Was it possible someone would recognize him? Would that bring back his memory? In fact, would he even be like the man whose name he carried?

He ran both hands through his light brown hair, fingers unconsciously tracing the long scar. *And what about Deborah?* he thought. *Is Mac right? I like her, but I can't imagine her liking me, a rangy old country boy like myself.* The thought stopped him. Was he a country boy? Where did that thought come from? Were there more? "Too danged many questions!" Hank said aloud, causing the men in the beds near him to turn and look. "Sorry," he said to no one in particular, "just thinkin' out loud."

"That can get you in trouble, Sergeant Remington."

Hank looked up to see the smiling face of Sister Deborah.

"You might not want everyone to know your thoughts."

He grinned at the trim young woman. "You're certainly right there. My thoughts are running into each other, trying to figure out where I should go or what I should do to figure out exactly who I am."

Concern clouded her expression, tiny wrinkles of kindness appearing at the corners of her soft brown eyes. She stepped closer and placed her hand on his shoulder. "I know you must feel a heavy burden, but please try not to worry. The doctors are trained to give you the bleakest outlook so you aren't disappointed, but I firmly believe you will regain your memory. It may take a while, but it *will* come back to you."

He had been watching her speak. High cheekbones framed a strong, caring face. Her nose, a little large for her face, ended above a wide mouth outlined by full soft lips and perched above a firm chin that, when she was angry, moved aggressively toward her opponent. When she smiled, two dimples leaped into existence, one on each side and slightly above the corners of her mouth. All of her features combined made her an attractive and desirable woman.

"Thanks," Hank said. "It helps to be reminded. Has the doctor told you about my discharge?" He watched a touch of sadness drift across her face.

"Yes, I'm sure you're excited. I'm glad for you, but I shall be sorry to see you go. I'll miss our conversations."

Hank stood and, smiling down at her, said, "I had hoped you'd be sorry for more than our conversations."

"Why . . . I . . ." Deborah, cheeks delightfully bright pink, pushed an unruly brown curl back under her nurse's cap, regained her composure, and looked into his eyes. "Henry, I shall be very sorry to see you leave, but very happy that you have done so well."

It was Hank's turn to be surprised. Could Mac be right? "Thank you. I'll miss you, too. I know the hospital is closing; have you made any plans?"

"I'm thinking about going to the Colorado Territory. I have an uncle there, and he has been trying to get me to spend some time with him and his family." Suddenly, she became conscious of the fact that they were standing in the middle of the hospital ward, with many of the sick men watching them. She pulled her light blue sweater tight around her and, holding it closed in the front, said, "Maybe we can talk before you leave. I've got to get back to work."

At that moment, Dr. James walked into the room and spotted Hank. "First Sergeant, could I see you in my office?" He then turned and started back down the hall.

Hank tore his eyes from the slim beauty in front of him and called, "Yes, sir. I'll be right along." He looked back down at Deborah. "Maybe we can talk later?"

Her soft brown eyes held him for a moment longer. "Yes, Henry, I'd like that." She gave him a quick smile. "Now go see what Dr. James wants."

Hank left her, reluctantly, and made his way to the doctor's office. The hospital was a bedlam of sound as patients, equipment, and supplies were being moved to other hospitals. Moans came from patients as their stretchers bumped into obstacles. Hank looked around, thankful he was leaving under his own power. He reached the office and knocked.

"Come in," was shouted from inside.

Hank pushed the door open and stepped into the doctor's office. Boxes cluttered the small space, leaving barely enough room to open the door and follow a narrow path to the man's desk.

"Ah, Henry, please sit down."

Hank had to tilt the chair to get past it so he could sit.

"Sorry about the mess. Moving is not going as smoothly as we had hoped. The other hospitals were supposed to be ready for these additional patients, but ..."

The doctor stopped, shook his head, and continued, "Not your problem. How are you feeling?"

"Feelin' great, Doc. I'm just glad I'm not one of those poor souls being rushed out the doors on stretchers. They look miserable."

The doctor shook his head again. "Yes, some are so serious they shouldn't be moved, but when the government says jump, the individual is quite often lost in the rush."

The doctor shook his head again. "I haven't much time, Henry, so let me get to it. Have you recalled anything new?"

Someone knocked and opened the door.

"Not now!" Dr. James shouted as the orderly quickly stepped back and closed the door.

"No, Doc, I haven't thought of anything else."

"All right, let me explain a few things. I was going to tell you this when I gave you your release and discharge, but your friends were with you." The doctor paused and looked straight at Hank. "You may never regain your memory. I've worked on many cases like yours, trying to find a key to memory return, and I've found none. Sometimes, for no reason, complete memory returns in an instant. Other times, it may return from a blow to the head. I've found nothing to indicate how, when, or why a person's recall returns."

The doctor, using his forefinger, tapped on the desk to emphasize his next words. "What I have found is that people who search for their past, forgetting the importance of living now, lose their future. I know you have a Southern accent. Obviously, you are from somewhere in the South. You can go back there searching, but it could become an obsession. You may or may not find connections or family, but the time you spend searching is gone."

Hank's head was spinning. That was exactly what he had planned on doing, searching Virginia, Tennessee, Kentucky, and Georgia. Somewhere, someone might know who he was. But now the doctor was telling him something different. He looked up at the ceiling in search of an answer. Nothing appeared.

"Henry, I know you may feel lost, but you could look at this lost memory differently. It could be a blessing. You are now unencumbered. You can start a new life. I'm not saying don't search. What I'm saying is that if you must search, make the search secondary. Your primary goal is living your life."

Hank shook his head, feeling almost like a physical weight dropped on his shoulders from a thought that had never entered his mind before. "But, Doc, what if I'm married? What if I have a wife and kids back home waiting for me to return? I can't just abandon a family. What will happen to them?"

"First, you don't know you are married, and I suspect you are not. Usually there is a ring. You had none. Or a picture. You had none. Letters. You had none. Hank, you are not married, but you could have other family members back home, wherever that is. Again, do you throw away your future searching, or do you go on with your life and, while living, search? That's what I recommend."

Dr. James let out a long sigh. "I know this isn't a perfect answer, but I find nothing in this life is perfect. We just make the best out of what we're dealt. Do you have any questions?"

"No, Doc, I guess I don't."

The doctor rose, and Hank followed. Extending his hand across the desk, Hank said, "I'm much obliged. From what I gather from Sister Deborah, I wouldn't be here today if it wasn't for you."

Dr. James grasped Hank's big hand in both of his. "Though you haven't regained your memory, you've regained your health. I am happy for you. Now get out of here and live a life we can both be proud of."

Hank nodded, squeezed by the chair, opened the door, and stepped into the hallway, almost knocking over an orderly who was rushing somewhere. The man tossed him a quick frown and kept moving. Hank turned to make his way through the crowded hall back to his packing.

"Hank!"

Recognizing the owner of the booming voice, he turned to see Mac, followed by Wade, making their way through the crush of people toward him. When the men drew close, Wade called, "Are you packed?"

"Mostly. I've got to—"

"Hang it, man!" Mac said. "We've got a wagon waiting to take us to Baltimore. There's a schooner leavin' on the evening tide for Galveston, Texas. 'Tis luck we've had findin' out about it. I've talked to the agent here, and he says there are four passenger berths remainin'. It'll save us at least two months, but we've got to be movin' now. We've gotten our discharges, Hank. We're free to go. We've picked up the gear we stored for you, and it's all in the wagon."

Hank was stunned. *I haven't even considered Texas seriously,* he thought. *What about my family? Where are they? Do I forget the search like the doc said?*

He had always been a man of quick decisions, but a drifting thought slipped through his mind. *Don't waste time making up your mind. Just do it! Where'd that thought come from? It's like I've heard it before.* He turned to the two men. "Where's Darcy?"

"On the wagon. The teamster has a load that's goin' to our ship. He won't wait long," Mac said. "Are ya comin' with us now?"

"Yes, I'll do it! I've got to get my gear and tell Deborah."

"Make it quick," Mac said. "The wagon's out front. He ain't waitin' forever."

The two men spun around and, in the crush of people, made their way toward the front door of the hospital. Hank turned in the opposite direction toward his ward. Fortunately, he was packed. He just needed to grab his bag, tell Deborah what was happening, and be on his way. They would miss the time together they had planned, but it couldn't be helped.

Reaching the ward, Hank picked up his bag, threw his overcoat across his arm, and quickly scanned the large room. No Deborah. Two long steps took him to one of the orderlies. "Do you know where I can find Sister Deborah?"

"She was here, but Dr. James sent for her."

Hank spun around and entered the congested hallway. "How did I miss her?" he said to no one in particular.

Several of those nearby turned and looked at him, but he ignored their stares and pushed on through the patients and orderlies who slowly flowed toward the front door. Finally reaching the doctor's office door, without knocking, he pushed it open—and was brought up short.

There stood Dr. James and Deborah in an embrace, her head on his shoulder. Neither of them saw him. Shocked, he stood for a moment, then quietly eased from the room and headed for the front door of the hospital. A myriad of thoughts clamored for his attention. *Why didn't I notice? I saw that they were friendly, occasionally telling jokes and laughing, her hand on his arm, but that's what friends do. I was a real pushover. I thought she might possibly like me. I guess you're never too old to learn.*

Hank shook his head, let a stretcher pass in front of him, and followed it out the door. He immediately spotted the wagon and laughed. How could he miss it with all three of his friends standing in it, shouting, and waving? The crowd thinned somewhat as equipment was taken to different wagons and patients were distributed among the waiting ambulances.

"How do?" the driver said as Hank walked up. "Name's Mitt Casey. You must be Hank. Toss your gear in the back and sit up here with me. The fellers were telling me about you, and I'd like to chew the fat on the way to the Baltimore wharf."

"Hi," Hank said. "I'm Hank Remington." He shrugged into his

overcoat, pulled his hat down over his eyes to keep it tight, and tossed his bag in the back. Scanning the wagon's crowded bed, he saw the rest of his gear and climbed aboard. The other three made themselves as comfortable as possible in the back.

The driver popped the reins and expertly guided the horses out of the press of ambulances, wagons, and people. He reached the street, waited for a moment to merge into the traffic on the busy street, and trotted the horses between a surrey and a loaded wagon, causing the other teamster to pull his horses up. An unintelligible yell issued from the man, but Mitt did a good job of ignoring it, just waved and continued north.

"With the government in session, it'll take us a couple of hours just to get out of Washington. Danged politicians, all they do is clog up the works and cost us money. But the *Swift* ain't scheduled to leave until ten tonight, so we've got time."

Hank nodded and turned around. "How you boys doing?"

Darcy spoke up. "I'm as comfortable as an old hound lying on a nail. It hurts enough to whine, but not enough to make him move. Reckon I may be stove up when we get to that ship, which I ain't real thrilled to be puttin' my trust in, if you want my two cents."

"We don't," Wade said. "We're fine, Hank. I think you'll like this sailin' thing. I've done it a couple of times and it sure saves time. Now that the war's over, you don't have to worry about gettin' sunk, and you're not stuck on a horse's back day in and day out."

"I don't mind a horse's back," Darcy replied. "In fact, I prefer it over all that water, and you cain't even drink it." Darcy took a breath. "And don't you go thinkin' that just because the war's over, ships don't sink. They sink when there's no fightin', too."

Mac was stretched out on several tarpaulins that were on top of boxes. "I'm thinkin' I just might take me a wee nap." He winked at Hank and pulled his campaign hat down over his eyes.

Mitt said, "With all the time we have, how about I take you by the Capitol Building and the Washington Monument? If you haven't seen 'em, of course."

"I'd like that." Hank started to turn to ask the others, but already could hear loud snoring coming from the back.

Mitt nodded and, a few blocks later, turned left onto Constitution Avenue and proceeded west. Hank was excited. This was something he could tell his children if he ever had any. With that thought, the picture of Deborah wrapped in Dr. James's arms struck him like a howitzer round, bringing deep pain, almost physical. He silently stared at the traffic going by, his eyes seeing nothing.

"There it is," Mitt said, pointing at the Capitol Building passing by on their left.

Hank could see people hurrying up and down the tall steps. "So all the senators and congressmen are in there right now?"

"Most of 'em, at least the ones who ain't out carousin'."

Hank soaked it in, remembering that Deborah had said to make new memories. *That's what I'll do,* he thought. *I'll fill my mind with new things. If I can't have my old life, I'll make a new one.* Turning, he continued to stare at the Capitol Building until he finally turned forward, and there in front and to his left rose a tall concrete monument that appeared to have had a giant axe lop off the top.

"What's that, Mitt?"

The mule skinner shook his head. "That there is folly on display. Oh, they had themselves a fine idea when they started it in '48, but I guess they run outta money. That, Sergeant, is a monument to the father of this country, George Washington, or at least it was meant to be. It was supposed to be four times that height, but you can see they ain't never finished it."

Hank's eyes were glued on the four-sided monument that thrust itself skyward until coming to an abrupt stop. "You think they'll ever finish it?"

"I doubt it. Reckon it was a good idea, but it's been like that since '54. It's a durned shame. General Washington deserved a lot more respect than that sore thumb is giving him. I remember my grandpa telling me stories of the great man. Why, if it hadn't been for him, we'd still be under British rule."

Hank searched his memory of George Washington, but though he felt he should know who the man was, his mind gave him nothing.

His thoughts wandered. *Did I have a grandpa who told me stories about George Washington, or brothers or sisters? What about a ma? Were we a close family?*

Before they reached the monument, Mitt turned right, onto an equally busy street. They rode in silence until another large white building came into view.

Before Hank could ask, Mitt said, "That there is the White House. That's where that useless Andrew Johnson lives. I can't wait until the next election so we can kick his worthless carcass out of there, but I figured you'd like to see the White House. Many a good man has lived there, and a few losers."

Hank watched the large white building as the wagon passed by. "So that's where the president lives. Mighty fine place."

"It is. At least we can be proud of the building and what it represents." The mule skinner popped the reins, and the horses stepped into a trot. "We won't be able to maintain this pace for long, what with the traffic, but we need to get on to Baltimore. I've got to get this freight and you there before the *Swift* sails."

"Thanks for the show."

The mule skinner nodded and kept his eye on his mules and the multitude of surreys weaving in and out of the traffic.

4

The gaslights pushed back against the darkness along the streets of Baltimore and around the wharf. In the shadowed light, Hank could discern the outlines of ships lined up at the docks and more sitting in the bay waiting to come in and drop their cargo, only to pick up another load.

He watched Mitt guide the horses through the organized bedlam. Men wheeled barrels and wooden boxes on huge handcarts, while others carried sacks over their shoulders. They came into the light, then disappeared in the holes of darkness that existed between the warehouses and the ships.

Finally, Mitt pulled the horses to a halt. "There she is, boys, in all her glory."

As soon as the wagon stopped, stevedores swarmed around, quickly emptying the wagon of its contents.

The four men grabbed their gear, climbed down from the wagon, and walked around to the left side, staying clear of the workers. In the dim light they watched as the dockworkers scurried on board with the cargo.

Three masts reached skyward, and the ship tugged at her

lines as if she were anxious to be on her way. She was a stream-lined, graceful ship, still a beauty, though the years were showing on her. But in the pale glow of the gaslights, Hank felt an ominous gloom surrounding the ship. Never a man to question his decisions, he now felt unsure. Was it right for him to be going west, or was the East where he should be, searching for his family, if he had any?

The activity on deck broke through his melancholy. There were shouts and curses as the men lowered cargo into the shallow hold. A large man, standing at the near rail, saw them and yelled, "If you're a-goin' with us, ya best come aboard, and step lively."

Hank, shaking the feeling, turned to Mitt. "Thanks for the tour and good luck to you."

"I'm thinkin' it'll be you fellers who'll be needin' the luck. You'd never catch me out on them big waters."

Darcy was eyeing the ship as if he were looking at his own coffin. Wade slapped him on the back. Darcy looked at him for a moment, shook his head, and turned back to the wagon.

The men shook hands with Mitt, and Hank, carrying his bags and rifle, led the way to the line of men who were hauling the final supplies on the ship. Stepping on board, Hank moved out of the way of the stevedores and, rifle in hand, dropped his gear in front of the big man who had yelled. He extended his right hand and said, "I'm Remington, and this is MacGregor, Dillon, and Smith."

The big man ignored his hand and looked at the papers he was holding. He squinted to read in the dim light, flipping through several pages. Finally stopping, he pulled a pencil from under his cap and made four marks.

In a surprisingly high voice for a man of that stature, he said, "You'll be in the after deckhouse. You need to remember this is a cargo vessel. We don't cater to passengers. Stay out of the way and we'll get along." He turned to an older man hurrying past with a slight limp. "Jacky boy, hold up."

The man slid to a stop. "Aye, Mr. Pitts?"

Even in the dim light, Hank could see the fear in the man's eyes.

"Take these landlubbers to their berths." He pointed at Hank's Henry rifle and the Spencers carried by the other men. "Take their guns to the master's quarters, and he'll secure them in the gun locker." Then he turned back to the four men. "No guns on the *Swift*. You'll get 'em back when we reach Galveston."

Jacky reached for Hank's rifle.

Hank yanked the rifle back. "Whoa, Jacky, not so fast." Turning back to the big man, he said, "You never said your name."

The man looked Hank over with an insolent sneer. "I'm the first mate. You can call me Mr. Pitts. Now give the man your rifle or get off this ship."

"Look, Pitts—"

"I said I'm the first mate. You will call me *Mr. Pitts*."

Hank could feel his anger beginning to boil. His scalp started to tingle on the left side, a telltale sign of his rising ire. He held himself back, for he felt like grabbing Pitts and throwing him over the side of the ship.

"I'll call you when I need you, Pitts. Where's the captain?"

The first mate's face grew red, and Jacky moved away. "In the first place, we don't have a captain on this ship. He's called master, and I don't care if you're a payin' passenger or not. I'll just teach you a little lesson right now."

Hank and the others were facing toward the bow of the ship.

"I'm right here, Mr. . . . .?"

Hank turned to see a broad-shouldered man of indeterminate age behind them, standing on a higher deck. "I'm Henry Remington, and these are my friends. Your man here"—he tossed a thumb over his shoulder, not even deigning to look at the first mate—"is telling me we must give up our guns."

"Mr. Remington, I apologize for Mr. Pitts. I am Master Ethan Powell, the master of the good ship *Swift*. Though Mr. Pitts makes a habit of being boorish and sometimes insulting, he is an excellent first mate. What he is telling you is the truth. If you desire to ship with us, you must give up your weapons for now. Upon reaching our destination, they will be returned to you."

"Master Powell, I'm not real comfortable giving up my weapons. I think I'll just wait and try another ship."

"That, of course, is your prerogative, but you should take two things into consideration. First, I know of no master who will allow you to keep those guns, and second, your money will not be refunded."

The master pulled his watch from his waistcoat, pressed the release, allowing it to pop open, and checked the time. He then closed it and slid it back into his pocket. "Mr. Remington, you must understand, it is impossible for us to fill those berths at this late hour. I understand you find yourself in a dilemma, but you must make a decision now, for this is the pilot coming aboard, and we must be on our way."

Mac leaned forward and, in a low voice, spoke in Hank's ear. "I know you have some extra money, lad, but me and the boys used almost all we had to buy these tickets."

Hank gave a short nod. "All right, we'll give you our weapons."

Master Powell nodded. "Jack, take Mr. Remington and his friends to their cabins.

"You've made a smart decision, sir. There is hot coffee in the galley. I'll speak to you later, and I hope all of you will join me for breakfast in the morning. We'll be eating at six." With that issue resolved, it was obvious the master had moved on to the immediate problem of getting the ship underway.

Hank turned back to Pitts, who had remained behind them.

The man was glaring at them. When Hank bent down to pick up his bags, Pitts followed him and, in a low voice, said, "I'll settle with you later, matey."

Grasping his bags, Hank rose back up and locked his eyes on the first mate. "Anytime, Pitts."

Before he could say more, Jack stepped in, taking Hank's rifle and bag, and led the men up the ladderway and to the hatch that opened into the after deckhouse. Hank had to duck his head. Once inside and standing erect, it looked like he had little more than a foot of space between his head and the ceiling. The single lit kerosene lamp in the hallway labored unsuccessfully to withstand the darkness, which covered a good portion of the corridor. Once inside, Jack said to Hank, "Don't mess with Mr. Pitts, sir. He's a mean 'un. He's killed more'n one man with his bare knuckles." He turned and continued along the passageway.

"He'll find no trouble from me unless he starts it," Hank replied.

Mac spoke up. "How long be the voyage, Jack?"

The man stopped again and turned to Mac. "'Tis ten days to Santiago, Cuba. We'll be there for two days, and then another eleven days to Galveston. Less than a month, it'll be."

Hank, surprised at the stop in Cuba, tossed Mac a questioning look.

Jack checked his list and turned to Hank. "This'll be your cabin, Mr. Remington. I'll show the other gentlemen to their berthing compartments and then be back to pick up all the guns you might have."

Stepping into the room, Hank looked around, or at least tried to. For a big man of at least two inches over six feet, and wide shoulders, when he took a breath, he felt like he was inhaling the room. At the end of the bed, standing at a right angle to the length of the little room, there wasn't sufficient width for him to stretch out his long arms. He tossed his bags on the bunk, couldn't help but notice the length of the bed, and shrugged his shoulders. The beds in the hospital had also been too short.

His larger bag had most of the gear Mac and the boys had stored for him. That was where his firearms, powder, ball, and ammunition for the Henry rifle were packed. The first thing he took out was the belt holding a knife and scabbard. The scabbard had a leather thong that slipped over the top, holding it secure. The handle was made from a large buck's antler, wrapped with tough cowhide that was shrunk to fit tight against the antler. The big knife fit his hand perfectly. Mac had called it a wicked-looking meat slicer, and it was. A long blade, he guessed at least a foot, maybe an inch or two longer, extended from the cross guard. The steel blade glistened in the flickering light of the kerosene lamp. He checked the edge, sharp, but in need of some work. He'd have plenty of time for that on this voyage.

In examining the belt, he found three pockets that had been painstakingly tooled into the wide leather. A leather flap over-lapped each pocket and held tight against the bottom edge of the belt, making it difficult, unless you examined it closely, to spot the pockets. In each space he found secreted, three double eagles laid side by side. *I like my planning,* he thought. *If I'm ever in a tight situation, I'll have the money to buy a horse, saddle, and guns—if need be.* He swung the belt around his waist and fastened it, the knife hanging below his right hand.

Next, he examined each Remington .44 revolver as he removed it from its holster. *Mac tells quite a story about these,* Hank thought. *I wish I could remember.* He hefted each one. *They're a snug fit for my hand, and they're in good shape, though the metal shows signs of wear where they ride in their holsters. Am I good with them? Can I hit what I shoot at? From the appearance, they've defi-nitely been used.*

Still staring at the revolver in his hand, he could hear yelling on the deck and felt the ship jerk as if a rope had become taut. The ship was moving. No turning back now. He slid the revolver back into its holster, fastened the flap, and placed it next to the other two. Next, he examined three extra, unloaded cylinders that obviously fit the Remingtons. Finally, Hank removed the .41-caliber Remington derringer. The weapon had two barrels, one on top of the other, and was small enough to slip behind a waistband and never be seen. He slipped the thumb catch, rotated the barrels up, picked up two cartridges from the small box he had opened, and dropped a rimfire cartridge into each chamber. Then he clicked it closed and slipped the tiny weapon into the pocket sewn into his wide belt behind the buckle.

He had wondered what the pocket was for until he found the derringer in his bag. It was a perfect fit. Next, he took the few clothes he owned and hung them on hooks inside the small closet. There was a bar across the top of the closet, but he had no hangers. He looked at the uniforms. He had put off buying new clothes too long. If he was going to use them, he'd have to remove the chevrons—time for that also.

There was a knock on the door. He turned, opened it, and found Jack, laden with weapons, standing there with a sheepish look on his face. "Sorry, I've got to relieve you of your firepower, Mr. Remington, but . . ." The man stopped, his eyes finding the big Bowie knife. "That's a king-size blade you have, sir."

"Call me Hank, Jack. I use it for slicing meat."

"As long as it's not my meat you're slicing. Now I'll need your bang sticks . . . Hank."

"It looks like you're loaded. Can I give you a hand?"

"That'd be right kind of you, sir, what with all I'm carrying. We'll be heading down this hallway to the master's quarters."

Hank gathered up his Remingtons and followed Jack down the hall. When they reached the end, they turned left. Another kerosene lamp provided faint lighting. Jack stopped and knocked at the door. When there was no answer, he opened the door, peered in, and, opening it wider, stepped into the master's quarters.

It was spacious compared to Hank's room, but smaller than he expected. The windows at the back allowed the master to see behind the ship, looking beneath the fly rail. There was a large bed, a table that could fit eight or double as a big desk, and a large closet.

"Nice closet the master has," Hank said.

"'Tis a locker, sir, and that there door is called a hatch."

Hank nodded. "I see I have much to learn, Jack."

Jack laid the guns on the table, standing the rifles in the corner formed by the master's bed and the back wall.

"It'll be easy, sir. By the time we get to Cuba, you'll be soundin' like an old salt."

"Well, I'd appreciate all the help you could give me, Jack."

"Aye, sir. Glad to do it. That there wall is called a bulkhead, the door is a hatch, and the ceiling here is the overhead."

Hank went over them in his mind. "Thanks."

They were about to leave when Pitts stepped into the room. "You've got a ship to tend to, Jacky. Your pay ain't for teachin' landlubbers, and by the by, what's he doin' in the master's quarters? You know this space is restricted."

Jack had paled at the sound of Pitts's voice. "Aye, Mr. Pitts. He was just a helpin' with the guns. They had quite a bundle."

"He did no harm," Hank said. "I offered to help."

"Get topside, Jacky. Now!" Pitts's voice went higher when he raised the volume. He turned to Hank. "I'll thank you to find your way to your own berth, and keep out of the master's quarters."

Hank ignored him and stepped past the broad man to exit the cabin. As he moved past the first mate, the man grabbed him by the shoulder.

"You acknowledge me when I speak to you, soldier boy."

Hank spun, his big right hand moving so fast it was only a blur, reaching and clamping on the first mate's throat. Both of the mate's hands clamped on Hank's wrist, but couldn't budge him. The man gasped for air.

In a low, chilling voice, Hank said, "Don't you ever put your hands on me, *Mister* Pitts." He held him for a moment longer, then released the man's throat, ripping his arm out of the other's grip.

Pitts leaned over, his hands on his knees, gasping for breath. As his lungs began filling again, he looked up from that position, poison in the glare he gave Hank, and in a hoarse voice cursed and then said, "You'll pay for this. You'll pay dearly."

"All I've seen or heard from you, Pitts, is threats. Come see me when you'd like to back that hot air up with something more substantial." He spun back into the passageway, almost running over the master. "Sorry, Captain, I was just helping Jack bring our weapons to your quarters. Pitts had a problem with it."

Master Powell stepped into his room, glaring at Pitts, who was busy rubbing his red neck. "Can you tell me what's going on, Mr. Pitts?"

"Aye, sir, I surely can. I found Jacky and this man in your quarters. When I nicely asked him to leave, he tried to choke me. If I didn't have the strength I have, he might have throttled me."

Hank stood listening to the lies told by Pitts, shaking his head. "Captain . . . I mean Master Powell, the man is a bald-faced liar. It is true he found us here, but as I mentioned, I was only helping Jack bring our weapons here. He was trying to get back outside to help, and he would have had to make two trips if I hadn't brought along my own weapons. As far as choking him, that is true. After listening to his guff, I was leaving the room and he grabbed me. That was enough. I throttled him to extend a lesson in manners." Hank raked Pitts with a disgusted glare. "Obviously, it didn't take."

The master turned to Pitts and in a hard voice said, "Mr. Pitts, you may take your leave. We'll be talking later."

When Pitts had gone, Powell closed the door and turned back to Hank, folding his arms in front of him. "Mr. Remington, I am sorry for the actions of my first mate. He is not normally on this ship, but my regular first mate is seriously ill, and the company replaced him with Pitts. I do not like the man, nor do I condone his actions. I assure you he will be removed upon our return to Baltimore."

There was a knock on the hatch. Powell paused and opened it to find the cook standing there with a tray containing a pot of tea, a small pitcher of milk, a silver bowl of sugar, two cups, and a plate of sweet shortbread biscuits. "Ah, Thomas, come in. Just place them on the table." The cook set the tray on the table and started to remove the items. "That's fine, Thomas. We'll take care of that. Thank you."

"Aye, sir," the cook said and quickly departed, closing the hatch behind him.

"Please join me, Mr. Remington. This is a special blend of tea I picked up on a voyage to India. I think you will enjoy it. I would appreciate some company."

The two men seated themselves at the table and the master poured tea for the two of them. He looked up. "Milk?"

Hank shook his head. "No, thanks."

"This is rather strong tea. I'd suggest two scoops of sugar."

Hank nodded and did as the master suggested. He stirred until the sugar was dissolved and laid his spoon down. Picking up his cup, he felt the ship heel slightly to the left, and the sound of the *Swift* cutting the water came softly through the hull.

Powell nodded. "The pilot is adding sail. We must be in the Patapsco River. As a young master, I was always so nervous. I would never leave the pilot until he had us into the ocean, which, if we make good time, will be tomorrow night about this time." He laughed at Hank's surprised look. "Chesapeake Bay, which we'll be sailing down, is almost one hundred forty miles long. It takes more time than most think to reach the ocean from Baltimore."

"I had no idea it would take a ship that long just to get to the ocean."

"Yes, it's quite a little voyage."

The master took a sip of his tea and set the cup gently back on the table. He picked up the tray of sweetbreads and, while holding it out to Hank, said, "Mr. Remington, I must point out a few rules of the sea that could impact you very negatively should you persist in your disagreement with Mr. Pitts."

5

"Mr. Remington, I must admit I find this difficult, for you are a paying passenger with our company, and I like you. Unfortunately, there seems to be some strife between you and Mr. Pitts. As difficult as he is, I cannot allow him to be assaulted by you. Therefore, this is a warning and a plea. Please resist the urge to strike this man. Should it happen again, I will be required by the law of the seas to have you detained."

Hank, sitting across from the captain, was shocked. He set his cup down and leaned forward in his chair. "Captain Powell, everything I have done has been in self-defense."

Powell held up his hand, palm toward Hank. "I understand. Please do not get upset. I am just giving you information to prevent future occurrences. Though he is an unpleasant man, he is my first mate, and due respect must be shown toward him."

Hank rose. "Captain, I give respect where it's due. Pitts deserves none. I am sorry he is the first mate, but if he makes any attempt to harm me or my companions, I will deal with it."

The captain pushed his cup aside and stood. "Mr. Remington,

this voyage has just begun. Please do not make it difficult for all concerned."

Hank turned for the door. "Thanks for the tea. I will create no difficulties for you, but I can't speak for Pitts. Goodnight."

As Hank was closing the door, he heard the captain respond, but the comment was unintelligible. *Well, you sure did it,* Hank thought. *Not on this ship for one day and you've already alienated the captain and have a problem with Pitts that will come to a head probably long before we reach Cuba.*

Mac and the boys were standing in the hallway when Hank turned the corner, their faces frowning with concern.

"Couldn't help overhearing you and the captain. Is there a problem?" Mac asked.

"You could say that." Hank explained the choking incident with Pitts and how Captain Powell came upon the two of them during the incident. "Then he invited me for tea and flat out told me any more problem with Pitts and I'd be getting the short end of the stick."

The three of them shook their heads. Darcy, his face pale in the lamp's light, asked, "What are you gonna do?"

"I'll do my best to stay out of his way, but I don't know how long that'll work. Bullies like Pitts love to harass folks. At some point, I'm going to have to straighten him out, and the captain made it clear what will happen when I do. For now, I'm putting it out of my head and hitting the sack. I suggest you three do the same. Breakfast is at six in the captain's quarters."

"You think he'll still want us there?"

"I'm sure he will. He invited us, and I don't think he would change his mind. He strikes me as a man who sticks by his word."

The three of them made their way to their separate quarters. Hank closed the hatch, leaned back against it, and shook his head. He was stuck here for the next twenty days or so, eleven to Cuba and ten to Galveston. He'd have to do his best to stay clear of Pitts. One month out of his life—not such a long time.

He undressed and crawled into bed, his mind going to Deborah. *I liked her—a lot. It's hard to believe I didn't recognize there was something between her and Dr. James. You'd think she would've told me when I asked to take her out. Oh well, she said I should be filling my mind with new things. That's just what I aim to do.*

The whisper of the water rushing past the hull seemed to increase in volume. *We must be picking up speed.* Hank lay there listening to it flow past, and his eyes drifted shut. His tall body relaxed, and moments later light snoring could be heard coming from his room.

Hank leaned against the railing, watching the fluorescent foam generated by the schooner *Swift* as it cut through the black water of the Windward Passage. The faint moon, occasionally hidden by the clouds that raced along with the ship, would be setting behind the island of Cuba in another hour. Cuba, no more than ten miles to the east, had several fires visible along the coast. Jack had told him those were set by landowners to clear jungle and undergrowth as the first step in clearing the land for cultivation.

This first leg of the trip had been fast and surprisingly pleasant. At least for everyone except Darcy. He had become seasick sailing down the Chesapeake, and it only worsened when they reached the open sea. Jack had tried to help with several cures. None worked. Darcy lay in his bunk with a bucket by his side. *I just hope he doesn't decide to stay in Cuba,* Hank thought. In reality, he felt sure his friend would continue to Galveston. But Hank knew that if it were him feeling like that, he'd seriously consider staying in Cuba rather than get on another ship, though that would only postpone the pain.

He had learned much from Jack on this trip. Hank couldn't stand to be idle, so after obtaining permission from the captain—

he hadn't been able to get this "master" thing down—he started working with the crew, even in the rigging. He was glad he had. Because of the work, he was getting stronger by the day. He could feel it in his arms and shoulders, but most of all in his legs. It felt good to work his body. The harder he worked, the longer he kept Deborah out of his mind. She had really fooled him. Shaking his head, he lifted his eyes from the foam and gazed into the dark night. The moon, now completely covered by thick clouds, did little to dispel the heavy darkness. He watched the fires twinkle in the distance while his mind worked, unsuccessfully, at pulling out memories.

He had a faint picture of a woman in his mind, but he couldn't place her. The image never stayed. It would slip in, unbidden, and then disappear before he could recognize her. He knew she was older. He felt more than actually saw her. A feeling of kindness and love came over him every time she appeared.

Frustrated with his memory, he reached up and bumped the scar on his head twice with the palm of his right hand. The wound no longer hurt, but there was a groove, bare of hair, cut in his skull where the bullet had tracked. Hair had grown back around the trench, but it was a white strip that would be his token for as long as he lived. *As long as they don't start calling me Skunk.* Hank grinned at the thought, his frustration evaporating in the cool spray from the bow.

Master Powell, Ethan, had said they were making excellent time. They would arrive in Santiago a full day early. That was good news for everyone, although bittersweet for Darcy. Their rapid journey was caused by a north and then northeast wind that drove them through the rough sea, so a day less in pain where Darcy was concerned, but more severe due to the excessive pitching and rolling of the ship.

Hank started to turn to look up at the sails and, too late, caught the movement of four men, including Pitts. Hank spun around to confront the men closing in on him, but realized he was too late. The belaying pin, clinched in the grip of the first mate, was already descending toward Hank's head. He only had time to move his head slightly when the club connected with the left side of his skull. Though he tried to fend the men off, he felt himself collapsing, his legs and arms no longer responding to his brain's commands.

He felt hands grasping his legs and upper body. A feeling of peace flooded over him as he floated through the air. He could feel himself turning over and over. Everything would be all right. A smile drifted across his face and he relaxed.

The *Swift* was traveling at thirteen knots. The bow was rising and falling, cutting through the dark water at an unusually high speed for the old ship. Its bow wave, pushed aside by the schooner, rolled out and away, growing smaller with distance. Since Hank had been standing near the bow, he fell directly into this wave. The wave enveloped him in its deadly arms, twisting and turning his body as he sank into the deep.

His euphoria vanished when he struck the water. Though only moments passed before he regained consciousness, some instinct of self-preservation kept him from gasping and drawing water deep into his lungs. His eyes flew open, only to be met by instant, burning blackness. His head felt as if it would explode, but for now that was the least of his worries. He needed air.

First thing, he must get to the surface, but where was the surface? Black surrounded him. There was no up or down. The bubbles weren't drifting in any discernible direction. They were rolling over and over with the wave.

He felt panic slip into his racing mind. He knew he had faced it before, and somewhere, someone was telling him that to survive, panic must be controlled and discarded. But he needed to breathe. He had not gone under the water with full lungs of air, and now they were reminding him—air. Not screaming yet, but insistent. With all of the willpower he could muster, he did two things. First, though it was one of the hardest things he could remember doing, he pushed panic from his mind. Then he relaxed. He stopped fighting the bow wave and rode with it.

His body kept rolling. He couldn't tell if he was moving vertically or not, but made himself remain relaxed. Now his lungs were becoming more demanding. They wanted air. They screamed for air. *Not yet!* he screamed back in his mind. Over and over. *Not yet!*

And then he burst to the surface, rising almost halfway out of the water, his mouth open, filling his starving lungs. He splashed back down, treading water while looking for the ship. There it was. His first instinct was to swim toward it, but in the time he had been underwater, the *Swift* had drawn away at least three hundred yards and was rapidly widening the distance. A feeling of dread washed over him. *I'll never catch it.*

Now was the time to check his head. He reached up and touched the new wound. He could feel the torn skin, and there was a knot the size of an egg. He felt for his knife. It was still there, along with the derringer behind his belt buckle. It wasn't much, but at least he wasn't totally unarmed. With one arm, he reached down and pulled his shirttail out. He needed a strip of cloth to tie around his head, hopefully to stop the bleeding. Hank started to pull out his knife and thought better of it. He didn't want to lose his knife in the sea. The bottom was a long way down. Ethan had told him it was deeper than the ship was tall many times over. He stopped treading water with his hands, leaving all of the work to his legs, took a deep breath, and while slowly drifting beneath the surface, tore a strip from the lower portion of his shirt and pulled back to the surface.

The waves had to be at least five or six feet high. They made it difficult to get the strip tied around his head and chin. Once satisfied it was tied as well as possible, he drifted to the top of a wave and spotted land. Cuba was west of him, and the waves were moving in a southwesterly direction, so he took up an angle across the waves and began to swim.

It was hard work. Up one side and down into the trough, quartering, repeated over and over again. He swam for what he figured was thirty minutes and stopped to rest, floating on his back. The fires looked no closer. Hank started off again. *Keep despair away. I can do this. At least I can swim,* he thought. *Another talent I was unaware I had.* He pulled for Cuba.

His mind worked overtime as he kicked and stroked his way west. He had plenty of time to play what-ifs in his mind. What if he hadn't been able to swim? He'd had no idea of his swimming ability one way or the other until he hit the water. What if he hadn't been shot in the head? Would he be home now? If so, where was home, and would anyone be there waiting? The kind woman's face that he kept seeing but couldn't quite make out, was she family? He continued to swim.

The sun was coming up; the warmth felt good on his back. At his last rest break, he had examined the coastline in daylight. Still too far to make out details, it looked like there were tall cliffs that came down to the ocean. Hopefully, there were sandy beaches. He didn't relish swimming all this distance to be smashed against a rock face. Hank could make out the green along the tops of the cliffs.

He was tiring. The past week of work on the ship had strengthened him, but he could feel the water sapping his strength. Time passed slowly, but it passed. He had no idea how long it was since he had been thrown overboard. Hank could feel the anger build in him. How could a man like Pitts develop such hatred? He hoped for the opportunity to confront the man, though he had to admit, the odds of that happening were pretty slim now. He kept swimming.

His back was hot through his shirt. To relieve the heat, he tried alternately swimming on his back and just floating, letting the waves carry him, but the waves were almost paralleling the shoreline.

He was close now, but was fighting exhaustion. He could

barely make his legs kick. He stopped to rest. The waves seemed to be getting higher. From the crest he could see where the cliffs rose several hundred feet. At the base, it looked like the waves, and they were getting bigger and breaking against a rock shelf.

It took him riding up on several crests before he picked out a small strip of beach. It couldn't be more than a hundred yards long, and at each end the rocky shelf disappeared into the smashing waves. With their direction, there was little chance he could reach the beach. There was a distinct possibility he'd be swept past it, only to end up on the sharp rocks. But even if he made it near the beach, his troubles weren't over. The waves appeared to be rising ten or fifteen feet above the beach before they crashed and rolled in, washing across the sand. But the beach was his only chance. He'd have to try.

Hank started out again. The sun was brutal. Even through the shirt, it felt like his upper back was broiling. Summoning the last of his strength, he began cutting across the waves at a wider angle in hopes of reaching the breach in the rocks.

He kicked hard to push himself forward and felt his left foot strike something. A moment later a shadow glided beneath him. It took forever for it to move past—at least twice as long as he was tall. Now he felt a strong surge of anger and adrenaline. He was almost there, and now this?

Moments passed, and the shadow again glided beneath him. He dug with all of his strength. He could feel his body propelled through the water. The shadow stayed directly beneath him until he started rising on one of the waves. Then it moved out to the side and drifted closer to the surface. He could see a huge fin rise out of the water and turn toward him.

The wave he was on had lifted him high above the beach. He looked down and saw he was going to make the beach if the huge shark didn't get him first. His last sight of the great predator was as he and the shark crested. It had a gaping maw that was moving toward him much too fast. With a superhuman effort, he kicked himself forward into the wave just as it broke.

Time stopped. He expected to feel the pain of the shark clamping down on some part of his body. At the same time, he felt like he was flying, for he had been propelled out past the wave and for a moment hung in space, until at last he fell into the rolling water below. Now he was being tumbled over and over, ground against the sandy bottom as he was pushed toward the beach. He felt the sand alternately being ground into his arms and chest, and then his head and back.

The water receded and he was lying on the beach. He summoned the last of his strength and dragged himself far enough up the beach to make sure neither the water nor the shark would get him. He raised himself up on his forearms, looked around, and collapsed.

6

He opened his eyes to the touch of a damp cloth moving across his forehead. His eyelids felt like weights were fastened to them. Hank battled to keep his eyes open to see who was holding the cloth that felt and smelled so good. In the darkness, he could make out a slim arm, but when he tried to focus his eyes, they rebelled, dropping shut. He reentered a deep sleep, brought to him by the exhaustion of his extraordinary swim and brush with death.

The next time his eyes opened, he lay still and tried to evaluate his surroundings. It was daylight and hot. If it wasn't for the breeze, the heat would have been nearly unbearable. Air coming from two windows in the hut allowed some cross-ventilation. He turned his head and examined the shelter.

There were four other pallets, similar to the one he was lying on, stacked against one wall, providing more room in the hut. Next to his bed was his belt, the derringer still in its holster. He could see the knife, pistol, and belt had been cleaned and oiled with some type of oil. *Good,* he thought, *the salt water would do terrible damage to my weapons.* Over the door hung a blanket, which provided a small amount of privacy inside.

As he was staring at the door, the blanket was pushed aside and a wiry man, appearing to be quite old, stepped inside. His wrinkled skin glistened with sweat. When he saw Hank awake, he turned to someone outside and spoke rapidly in what was an unfamiliar language to Hank. The man stepped back inside the hut and squatted down beside him.

"You feeling better?"

"Other than a little skin lost, I'm feeling pretty good."

"You were very lucky, at least three times over." The man held up three fingers.

Hank frowned at the man's response. "How do you mean?"

With this, the old man grinned, showing blackened and broken teeth. "My son and I saw you before you reached the big wave. We were standing on the cliff above the beach. We watch you swim in from long ways. You real lucky you land on the beach. Not much beach on this side of the island, just rock. You want beach, you must go to north side—pretty."

Hank started to throw back the light quilt and get dressed when he realized he had nothing on under the covering. He rose up on a forearm and looked around for his clothes.

The old man watched him closely, then yelled something. A moment later a woman who looked to be about Hank's age came into the hut carrying his clothes. Her black hair, streaked with gray, was piled high on her head. Dark eyes glinted at him and white teeth flashed in a friendly smile. "Would you like your clothes, Señor?"

Hank nodded to the woman. "Thank you."

She smiled again. "I am sure you are hungry. Dress and come outside. We'll eat." She turned and, pushing the blanket aside, exited the hut.

Hank picked up his underwear and sat up, waiting for the man to turn around, but he did nothing except watch. Hank shrugged, tossed the blanket off, and slipped into his clothes.

Once Hank was dressed, the old man stood, inhaled audibly,

and pressed both hands to his back, stretching. Several loud pops came from the man's back. Then he moved slowly through the opening, one hand on his back, the other motioning for Hank to follow. The woman was stirring a large black pot, a plate in her other hand. She looked up at Hank and said, "You are a big one."

"Thank my ma for that. She fed me well."

Whatever's brewing smells good, Hank thought. *I need to build my strength back so I can return to the ship.* He turned back to the old man. "So, I was lucky I made it to the beach. What are the other two reasons?"

"Number two, you are very lucky the wave did not kill you. There is a storm to the east, I am sure. For when we have such a storm, the waves grow to what you just rode. They are very dangerous, but lucky again, it no killed you."

There were some intricately woven cane chairs around the fire. The old man sat and pointed to one. Hank followed. The woman handed Hank a large wooden plate. On it were what looked like cooked bananas and a large pile of rice smothered in stew. He recognized what he thought were big pieces of chicken and chunks of tomato and other vegetables. Hank realized he was ravenous. His stomach growled like a dog attacking a bone.

The old man laughed and said, "Eat."

Hank grinned an apology and overfilled a wooden spoon with food. Before shoving it all into his waiting mouth, he said, "The shark was the third?"

"Si! The shark was number three. It was very big. You had to have seen it following you for much distance."

Leaning over his plate, Hank quickly shoveled two more spoonfuls into his mouth before saying, "I saw it, but there wasn't much I could do about it except swim as fast as I could. If I'd slowed down, the wind would have blown me past that narrow beach, and I wouldn't be sitting here now."

The woman stood next to the old man. "The sharks are very dangerous. You were most lucky."

"I agree," Hank said. "My heart was in my mouth when it made the final run on me. I knew it had me."

"I knew—" the old man paused for effect "—the shark would miss you. He waited too long, and the wave took you away."

The woman handed the old man a plate similar to Hank's. He took it without a word and began to eat.

Hank again lifted the spoon to his lips. He was starved, but the chicken and tomatoes, combined with the rice and vegetables, were beginning to take the edge from his hunger. At that point he realized he hadn't introduced himself nor did he know their names. He looked up from his plate.

"I am sorry. You have been so hospitable and I haven't even taken the time to tell you my name. I am Henry Remington, but people call me Hank."

The woman smiled and said, "It is nice to meet you, Señor Hank Remington. I am Tasha Felipe Pinto, and this is my father-in-law, Señor Riel Torres Salgado."

Hank inclined his head to each and said, "My pleasure. Thank you for saving me." He then looked down at his empty plate and then to Tasha. "And thank you for feeding me. It was the most delicious meal I've had in a long time."

Tasha stood and smiled at Hank, taking his plate. "More?"

"If I'm not being too much of a pig, that would be great. Thank you."

The chatter of children could be heard approaching, along with a male voice. A rather short man, not much taller than Riel, but with wide shoulders and a thick chest, wearing pants that came to his calves, and no shirt, was followed by a boy and girl. He walked to a tree limb well above the ground and hung a string of large fish. He turned to Hank and said, "He's awake."

The boy, approaching his teenage years, and a little girl, who looked to be about six years old, came to a sudden halt and stared at Hank.

Tasha walked over to her husband and gave him a kiss on the

cheek. Then she indicated Hank. "This is Señor Hank Remington, Maceo." She looked at Hank and said, "This is my husband, the one who carried you back from the beach, Señor Maceo Torres Velasco."

Hank strode to Maceo and extended his hand "Señor Velasco, I'm much obliged to you for saving my life."

Maceo, a frown across his dark features, accepted Hank's hand. He examined Hank carefully, then said, "Not Velasco, Torres. You have many wounds."

As soon as the man entered the clearing, Hank began evaluating him. On his chest and massive arms were several old gunshot wounds. The gunshot puckers weren't the only injuries his shirtless upper body showed. A long scar, from a large knife or sword, ran from the top of his shoulder, through his immense left bicep, and across his forearm. Fortunately, it looked like he still had full use of the arm.

Hank grinned back at the frowning man. "Sorry, Señor Torres, I'm not well-versed with the Spanish names. By the way, it looks like you've engaged in a few actions."

Maceo released his hand and turned to his wife, who was now frowning at his rudeness. "I'm hungry."

Ignoring her husband, she motioned the children over to her. Her son was slightly taller than his mother, and the daughter's head reached her waist. She put one arm around her son, who was now frowning like his father, and the other across her daughter's shoulders. "The boy with the frown on his face is my son, Anton Torres Pinto, and this little beauty is Liliana Torres Pinto."

Her son's frown deepened and he pulled away from his mother, while her daughter giggled at her comment.

Now Riel was frowning at his son, who had gone to the fire and was helping himself.

Hank didn't know what strife he might have caused the family by being here, but he needed to get to Santiago to catch his boat. He walked back into the hut, picked up his belt, and swung it around his waist. Looking around the small home, he took a deep breath and stepped back outside.

"I must be going. Thank you all for your hospitality. If someone can start me in the right direction, I have a ship waiting for me in Santiago."

All of the family looked toward Maceo. He stood and pointed west. "Go west until you hit the road, then turn left. It will take you to Santiago."

"Maceo!" Tasha began.

He spun on her. "Say nothing, woman. It is up to me to protect this family. This man is a gringo! We cannot trust him." Maceo faced Hank. "It would have been better if the shark had gotten him."

"West," Hank said, ignoring the outburst, and started off. He glanced at the children, whose eyes were wide with confusion and fear. He gave them a kind smile as he passed.

"Wait!"

Hank turned around to see the old man standing. His son glowered at him. But the old man's scrawny chest was expanded as he stood straight in his anger, facing his son. "Maceo, how can you do this? Would you send a man to his death? This man has done nothing to us. It is for us to help our neighbor, and he is our neighbor. If he goes, I go." The old man picked up a sack and began putting items into it.

Liliana ran to her grandfather and threw her arms around his waist. Tears ran down her face as she spoke rapidly in Spanish. Hank understood nothing except for the "no" repeated several times.

He watched the sad sight. "I don't aim to cause you folks any trouble. Señor Riel, I can find my way. You folks have done more than required. Stay here with your family. I'm obliged for your offer."

"No! I go." Riel lovingly removed his granddaughter's arms from around his waist, bent, and kissed her on the cheek. Tears

flowed freely from her unhappy eyes, but her arms hung help-
lessly at her sides.

Tasha stood with hands on her hips and her jaw set, glaring at
her husband. Finally, as Riel started to lift his bag, Tasha said
something in a low, harsh tone to her husband. He gave his head
a hard shake. She spoke again, her voice cutting like a knife. This
time she was pointing at Maceo.

The angry husband raised his head and stepped toward his
wife. His face was hard and menacing, but she flung her chest out
and crossed her arms, never moving her eyes from his.

Maceo looked at his father, then his son and daughter. He
looked over at Hank with a disgusted look, then turned back to
his wife. In English, he said, "It is fine, he can stay, but only until
he is well enough to travel." Immediately he switched back to
Spanish and laced into his wife, pointing at her and waving his
arms.

She listened calmly until he was finished. After he had
stopped, she spoke, again in English. "Yes, I understand you.
Maceo, you are a good man. I have much respect for you. But
you can be wrong, and when it affects this family, I will not be
quiet, no matter what you threaten, and do not threaten to hit
me. It may be alright with our neighbors, but it is wrong. You hit
me, and I leave with Anton and Liliana. Do you understand
me?"

Maceo glared at her for a few more moments and nodded.

Hank felt a wave of relief. He didn't want to go because, with
the little movement he had made, he realized how exhausted his
body was. In his condition, he certainly didn't want to be responsible for the old man.

Riel motioned to him. "Come, sit back down before you
drop."

Hank moved to the chair he had previously sat in. "Thanks, I
don't think I could have made it very far."

"Now that you've eaten," Tasha said, "you need more sleep.

Please go inside and rest. When your strength returns, it will be time enough for you to leave."

"But," Hank said, "I've got to make my boat. It's only going to be in Santiago for two days."

Riel shook his head. "Impossible. You have been out for almost two days. There is no way to get there before it leaves. Perhaps you can catch another."

Hank considered that option. *Perhaps I can, and I do need rest.* "That's a good idea, Señor Riel. I think for now I will rest." He turned to Tasha and Maceo. "Thanks for the help. As soon as I get my strength back, I'll leave." With that, he stood and slowly made his way back inside the hut. After removing his belt and laying it next to the bed, he lay down, stretched his long legs out, and was immediately asleep.

HANK WAS JARRED from a deep sleep. He looked around the darkened hut. Liliana and Anton were sitting on the edge of a bed, his arm wrapped tight around his sister and her back pressed hard against his side, her legs shaking and eyes wide.

The harsh voice that had awakened him spoke again. Hank could understand Maceo's name being used, but he understood nothing else except the harsh tone of the voice. He quietly slipped his belt on and checked the loads in his derringer before silently snapping it closed. Standing, he loosed his knife and moved to the back window, stopping on his way to lean over Liliana and whisper, "It'll be all right. Don't you worry."

It was difficult for him to slip out the window, and in the process, he stepped on a twig, snapping it. To him it sounded like he had felled a tree. He froze. But there was no indication of anyone hearing him. They were all focused on Maceo, who was speaking. Though Hank could not understand a word, he could tell that Maceo's voice was just as harsh as the stranger's.

The next sound to reach Hank's ears was the sound of an open hand striking flesh, followed by the gasp of a woman. By now, Hank had slipped through the trees to where he could see, by the firelight, what was happening.

An officer, probably Spanish, had dismounted and had just slapped Tasha. The man reached to his right hand and, nonchalantly, pulled his glove tight, then looked at it as if to ensure it was clean. He was accompanied by five men. Two remained mounted, one with a lance threatening Riel, and the other with a rifle drawn and ready. A sergeant, saber drawn, stood behind and to the side of his officer, watching him work. Occasionally, he would glance at the two remaining soldiers holding tight to Maceo's arms. However, it was Tasha whom Hank was most concerned about. To torment or possibly persuade Maceo, it seemed the man was concentrating his efforts on Maceo's wife. Hank had been able to see the Spanish officer's expression when he turned toward her. The man was enjoying himself.

From where he had struck her mouth, a small trickle of blood escaped and flowed down her chin. He reached out and, with the back of his hand, softly rubbed her cheek above the injury. Tasha drew back from his touch. A frown spread across his handsome face, and he drew a small dagger from his belt, cutting his eyes toward Maceo in an evil grin.

Maceo struggled with his captors, but they held him tight. Unable to loosen the soldiers' grip, he screamed at the officer.

Smiling at Maceo's reaction, the man turned back to Tasha and slowly caressed her cheek with the flat edge of the glistening blade, at the last moment turning it only slightly to leave a fine line of blood.

Tasha gasped at the pain, but said nothing. In the firelight, Hank could see tears glistening on her cheeks as she battled her emotions, holding her head high.

The officer smiled, turned back to Maceo, and in a soft,

threatening voice said something to him, then placed the glistening point of the dagger against Tasha's neck.

Maceo almost threw one of the men to the ground, but the soldier retained his footing and grip on the man. Now the officer laughed, removed the point from Tasha's neck, drew a handkerchief from his breast pocket, and wiped the blade clean. Then he slid the knife back into its scabbard and stepped closer to Tasha.

Hank had slipped behind the mounted men and now moved out of the shadows just enough for Maceo and Riel to see him. They both made imperceptible nods to indicate they were aware of him.

Hank wanted to save the two bullets in the derringer, for those were the only two remaining. When he had slipped just behind and between the two mounted men to where he could almost reach them, he slipped the derringer back into its holster. At that moment, possibly the horse on the left heard him, but for whatever reason, the animal started to shy away. His rider, who was holding the lance on Riel, turned. His face contorted with surprise and fear at the sight of the big knife and the bigger man.

7

H ank stepped forward and drove the heavy blade to the hilt into the man's side. Angling upward, the blade cut through the man's diaphragm, driving across and skewering his heart. The soldier collapsed, and Riel wrenched the lance from the hands of the dying man. While this was happening, Hank's long right arm reached out for the man's companion. He grasped the man's highly polished belt and ripped the soldier from his saddle. At the same time his left hand yanked the bloody knife from the dead man's side. The soldier hit the ground hard on his back, violently emptying the air from his lungs. His gasping was cut short by Hank's Bowie knife, which was driven into the man's chest with such ferocity that it drove through the protecting ribs to find its target.

Hank yanked the knife out and pushed the horses away, drawing a saber from the saddle. With the saber in his right hand and the knife in his left, he stepped around the horse to be met by the rushing Spanish sergeant. The man was taken aback momentarily at the size of Hank. But assuming the big man had little experience with a bladed weapon, he confidently stepped forward, swinging a hard slash from right to left. If it had reached its target, Hank's head would have been rolling on the ground. He parried easily, driving the sergeant's blade to the ground. With the saber down, he used his left hand to plunge the knife deep into the man's neck, severing the jugular.

The sergeant's eyes registered shock at the pain and being bested by a wild-looking gringo. He stood staring at Hank, his saber forgotten as it fell to the ground. Hank put his hand on the man's chest and shoved him off the blade, allowing him to collapse, dead.

His hard eyes searched quickly for another target, only to find Riel and Maceo had also been busy. One of the soldiers lay on his side; the full length of the lance tip protruded from his chest. Another lay on the ground, his neck twisted grotesquely. The officer lay dying, the dagger buried in his chest. Maceo stood over him, holding the officer's saber, the point inches from the man's face as he berated the dying man.

Tasha stood with the officer's revolver, hammer back and finger on the trigger. The muzzle was pointed at the prone officer's head. Hank marveled at how steady her hand was. The muzzle never wavered. Finally, she removed her finger from the trigger, lowered the hammer, and reached for her husband.

Maceo stopped yelling at the dying man and turned to his wife. Then he turned back and ripped the handkerchief from the man's tunic. He stepped close to her and gently wiped the blood from her mouth and cut. He embraced her long and hard before turning back to Hank.

"I misjudged you, Señor Hank. If it had not been for you, we would have been captives of this Spanish pig." At that he turned, kicked, and spit on the dead officer. "He has been looking for me for months. I don't know how he found us here. Maybe he was just lucky, but I suspect someone told him."

Tasha turned and quickly entered the hut. Inside, Lily could be heard crying while Tasha soothed both of the children.

"You need to clean up, Hank," Riel said. "I think there is not much space on your body that is not splattered with blood."

Hank looked down. His arms and hands were covered, and it was already starting to dry. The sight registered with him. It was as if he had seen himself like this before. He didn't care for that idea, but he would like to have any memory, even if it was bad. He stared a moment longer, but nothing came.

"Knife work can be bloody," he said.

Riel nodded. "Yes, that is true, and it appears you are on a first-name basis with it. I could not believe how efficiently you took out those riders, and then the one with the sword. You know how to use those weapons. That is for sure."

"I guess," Hank said, "but I've got to get cleaned up before the kids see me. I'll scare them to death."

"Come with me," Maceo said. "There is a stream a few yards from here. You can wash up. Since it hasn't dried yet, maybe you can get the blood washed from your pants. I'll bring a pair of mine. They'll work for you while yours dry."

Maceo started through the jungle with Hank following. "Señor Hank, how is it you are such a fighter? I see the bullet holes in your body and the knife wound in your side. You were in the American war?"

Daylight was slowly coming to the depths of the trees as the two men moved through the thick vegetation.

"Yes, Maceo, I was, and I'd appreciate it if you'd just call me Hank."

"*Gracias,* Hank. How long were you in the war, and if I am not being offensive, for which side did you fight?"

"I fought for the North, and I'd really like to tell you how long I was in the war, but unfortunately, the ball that hit me in the head took my memory with it."

"You remember nothing, not even your family?"

"That's right, I have no memory past the time I woke up in the hospital. I don't know if I have a family or not."

"You do have a family, Hank. You may have a family back in America, but you will always have a family here." Maceo stopped and turned to Hank. "If you will accept us after my terrible behavior."

Hank looked at the stocky man for a moment, then thrust his hand out. "I'd be almighty pleased to be part of your family. Thank you."

"Good. Now here is the stream."

The water was dark, obviously stained by the profusion of limbs and leaves falling into it, but it was wet. Hank waded into the stream up to his waist. He slipped his pants off and scrubbed the blood from his hair and face. Then he worked on his arms and finally his legs and feet. When he felt clean again, he walked out of the water. Maceo handed him the pair of cutoff pants. Hank studied them for a moment and then pulled them on. Though they were shorter on him, he was surprised to see they fit in the waist and thighs.

"Let's head on back before your kids start worrying about you."

Maceo held up Hank's pants. "I think I have most of the blood out. Tasha will be able to get the rest." He tossed them to Hank, and the two of them headed back.

When they arrived at the camp, the bodies had been laid out in a row, and all of their weapons had been removed. The children were busy packing what little the family owned in burlap sacks.

"You're leaving your home?" Hank asked Maceo.

"We must. It has been found once, and the Spaniards will surely find it again."

Maceo hurried to his wife and father, helping them finish packing the cooking utensils. Time had hardly ticked by before they were ready.

"That was fast," Hank said to Riel.

The old man smiled and said, "It is easy to be fast when you have little."

Tasha walked up to the two men and stopped in front of Hank. "You are a brave man. If it had not been for you, I am afraid we would be dead. Maceo would have fought, but there were too many for him." She stood on tiptoe and kissed him on the cheek. "Thank you for saving my family." A tear slowly slid down her cheek. She brushed it away impatiently and turned back to her husband. "We are ready, Maceo?"

His eyes were sad when they looked at his wife's cut and swollen face. "Yes, we are packed. We must load the bodies on the horses and leave, now."

Hank stepped forward, picked up one of the men he had killed, and carried him to the man's horse. The blood smell was heavy in the small clearing. All of the horses were edgy. When he tried to put the body on the horse's back, the animal sidestepped away from him. He put the man down, grasped the reins, and began to stroke and talk to the horse. After a few minutes, he tried again, and though the animal was obviously not happy with the smelly weight on his back, he accepted it.

With some effort and persuasion, all of the bodies were soon loaded on the remaining horses.

"We will walk and lead the horses until we hide the bodies. Then we can ride for a ways. Follow me," Maceo said, leading two of the horses. Lily was sobbing at leaving her home, and though Anton was silent, his eyes were red. Tasha put her arm around the little girl and, gripping the reins of one of the horses, followed her husband.

Maceo led them toward a massive boulder angling to its south side. Drawing even with it, Hank saw the trail behind them. Once they had traveled down the trail for a short distance, Maceo held up his hand and stopped the small caravan. He gave the reins of his horses to Tasha, and he and Riel jogged back and disappeared around the boulder. After a short time, they reappeared, brushing out the tracks. Once the tracks were gone, they moved a pile of brush that had been stacked by the trail, to the edge of the boulder, where it now completely blocked the trail from view. Then they covered the tracks as they made their way to the waiting group.

"So you had planned for this," Hank said.

"Not exactly this, but the need to escape. I will tell you why later. Now we must be on our way. We must get a far distance from here quickly. The soldiers will be missed, and others will be sent to find them."

Without another word, Maceo ran to the front, took the leads from Tasha, and started off.

Hank marveled at the huge trees, many of which were palms that pushed against each other for the sunlight filtering down to the forest floor.

"We are lucky," Riel said, bringing up the rear and standing directly behind Hank. It was obvious he had observed Hank's interest in the surroundings. "Now it is not the rainy season, for then this trail would be impassable. All of the plants you see scattered around, though they may look thick now, during the rainy season they will completely cover the trail."

At that moment, two birds flew over, making loud flapping noises. When Hank looked up to watch them pass, Riel chuckled. "That is the tocororo. It is not the best flyer, but it is a beautiful bird."

The two birds lit on a bush not far from the trail. *Riel is right,* Hank thought as he took in the brilliant green back, scarlet belly and beak, and white throat and chest. The two birds looked to be nearly a foot long. The caravan passed and Hank heard from behind a melodious "toco-toco-tocoro-tocoro."

"It is the tocororo saying goodbye to us," Riel said.

"Mighty pretty birds," Hank replied. "I have never heard or seen a bird like that."

"You do not have them where you come from?" Riel asked.

"Nope, never seen such."

The men continued on the jungle trail, following Maceo and the rest of the family. Time passed quickly for Hank. He knew he wasn't fully recovered, but he was at least able to keep up.

Ahead, Maceo stopped. They had been climbing almost continuously. Off to their left was the edge of a steep drop-off of at least five hundred feet. A ribbon of water could be seen through the treetops they looked down upon. Directly beneath the treetops was thick brush.

"Here is a good spot to get rid of the bodies," Maceo said. He pulled one from a horse and launched it over the edge. It disappeared under the canopy below and could be heard crashing into the brush. Hank stepped up, grabbed the next one, and tossed it over. Quickly they relieved the horses of their burdens.

"There is a small stream ahead that runs into the river below. It is only a short distance. When we get there, we will stop to allow the children to rest. We can clean the blood from the saddles and horses once we are there."

Hank nodded and moved back to his animal. They continued following the trail while Hank's mind worked on his situation. *Though the* Swift *is probably gone, I can still catch the next ship to Texas.* He watched Lily walking hand in hand with her mother. Anton had moved up with his father. *But what are these folks going to do? They might have been able to talk their way out if I hadn't killed the soldiers. Now they're marked. I owe them. Plus, they saved my life.*

Hank continued to concentrate on the situation as they traveled along the trail. At one point they passed another pair of tocororo, but he didn't notice, so deep in thought was he.

Maceo pulled up, motioning them to bring the horses forward. Once there, Hank could see the trail had opened into a small glade surrounded on three sides by the jungle. The fourth was the cliff that dropped off even farther now. Cutting through the clearing was a small stream that rushed toward the edge of the precipice and cascaded down the mountainside. It was shallow and almost narrow enough to step over, but the water that raced by was clear and inviting. He brought his horse to the water. Along with the others, the animal thrust his muzzle deep and greedily gulped the foaming water.

Tasha had taken some large leaves from a long-stemmed plant and passed them around to everyone. She then knelt by the stream, wet the leaves, and started cleaning the saddles and horses.

Hank and the others followed her example. It wasn't long before there was no blood remaining on the horses or tack. He spoke to Maceo. "You know that cleaning them up will not protect us. These are military animals in military rigs. They'll be immediately recognized."

"Yes," Maceo said, "but where we are going, they will not be seen, at least not until it is too late."

Riel helped remove one of the bags with the cooking utensils, then motioned to Anton and Lily to help. They moved to an area that showed signs of heavy use, cleaned it off, and started gathering wood and kindling.

While Riel and the children were getting the fire ready, Tasha took utensils from a sack and began mixing several items into one of the pots for a meal.

Maceo found a long straight limb nearly the size of his wrist. Using his knife, he rapidly sharpened one end and, before he disappeared into the jungle, said to Hank, "Would you take care of the horses?"

With little chance that a horse in the jungle would wander off, Hank led them to a grassy spot on the side of the glade opposite the camp, unsaddled each, and released them. They immediately began to feed on the rich grasses.

No more than twenty minutes had passed before Maceo returned carrying a small furry animal. Tasha saw her husband and clapped. "Clean it quickly," she said, adding nuts to the mixture in the boiling pot.

Hank walked over to get a look at the animal.

"It is called a hutia," Maceo said. "You will find it tastes very good." Finished with the cleaning, he handed the carcass to Tasha. She butchered it quickly and dropped the pieces into the pot. She smiled at Hank. "Now we relax."

While he had waited for Maceo, Hank, with the help of Anton, pulled several large logs into the clearing for everyone to sit on. Now he and Maceo joined Riel and Anton on the logs.

"I think we owe you an explanation of what happened," Maceo said.

"You owe me nothing. It looked like you were in trouble, so I helped—end of story."

Both Maceo and Riel shook their heads, and Riel spoke up. "Unfortunately, Hank, it is not the end of this story. They have been hunting us for many months. I was beginning to think we had finally found peace."

Maceo shook his head violently. "No! We will never have peace until the Spanish are gone—or dead."

Riel looked sadly at his son. "You cannot kill them all, Maceo. They will only send more. They make millions from the sugarcane and coffee. They will never let that go."

Maceo glared at his father for a few ticks of time; then his face softened. "I know, Papa, but we must fight back. Look what happens when we do nothing."

Hank's mind raced. *Have I jumped from one war to another? All I wanted to do was get to Texas and put together a herd. Can I make it out of Santiago? I guess the bigger question is should I leave these folks stuck with the Spanish Army after them? And what about me killing those three soldiers?* His mind pictured the gruesome sight of his own body after the fight, bloody, but none of it his. *That skill had to come from somewhere. Is that who I am? A killer?*

8

Maceo continued his story. "We lived in Santiago." He nodded at his father. "Papa owned a medium-sized sugarcane plantation worked by freemen. As a young man, I attended a private school. That is where I met my Tasha. She was from a very wealthy family."

He stopped for a moment, watching his wife. The heat in the afternoon jungle was intense, and she was preparing the meal near the fire, oblivious of the men watching her. She glanced up for a second, caught Maceo's gaze, and flashed him a brilliant smile.

The smile he showed his wife disappeared as he continued, "She deserves better than this. She is my princess, meant for grand balls, not jungles and death."

Riel shook his head. "She is stronger than both of us, Maceo, and she is happy with you. Do not take that away from her. She would not choose to be anywhere else but beside you."

Maceo nodded his head. "I suppose you are right. The school is where Tasha and I learned English. Papa used it in his business and insisted I learn, as we have insisted our children learn. Everything was fine until Comandante Perron saw my mother. By that time Tasha and I were married, and Liliana, our youngest, had just been born. We had built our own home on the plantation near my parents."

The conversation was interrupted by Tasha's call. "Come, the food is ready."

Laughing, Anton and Lily raced to their mother's side, and each picked up bowls, raced back, and handed one to their father, grandfather, and Hank.

"Thanks," Hank said.

The kids grinned at him and picked up bowls for themselves and their mother. Starting with Riel, she filled each bowl, hers last. Then she moved over to sit by her husband. Talking had ended. It had been many hours since their last meal, and silence pervaded the glade except for the horses tearing and chewing the grass.

Finishing first, Hank said, "Tasha, that was mighty good, thank you."

"You are most welcome, Señor Hank."

Anton spoke up. "Mama, he doesn't want to be called Señor. He said just call him Hank."

"Anton's right, ma'am. I'm not much with formality. Reckon I'm just an old country boy at heart."

"Thank you, Hank. As are we." She smiled at her husband, then grew serious. "Where are we going?"

Maceo gazed at his wife. "I think it is time we joined the Resistance. We will go to the main camp."

Worry fell across her face. "What about the children? The camp is not a good environment for them."

"I, too, am concerned for them, but I believe we should no longer avoid the fight. They searched us out and were going to kill us. We must fight them."

Anton spoke up. "I can fight too, Papa. I know how to shoot, and we captured all of their weapons."

"No!" Tasha said, pointing her spoon at her son. "You are too young. What would I do if you were killed? You cannot."

The boy turned to his father and in a wheedling voice said, "But, Papi, I'm old enough. I won't get killed."

Maceo shook his head. "Not yet. Your mama is right. You are too young. If the fight continues, your time will come, but not now."

Anton's disappointment and anger were clear for all to see. Quiet, he leaned over his stew and stared into the bowl. Silence followed Maceo's last statement. Finally, Hank looked around. "Y'all mind if I put in my two cents?"

Maceo and Tasha dipped their heads toward Hank, in consent.

Hank stood and walked to Anton. The boy also stood as he approached.

"Anton, give me your hand."

The boy complied, and taking his hand, Hank guided it to the long depression in his skull. "Feel that?"

Anton ran his fingers gingerly over the wound. Then Hank let him feel the wound in his arm and side. The boy stepped back, eyes wide.

"That's what war gets you," Hank said. "If you're lucky. Your folks care about you and they're both right. You're too young. I don't know anything about a war here, but I suspect it will be plenty long enough for a lot of young men to get into it." He turned and went back to his seat.

Maceo stood. "We should get moving."

"If you don't mind my asking," Hank said, "what are you planning for their guns?"

"I thought I'd give them to the Resistance. If we're found with them, they will kill us."

"You didn't have any this morning, and it sure looked to me like they were planning on killing you anyway." He looked at Tasha and then little Lily. "Or worse."

Pain and fear leaped into Tasha's face as she looked at her sweet daughter. "Are you serious, Hank? You think they would harm . . . us?"

"Yes, ma'am, I have no doubt."

She turned to her husband, her face set. "We must arm ourselves. As you said, it is time to fight. I say it is time to be armed for our own protection."

Maceo looked to his father. The older man gave him a solemn nod. "Then we must distribute them now."

They collected the six rifles and eight handguns; both the sergeant and the officer had hideout guns. The sergeant's could have been the twin to Hank's derringer, which was good news. He only hoped the man had extra rounds in his saddlebags. Except for the two hideout weapons, the rest of the handguns had been in saddle holsters.

"Maceo," Hank asked, "could I speak with you?"

Maceo looked up and followed Hank toward the horses and away from the group.

Hank stopped and in a low voice spoke to Maceo. "I noticed there are two .36-caliber Navy Colts in that stack of weapons."

"Yes, would you like them?"

"No, no, that's not my idea. I'm sure you'll agree with my first suggestion. The Navy Colt is an effective weapon. It's lighter and has less recoil. I think the short-barreled Police model should go to your wife."

"Yes, I agree, but we didn't have to come over here for you to tell me that."

"You're right. There's something else. You might disagree, but I'm thinking Anton should have the other Navy."

Maceo shook his head. "No, his mother would be very upset. He is too young."

"He's not too young. He's taller than his mother, and his wrists are huge for his size. He can handle it."

Maceo continued to shake his head.

Hank held up his hand. "Now, hear me out. As young as he is, he will probably have no need to use it. But what if today repeats itself? Do you want him hiding in a hut or defending his family? With what you're doing now, he needs to be prepared. He could be just what your family might need to survive."

Hank couldn't believe what he was saying to Maceo. He was talking about a young boy not yet in his teens shooting someone. What would that do to him? But even as he considered the negative aspects of arming Anton, something in his past that he couldn't put his finger on made him know he was right. The government could well be after this family, and they needed every defensive option they could come up with.

"I don't like it," Maceo said, "but, Heaven help us, I know you are right." He watched his family through sad eyes. The kids were laughing and joking with their grandfather and mother. "This will break Tasha's heart."

"She might hurt for a while, but your wife is an intelligent woman. In time, she will see the wisdom of this decision."

As the two men walked back to the group, Maceo sighed and then said, "I hope so."

When Maceo explained what he was doing, Tasha was appalled. She argued with her husband, coming up with all the protective reasons she could muster. Finally, her eyes full, she realized his mind was made up. She grew silent. When he gave her the Colt Police model, she looked as if he were giving her a snake, and dropped it quickly into a big pocket of her dress.

Anton tried to hide his elation, unsuccessfully. Every few minutes Tasha, who was now cleaning the pots along with Lily, would look up and throw Anton and his father a dirty look. Then she would go back to her work.

Riel had decided on a Barnes .54-caliber carbine, along with a Colt. Hank showed him how to squeeze the trigger guard, of the Barnes, to unlock the breech, then lower the guard, opening the breech wide so that a cartridge could be inserted, followed by closing and locking the guard. After a few practice runs, Riel caught on.

Hank picked up one of the Henrys and worked the action, tossing out a live round. He pulled the lever back into place and, with a practiced hand, opened the tube and dropped the round back in. He listened to the round make a short slide and come up against the next load. Gently lowering the hammer, he swung the rifle into the crook of his right arm. It felt natural.

He looked around the camp. Tasha had loaded up the utensils and the fire was out. The men took only minutes saddling the horses. The extra weapons had been placed in their scabbards, where they would ride until they could be distributed to the other Resistance fighters. It was time to be moving on.

Everyone mounted. Maceo and Hank took the lead with Anton just behind, followed by Tasha. Lily's little arms encircled her mother's waist. Riel brought up the rear, leading the extra horse. They eased out into the wide trail.

"How long till we meet up with your friends?" Hank asked Maceo.

"Tomorrow, we will see them tomorrow. This trail will take us deep into the mountains where the Spaniards will not ride. Also, we will be climbing. It will feel cooler tonight."

"I'm looking forward to that. I'd like to find a place where I can buy some clothes. The sun's going to roast me if we ever break out of these trees."

"Many people are where we are going. Clothes will be available for you there."

They continued to ride most of the time in thick trees, only occasionally breaking out into small meadows. Riding through the pastures, Hank looked up at the mountains around them—tall, green, and rugged. It was impossible to picture anyone else being near them in this wild country.

They came to another spot where the trail widened and

remained that way far into the distance. Maceo motioned for Hank to ride next to him.

Once there, Maceo continued his story again. "So, Perron saw my mother. I can only assume he wanted her. He visited us and began inviting Mama and Papa to his big celebrations in Santiago at the government house. These were gross extravaganzas where there was always dancing and wine. I do not know how much he spent, but I am sure the amount was, like him, obscene." Maceo's body screamed of the contempt he obviously felt for the man. He could hold it no longer. He cleared his throat and spit.

They came to a clearing, and the path cut around the eastern edge. The clearing contained what appeared to be an orchard. Trees of uniform height standing no more than four or five feet tall, but bushy. The small trees were covered with berries that grew in pods along the limbs. The large dark green leaves contrasted with the colored berries varying from deep purple to red or pink and green.

Hank looked over at Maceo with a questioning look.

"Coffee," Maceo said. "We are not far from the road we must cross. *La cereza,* ahh, how do you say?" Maceo thought for a second. "Ah yes, the cherry of the coffee bush is ripe and must be picked. You will find small farms like this one located near a road, for they must transport the bean quickly to Santiago for sale and processing. The cherry spoils fast. Anyway, inside the cherry are the coffee beans, usually two. There is a long process the cherry and beans must go through before they are ready to be ground and drunk. Cuba produces a deliciously strong coffee called Arabica. I am told it is the finest in the world."

Hank scanned the field and the trees surrounding it, looking for any type of human activity. "I don't see anyone in the field. I'd think if the cherries are ripe, the people would be picking."

"Yes, this is a nice-size field of about three hectares. That would be around seven of your acres. They should be picking unless they have already taken a load into Santiago." He turned and called to Anton, "Go check and see if any have been picked."

Anton jumped down from his horse and raced into the field. After examining several trees, he ran back to his father. "No, Papa, nothing has been picked. If they are not picked soon, they will start losing some of their crop."

"Thank you, son. Go mount up."

Anton dashed back to his horse while Maceo turned to Hank. "This is puzzling. There should be men in this field. The cherries grow only once a year. The coffee plant takes time to grow and produce. The owner of this field has invested at least three, probably four or more, years cultivating these plants. He would not waste this crop."

Riel had ridden up behind them. "If he is dead, he would not worry about his coffee trees."

Maceo nodded. "That is true. Perron is a devil. He is taking over everyone's fields. If he can't use the law, then he uses the knife or gun." He looked up the trail nervously. "We must continue quickly. If Perron has stolen the field, he will have his pickers here soon. We must get to the highway and cross it—now." He kicked his horse in the flanks and jerked forward.

Hank followed him, checking the Colt in the saddle holster. He watched Maceo pulling away. Turning, he could see Lily holding desperately to her mother. Anton was riding comfortably, as was Riel, who was bringing up the rear. Once assured everyone was keeping up, he turned and raced after Maceo. *I just hope he doesn't ride headlong into Perron's cavalry. If he does, we're all in big trouble. I wish I knew how far it is to the crossing.*

They had been racing along the narrow trail for at least ten minutes when Hank rounded a bend and saw Maceo stopped ahead. He slowed his horse and pulled up alongside him. There, through the trees, was what must be the highway. He had expected a wide, heavily trafficked road. In front of them was a two-lane track that showed signs of wagon travel, but not much else.

"We must cross now," Maceo said.

"Let's go. No reason to wait. You lead and I'll bring up the rear."

Maceo nodded. Everyone had caught up. After checking the road in both directions, Maceo waved his family across. Once they started, he galloped across and looked for the trail on the other side of the road; after a few moments, he found it and led them away from the highway.

Hank let Riel pass and fell in behind him. Reaching the road, he swung down and picked up a broken limb with a few leaves still remaining. Holding onto his horse, he walked into the road and swept away their traces. His work would do nothing to fool a professional tracker, but at least there would be no foot or hoof-prints running cross-traffic.

Once finished, he tossed the limb, swung back into the saddle, and eased the horse up the trail. He hadn't traveled ten feet before he heard the sound of equipment rattling and men talking. He urged his animal farther up the trail, where he could hide from prying eyes, and dismounted. Just as his feet hit the ground, his horse's sides expanded and filled with air. He managed to get his hand over the animal's muzzle before it neighed, and talked to him softly. He and the horse were well hidden in the thick jungle, but by bending low and peering around the base of the tree he was behind, he could just make out what was happening.

A group of ten men rode into sight, four cavalrymen and six laborers, and a donkey pulling a cart. At the last moment before they reached the trail, Hank thought, *What if there's another field in this direction?* With that dancing around in his brain, he anxiously waited for them to reach the trail. When they turned toward the coffee field, he released a long sigh and realized he had been holding his breath. He watched until they disappeared; then he mounted and headed after the family.

They were dismounted and waiting less than a half mile from the road. When they saw him, they started laughing, cheering, and clapping. He raced forward and chastised them in a hoarse whisper, "Quiet down! Soldiers are close."

With his frightening statement, all signs of humor disappeared.

"What did you see?" Riel whispered.

"Soldiers. Cavalry. Four of them. They were accompanying six workers and a mule-drawn cart. They turned down the trail to the coffee field. As far as I could tell, they saw and suspected nothing."

Everyone breathed a sigh of relief.

"But," he continued, "we've got to be quiet."

"Everyone, mount up," Maceo said. He helped his wife into the saddle and started to hand her Lily.

When he had his daughter in his strong arms, she said, "Papi, I'm hungry."

"I know, baby, it won't be long." He gave her a kiss and set her behind Tasha.

Hank watched the exchange of feeling between father and daughter. He looked away when Maceo placed his hand on Tasha's leg, and she, hand on his face, leaned down and kissed him. He could hear her saying, "I love you," to Maceo.

When everyone was mounted, Hank moved back behind Riel and rode, deep in thought. Maybe Dr. James was wrong. Was it possible he was married? He couldn't believe it so, for he felt sure if he was married, especially if he had children as sweet as Lily, he couldn't forget them. The face that kept appearing to him was familiar. He couldn't remember from where, but he was certain he knew her. Was she his mother or an aunt? Whoever she was, she had a kind face. He had to get back to the States, but how could he leave these folks? He knew that if he hadn't been in that camp, those soldiers would have killed them. For now, they needed him.

He would go when—

Suddenly, armed horsemen appeared out of the jungle and blocked the trail—all were fierce and angry-looking men. Hank reached for the Colt as more rode in behind them.

He heard the sounds of weapons cocking, accompanied by, "*No bueno, gringo.*"

iel said, "Do not worry, Hank. The ugly one with the big mustache is another of my sons. He is, as you *Norte Americanos* say, the black sheep."

This son was totally different from Maceo. He was almost as tall as Hank, but slim, although he did have wide shoulders and a big head. On that head he wore a wide-brimmed straw hat that had seen better days. At his father's words, his lips, almost totally hidden behind the huge mustache, pulled back in a wide grin, showing sparkling white teeth, very dissimilar from his father.

"*Mi nombre, Señor—*"

"Speak English!"

"Yes, Papa." If it was possible, the grin grew even larger. He swept his straw hat from his head, releasing the long black hair that fell around his shoulders, and bowed to Hank. My name, in English, is Rodrigo Torres Velasco, and I think I am pleased to meet you."

By now, Tasha had ridden back, along with Maceo and Anton. Tasha had a big smile on her face, as did her husband and son. Lily was kicking and holding her arms out to her uncle. When Tasha rode sufficiently close, Lily stood on the horse's back and leaped into her uncle's arms. Her little mouth chattered like a Gatling gun. When he caught her, she threw her arms around his neck and gave him a huge hug. After a moment she leaned back, wrinkled her nose, and said, "Uncle, you stink."

He tweaked her little nose, then kissed it. "You are the first to complain, my little beauty, but you smell like sugarcane."

She made a fist and punched his big arm with her delicate little hand. "Sugarcane stinks. It doesn't smell sweet like me."

Everyone laughed. Rodrigo slid back in the saddle and sat his niece in front of him. "Come, we must move on. We can't stay this close to the highway." He turned and rode in the direction Maceo had been traveling.

THE SUN WAS SETTING behind a green bluff that reached more than five hundred feet above the riders. They were now riding along a fast-running river, the water crashing against huge boulders and rocks. Rodrigo had taken pity on Hank and loaned him a worn poncho. Though it was hot beneath it, Hank was thrilled to have the protection from the sun. They had climbed higher and the trees were becoming more scattered. The sun had begun to take a toll on his body.

There had been little talking as the group rode deeper into the mountains. At times the trail narrowed and their legs extended over a precipice, while in other parts of the trail, trees surrounded them with lush greenery. Now, as darkness was about to envelop their second day of travel, they rode into an elongated basin that followed the river. In the flat, open area, surrounded by cliffs on three sides, numerous huts sat, with small fires burning in front of them.

Hank quickly assessed the people. There were at least two hundred of all ages. If he had to guess, at least twenty-five to thirty men were waiting in the village. He heard a scream, and a woman, quite a bit younger than Tasha, broke away from the crowd and raced toward her. Tasha jumped down from her horse, and the two of them met in the fertile meadow. They embraced with abandon, laughing and crying at the same time.

Rodrigo had lowered Lily to the ground, and she too ran toward the woman, bounding into her arms.

Riel pulled up beside Hank. "It is Tasha's younger sister. They have not seen each other for years. This is a good day." However, his sad face belied his statement. "Let's take care of the horses."

Hank swung down and stretched. His body, long in the hospital and then aboard the ship, was not yet used to being on horseback for this many hours, and it was complaining to him. Ignoring the aches, he led his horse to the big corral. It was built into a corner of the stream where there was an eddy, allowing the horses to water anytime they felt like it. Piled at one end was a stack, at least two feet high, of fresh-cut grass. He looked it over and thought, *Somebody put a lot of work into this. It can hold a bunch more horses than I'm seeing.* Rodrigo walked up as he was pulling the blanket and saddle from his horse.

"What do you think?"

"Nicely built. Someone spent a lot of time planning where they wanted this corral. Using the vertical bluff as one side was smart."

Rodrigo nodded and then grinned through his mustache. "Thanks, it took some work."

"You did it?"

"I planned it; then we all pitched in to build it. It didn't take long."

Darkness had slipped silently across the little valley. It was a clear night, but no moon yet.

Hank looked around. "It gets dark quick here."

"The mountains hasten darkness," Rodrigo replied. "It is not like the slow creeping night of the ocean. There is no water here to reflect. The trees and hills absorb what little light there is. If you are caught in the jungle at night, the best thing to do is find a spot and sit. Wait until morning. Otherwise, you could break a leg or worse, step off a cliff."

After pulling a handful of grass, Hank wiped down his horse. Once he had him dry, he gave the horse a pat on the neck and slapped his rump. The horse headed for the water, and Hank picked up his gear. He was anxious to find out what was in the soldier's saddlebags. Anything might help since he had almost nothing.

"Come with me," Rodrigo said as he led Hank to one of the fires.

Around the fire sat Riel and the Torres family, plus, sitting next to Tasha, her sister. They stood as Rodrigo and Hank approached.

"Hank," Tasha said, "I want you to meet my little sister, Angelita. We call her Angel."

"Angelita," Hank said, "that is a beautiful name." *A beautiful name for a beautiful girl.*

"Why, thank you, Señor Hank."

He watched as she turned and said something in Spanish to her sister. They both laughed, even the men, shaking their heads. He could feel his sunburned face turning redder. He was too old to be letting some young woman get under his skin. He cleared his throat and Maceo came to his rescue.

"Sit down, Hank." Then he turned to Rodrigo and Angelita and said, "Hank saved us all. It is thanks to him that we are still alive."

Riel spoke up. "My son is speaking the truth. We were about to be killed by Perron's lackeys when like an avenging angel Hank descended on them. You have never seen such destruction."

Others nearby moved closer to their fire and were urging Riel to tell them the tale. He looked at Hank with a nod of apology and launched into a detailed and gory description of what took place.

Though it was being told in Spanish, Hank's discomfort grew. Men were looking at him in disbelief and the women in awe, some with fright and others . . . he couldn't tell, but it was disconcerting. Angelita must have picked up on his feelings. She stood and started walking toward him. He quickly came to his feet as she approached.

"Will you walk with me to the river?" she asked.

He cleared his throat and in a gruff voice said, "I'd be happy to." He pulled the Colt .44 New Army from its holster and slid it behind his waistband and picked up his Henry.

Angelita looked at the guns and flashed her teeth in a grin. "You must think I am very dangerous."

He smiled back. "I try to be prepared for whatever happens. I imagine not all of the folks in these mountains are friendly."

The tinkle of her laughter drifted across the mountainside. "Then I feel well protected."

After a few more steps, she slipped her arm around his. "It is hard to see with no moon."

"It sure is," Hank said. "You hang on tight. I wouldn't want you to trip."

She giggled at his comment. "How old are you, Señor Hank?"

He thought about the question for a moment. "I don't rightly know."

She stopped, pulling him to a stop, and looked up into his eyes. "You don't know how old you are?"

"Angelita, I haven't the slightest idea."

"How can that be?"

By this time, they had reached the fast-running river. Hank found a comfortable log and, after helping her sit, joined her and went into the explanation. He told her everything up to being found by Riel and Maceo. He then said, "That's all I know. My nurse in Washington, DC, said not to worry about the memories I don't have, just make new ones. That's what I've been working on." Hank chuckled and said in a wry tone, "I've actually gotten more than I bargained for." He looked down at her black hair glistening in the rising moonlight. "Some of them mighty nice."

"Goodness, your story takes my breath away, but I think the nurse is right. I would add only one thing. Make enough good new memories to outweigh the bad." She smiled up into the big man's face, reached up, and pressed her soft lips to his cheek.

The warmth of her lips stirred yearnings he had not felt since Washington. Hank turned to her and grinned. "Ma'am, that was mighty nice. I thank you. I can't remember when I last felt something like that."

Her laughter was soft in the mountain air. "It *was* nice." She placed her hand on his thick forearm. "You may not believe it, but I haven't *done* that in quite a while."

The sky had started lightening in the east. Hank glanced in that direction. "Looks like we'll have some light to go back by."

"Yes," Angelita said as her eyes followed his, "a little moonlight always helps to chase away the darkness."

The sadness in her voice caused him to turn on the log so he was facing her. In the growing moonlight, he could see a lone tear glisten on her cheek. When she saw he had noticed, and before he could say anything, she stabbed at the tear with her left index finger, flicking it to the ground. "It is a feeble mind that dwells in the past. We are alive and strong here, now. That is where our minds should be."

Hank nodded. "That's true, but it has to be awfully hard to be hiding out like you folks are doing. I'd say you've been dealt a pretty sorry hand."

A melancholy smile crossed her lips before she said, "It is different from the life we knew, but this government will not always be in control. There will be a day when the Spaniards are gone, and freedom will come to our country. It may not be tomorrow or next week or even next year, but it will happen."

"I wish you luck. This is a mighty pretty country. The people deserve to be free."

Almost as if to punctuate Hank's words, shots could be heard in the distance. Hank reached for Angelita's arm, but she was already on her feet. The two raced back to the encampment.

They were met by Riel. "We must hurry. The outpost is under fire. We must move quickly."

Everywhere people were loading horses, mules, and donkeys. Younger children were crying while the older ones raced to help.

Angelita turned to Hank. "*Vaya con dios,* Hank. May your past return to you." She spun and ran into the darkness.

"Come," Riel said, "we must hurry. If it is the *soldados,* our guards will not be able to hold them long." As if to emphasis Riel's words, the firing increased.

Maceo had Tasha and the children packed and mounted when Hank and Riel reached the corral. As Hank leaned down to pick up his saddle, Rodrigo ran up. "I've just had word. It is a large force of Perron's soldiers. We need men to fight while the women and children escape." He looked pointedly at Hank.

"Count me in," Hank replied.

"Good." Rodrigo turned to the young man holding the reins of two horses, placed his hand on the man's shoulder, and spoke to him in Spanish. Immediately the man thrust the reins of one horse in Hank's hand while giving the other to Rodrigo.

Hank said, "*Gracias,*" and swung into the saddle. Rodrigo spoke quickly again and hugged the man, then leaped into the saddle.

Immediately, they were off, followed by at least twelve additional men, including Maceo. Thankful for the faint moonlight, Hank rode at Maceo's side as they raced through the jungle, only occasional spots of the trail illuminated through the thick foliage.

Nearing the fight, Rodrigo signaled a halt. The men leaped from their horses and continued through the trees. Now the firing was subsiding. Concern clutched Hank's heart. *If we don't reach them soon, they'll all be dead or captured.*

Rodrigo held up his hand and motioned for the group to

spread out and for Maceo and Hank to stay with him. He leaned near Hank's ear. "We are about to move into an area of low brush and many boulders. This overlooks the trail below. If we can keep them from getting by us or climbing above us, we can stop them."

Hank nodded, then moved to Maceo's left, who had eased up next to Rodrigo. Hunched over, the men moved into the open area and came up behind the trail guards, who had barely managed to hang on. Reaching the three men, they found two dead and the third wounded. The injured man spoke anxiously to Rodrigo, pointing to the steep ridge above them and signaling for them to get down.

No sooner had he finished speaking than gunfire burst from the ridge, followed by shooting from the soldiers on the trail below. Two of the men who had ridden to help slumped to the ground. Now the moon favored those at the top of the ridge.

Hank turned to Rodrigo. "We've got to stop those men or they'll cut us to pieces. Let me take two good men."

Rodrigo nodded and spoke quickly to two men. They both jumped up and ran to Hank.

Maceo shook his head.

"No. I will go."

Rodrigo stared at his brother. "You stay. You have a family."

"So does everyone else. Besides, I speak English. That will be needed. I am going!"

"Make up your minds," Hank said. "If we don't get moving, those men on the ridge will kill us all."

Resigned, with no time to argue, Rodrigo said, "Then go, but be careful. Antonio, you stay. Carlos, go."

Obviously disappointed, Antonio slipped back behind his boulder.

Hank, with Maceo and Carlos, dashed back into the thick cover provided by the trees. Once there he stopped and turned back to the two men. "It looked to me like these trees run up and over the tree line. I don't know why those shooters didn't slip down here; maybe they were just too anxious, but we can follow the trees right to the top."

Hank stopped while Maceo translated for Carlos. Then he continued, "We go up and over. That way we'll be out of their sight until we're right on top of them. Don't shoot until we are directly behind them; then blast away. Let's go."

He waited again until he was sure all three of them were in agreement; then he started up. At first it was easy; then the slope steepened. It was necessary to grab low-hanging limbs to pull themselves up, which made it even more difficult to keep quiet.

The urgency was pressed home by the firing from the top of the ridgeline. It sounded like it was growing heavier. Maybe others had survived the steep climb to join their compatriots, who now had the rescuers pinned down between their fire and that of the soldiers below.

Hank grabbed a thick limb and pulled himself to the crest, where the ground leveled for a few feet. Once there he turned and extended his hand first to Carlos and then to Maceo. He whispered, "Very quietly we will slip along the ridge." With that he pointed to the back side of the ridge, which fortunately, wasn't quite as steep as the side they had just climbed.

He could tell he was almost completely recovered from his injuries and his swim. Though he was still breathing hard from the intense climb, he wasn't gasping. His body felt strong again.

They moved along, testing each step. Though the firing had become intense, they couldn't rush. It sounded like there were several shooters. Hank knew they had to be sure when they came over the crest. There would be no second chance.

They had broken out of the tree line. The moon was higher, and in the light, he could see to the bottom of the canyon on this side. The slope was shallow at first, then it steepened. The brush grew out of rocky ground that was covered by loose pebbles. Maybe two hundred feet down, the slope ended in a drop-off, and, in the faint moonlight, it was impossible to tell how long a fall it would be—long enough to end a life with a smashed and broken body.

The shooting was now coming from the other side of the ridge crest. It was time. Hank looked at the two men. Determination hardened the faces of Maceo and Carlos. Their weapons were ready. Both men watched Hank. He listened once more to make sure they were in the right place, waited for a moment, and nodded. The three men leaped over the crest.

10

F our soldiers were in front of them, concentrating on their downhill targets. They heard nothing.

Hank swung the muzzle of his Henry and centered it on the back of the farthest man. Carlos and Maceo had done the same thing, and when Hank pulled the trigger, so did the soldiers. It was one reverberating blast. All three of the men slumped forward; all three died instantly.

The fourth man, obviously an experienced soldier, never hesitated in his rate of fire. Though the blast was loud and his friends were dead, he spun around, perhaps knowing he was a dead man, but still followed his training. Unfortunately for him, three rifles again barked at the same time, and three forty-fours plowed into his chest and drove him back against the boulder he was using for cover. With the last ounce of strength in his body, he struggled to bring his rifle to bear, but he was done for, and the weapon clattered to the ground.

Ears ringing, Hank looked around to make sure there were no other enemies near. About to let out a long sigh, he heard the distinct sound of a Henry's lever working, spun farther to his left, and saw a fifth soldier with his sights centered on Maceo.

Without thinking, Hank jumped between Maceo and the shooter, knocking Maceo to the ground. Simultaneously, he gripped his Henry like a handgun, fired from his hip, but knew he was too late. The blossom of flame from his enemy's barrel was blinding, instantly accompanied by a sharp pain in his arm. He fell hard, along with Maceo, both brought up short against the boulders, but his eyes stayed focused on the soldier.

Hank's bullet had caught him in the side, turning him slightly, but Carlos followed with three shots to the man's chest. The soldier's tunic was covered with his life's blood, and his eyes slowly glazed over. But the firing from the ridge had stopped, and the Resistance fighters below no longer had to contend with snipers.

Hank tried his left hand. It was working. Then he moved his arm. Everything functioned properly. That was the important thing. Carlos extended a hand to help him up. The Cuban had a big grin on his face. Hank grinned back and nodded to him. Turning to check on Maceo, he found his friend was bleeding from the head. Hank's first thought was that when the bullet cut through his arm, it had continued and struck Maceo in the head. Then he moved, opened his eyes, and said, "You are as dangerous as a bullet."

A grin took the sharpness out of Maceo's words. He extended his hand to Hank, who helped him up and took a look at his head. The cut above the man's ear was bleeding profusely.

"When you shoved me," Maceo said, "I fell into the boulder and hit my head, but, *amigo*, you saved my life. I saw him just before he fired. He had his rifle centered on my chest. I was a dead man except for you. That is twice you have saved my life. I guess I was wrong. There is at least one good gringo—but look, you are shot in the arm!"

"Nothing," Hank said, glancing down at the wound. He'd need to clean and bind it, but the bullet only creased him.

The firing from the Spaniards below had slowed. To change

the subject, Hank said, "We'd best get back to Rodrigo. Carlos, will you stay here until we signal? Just in case they try to send up more snipers?"

Maceo translated, and Carlos said, "*Si, Jefe.*"

Hank looked at Maceo. "*Jefe?*"

"Boss."

Hank turned back to Carlos and extended his hand. "*No Jefe. Amigo.*"

Carlos grinned, nodding his head enthusiastically, took his hand and said, "*Amigo.*"

Hank and Maceo slapped Carlos on the back and then turned to make their way down the slope. Going down was a lot quicker, though not any easier. They had to hang onto the bushes as they slid past, finally reaching a gentler slope where they could walk; the boulders protected them from the searching rounds below.

Upon reaching the waiting men, Hank explained what had happened to Rodrigo, but didn't mention the part about saving Maceo. While he had been on the ridge, he had surveyed the surrounding area. There were two boulders slightly forward of their position. It looked like one man could cover the trail and be protected from fire coming from the ridge above, if they sent anyone else up.

He moved forward to the boulders, checked them out, and returned to Maceo and Rodrigo. "One man, using those two boulders for cover, can hold that bunch off for quite a while. I'm thinking that all of you should get back to your families and help them disappear in these mountains. You leave me another rifle and plenty of ammunition and I don't think they'll ever get through."

"While you were gone, Maceo told me about you saving him. *Gracias.* He's not the best brother in the world, but I'd still hate to lose him."

"I was afraid of what Tasha would do to me if I let him get shot."

They laughed. "Yes," Maceo said, "she can be a handful."

Rodrigo turned serious. "Hank, you have already done too much. I will stay. I know where to go to escape the devils. I can do this. You must go with Maceo."

The two brothers argued in Spanish, but Hank finally stopped them. "No. I have no family here. Both of you and every man here does. I couldn't ride out of here knowing I contributed to a family losing their husband or father. You both know I'm the perfect one for the job."

Rodrigo thought for only a moment. Then he motioned to the men closest to him and had them pass the word—they were leaving. He then waved to Carlos on the ridge and motioned for him to come down. Everyone watched as the one man protecting them from ambush from above slid down the steep incline. A few shots rang out, but nothing came close.

Maceo handed his Henry to Hank. "Do not wait too long, my friend. If they are determined, there are ways for them to get up here. Hold them for a while. That will give us time to rejoin the others and ensure we all disappear. I will wait awhile at the end of the valley where we camped. Come soon."

Rodrigo handed Hank a burlap sack that contained several boxes of Henry .44 ammunition, and he repeated Maceo's entreaty. "You don't have to hold them indefinitely. Just for a while, then ride like the wind. Do not let them capture you. They will not be merciful." He looked at the big man towering over him, then finally thrust out his hand.

Hank shook hands with Rodrigo and then Maceo. The other men sat their horses, watching. The two leaders could wait no longer. They turned and swung up into their saddles. All the men waved as they galloped down the trail, swallowed up quickly by the jungle. He was now alone.

Moving quickly to the boulders, Hank peered over the edge to find the soldiers running from their positions to mount their horses. They must have heard the Resistance fighters galloping away and assumed everyone had left.

Bad assumption on your part. He settled the bead front sight on the chest of the first soldier. Because he was shooting downhill, he lowered his aim point halfway between the man's chest and his belt buckle, then squeezed the trigger. At the report of the Henry, the soldier slumped from his saddle. Hank swung his rifle to another man who had made it into his saddle, slammed the lever forward and back, ejected the fired round, and loaded a fresh one into the chamber. He repeated his action and watched the second man fall.

The remainder of the soldiers had scattered and returned fire. Hank slid behind the boulder, listening to the slap and whine of the bullets as some slammed into the rock while others ricocheted in all directions. He waited until the rush of fire subsided, then lying on his belly, eased from behind the boulder. Before he had an opportunity to view the lower trail, the huge amount of fire forced him back behind the boulder.

This isn't working as well as I thought it would. He leaned against the boulder, thankful the rock was between him and the heavy fire. He would be riddled with holes if he didn't have the cover. Finally, it slowed again. This time he eased to the other side and spotted a portion of a soldier's rear sticking out from behind cover. He grinned to himself. *That fellow's gonna wish he had listened to his sergeant better.* He squeezed the trigger. The blast was followed by a howl that echoed throughout the mountains. The man leaped up, giving Hank a clear shot.

He laughed and howled back, mimicking the man, but did not fire. Several of the man's companions yelled back at him. Hank was sure there was nothing complimentary in their comments even though he couldn't understand them. Hank eased back against the rock and glanced at the moon's position. Still a few hours of moonlight left, but when it set, he would be in more danger.

Firing had slowed through the early morning. Hank would occasionally ease out and fire a couple of rounds, but he wasn't receiving much return fire. He leaned back against the rock again. He knew he was in big trouble. Yes, he had already killed Spaniards, but they didn't know. Now, if they caught him, he would be treated as a combatant and probably shot. *I would've really liked to have found out who I am. I imagine after I'm dead I'll know. That'll be something.*

Hours had passed. *Maceo, Tasha, and the kids, along with everyone else, should be gone and well hidden.* Holding the Spaniards here had worked. With the moon disappearing, now would probably be a good time for him to get the heck out of here. He had no intention of becoming a dead hero.

He stood, leaned around the boulder, and noted this time there was no firing; it must be getting too dark. He knew he could barely make out their horses. Swinging the barrel away from the animals, he opened up with several rounds just to let them know he was still here. Return fire erupted from below and lasted a while. When it died down, he picked up the other Henry and the ammunition bag and trotted back to his horse. He slid his rifle into the scabbard and tied the bag around the saddle horn.

Under the trees where the horse was tied, it was almost pitch black. *I hope this horse can find his way.* Hearing a sound he could not identify, he stopped and listened, his foot halfway to the stirrup. Reaching for his Colt, he slowly turned his head to look over his left shoulder. The movement caused pain in his left arm, but he ignored it while scanning the darkness. A shadow disturbed him. He slowly eased his foot to the ground and focused to the side of the shadow, knowing that peripheral vision could sometimes pick up something better than looking directly at it, but nothing. Just a shadow.

He let out a small sigh, trying to relax. Thinking that as tired as he was, his ears and eyes were playing tricks on him, he swung back around and lifted his foot to the stirrup.

"Buenas noches, gringo."

Shocked, he tried to spin around, but his toe was in the stirrup, which stopped him. He reached for the Colt, and in the darkness just before it hit, he made out the butt of a rifle swinging to his head.

The impact collapsed him to the ground. Faintly, as he settled into a welcoming unconsciousness, he felt blows to his side and head, but it didn't matter, he was in a wonderful warmth of darkness. The last jolt was a metal-toed boot to his head, and then he was gone.

IT WAS SO warm and comfortable here. His body was awakening, but he didn't want to go. He felt so good, and he knew consciousness would bring pain. He'd had enough pain, he didn't want any more, but his body wouldn't listen. Though he struggled to stay where there was some peace, the pain relentlessly dragged him back to reality.

His head lolled on his chest as he shook it slightly and licked his lips. He was thirsty.

A sharp voice came from in front of him. He tried to open his eyes, but they were so heavy. He didn't understand what the man was saying.

"Wake up, gringo! I am growing impatient."

He heard steps in front of him, and then his eyes were yanked open by the pain of an open-handed slap that snapped his face to the side. Hank brought his head forward to examine the man who had hit him.

He wasn't big, maybe five feet five inches at the most. Straight as a stick, the man's shoulders were barely wide enough to hold the red tunic on his body. A number of medals hung on his chest, and a gold-hilted sword swung from a brilliant white leather belt. The man's boots were shined to a luster seldom seen. Hank absently wondered if he were close enough, could he see his reflection in the polished toes.

The little man wore a short, thin mustache that did nothing to hide his huge lips. Above his mouth was a tiny nose that would look out of place on the smallest child. However, it was his eyes that were most distinctive. They were so light, they were almost white.

Hank couldn't help but stare. He had never seen anyone who looked like the officer. Where the thought came from, he had no idea, but he wondered if the man could smell anything with that tiny nose. Without realizing it, he found himself smiling.

"Are you smiling at me, Gringo? Do you understand who I am? I could end your life like that." The little man tried to snap his fingers, but no sound came out. He tried again with the same result.

Hank knew his life was in jeopardy, but couldn't resist. Though his hands were tied behind him, he said, "Do you mean like this?" and snapped his fingers. The little man had been pacing in front of Hank as he spoke. At the sound of Hank snapping his fingers, he whipped around and slapped him again. This time Hank could taste blood and was starting to get angry. "Mister, I don't know who you are, but I'm an American citizen. You can't hold me against my will without first contacting the American Embassy."

The man's face turned livid. "What? You speak to me with that tone?" He drew himself up to his full, short height and said, "I am Captain Manuel Osvaldo Bacayado Santibanez. You will show me the respect I deserve, or I will have you whipped until dead."

Hank looked at the man, never doubting that he could and would do exactly as he promised. His head hurt from the butt stroke and his ribs were sore; luckily, he felt no sharp pain. Maybe no ribs were broken. He took a deep breath and said, "Sorry, Captain. I think I'm still a little groggy from the blow to my head. Would it be possible to get a drink of water?"

"That is more like it. Yes, that can be arranged." He stepped back to the desk and poured Hank a glass of water, and held it to his lips.

Though room temperature, the water felt wonderful going down. "Thank you, Captain," Hank said. Somehow, he knew it was better to humor this fop than cause him further anger.

"Now, what is your name, and what are you doing in Cuba?"

"My name is Henry Remington and I fell off the *Swift*, a cargo ship bound for Santiago and on to Galveston."

"You fell from the ship?"

Rather than tell the complete story, Hank said, "Yes, and I swam to shore."

"That doesn't explain why you were shooting at my soldiers. Are you a spy?"

At the question the captain had turned and was staring at Hank, waiting for an answer.

Hank tried to think of something that would persuade the man not to hang or shoot him, when the door suddenly opened.

The little captain turned, his mouth open, obviously ready to berate anyone junior to his rank for entering while he was questioning a prisoner. When he saw who had entered, he immediately gave a short bow and spoke respectfully to the older man in uniform.

Hank picked up the word *Perron*. One look at him and he could tell here was a man who was used to command. Men would jump to comply with anything he might say. This was the man who had killed so many people and was hated by Hank's friends. He waited quietly while the two men conversed in Spanish. *I have got to learn this language if I am going to be around here long. I have no idea what they are saying.*

After waving off the captain, Colonel Perron stepped forward, placed his finger under Hank's chin, and lifted his head so the two men could look eye to eye. He held this pose for a few moments. Then he turned to the captain and spat an order. In the same tone the captain turned and snapped at the guard. The man jumped to the back of Hank's chair, bent over, and removed the hand shackles, leaving the ones fastening his ankles to the chair.

Hank rubbed his wrists and moved his sore left arm. The gunshot had not been cleaned, and he was concerned about it, for the soreness in his arm was increasing.

"Now, Mr. Remington," Colonel Perron, in perfect English, said, "I would like to know how you have gotten yourself mixed up with such brigands."

11

The clock on the captain's desk ticked loudly as Hank stared up at Perron. The man was an imposing sight, not just from his uniform resplendent with medals, his polished, black riding boots, or the shining sword hilt. Any man could dress like a military peacock, but this man wore it well like he had earned it. His bronze skin emphasized the sharp cheekbones and wide-set blue eyes. Eyes that were hard as the glass pitcher on the table. His tunic was impeccably tailored, emphasizing what had once been narrow hips and waist, now grown thick with easy living, tapering up into wide shoulders. His large hands hung relaxed at his sides.

Hank worried about his friends, for this man would be a formidable enemy.

The clock's tick was the only sound in the room. The young captain was becoming nervous in the silence and moved as if to step forward.

Perron turned his head like a hawk, stopping the man with his glare, then turned back to Hank, a small smile lifting his trim mustache.

"They rescued me," Hank finally said. He nodded toward the pitcher and glasses sitting on the desk. "Now, how about a drink?" Before Perron could speak, the captain blurted out, "Don't be impertinent, gringo."

Perron again turned to the captain and in a soft voice spoke quickly in Spanish.

The captain's face blanched. He nodded several times, saying, "*Si, comandante, si.*" Then he walked to the side of the guard and stood at attention.

Perron showed white, even teeth in an indulgent smile. He stepped to the desk, poured two glasses of water, and handed one to Hank. "You were on the schooner *Swift?*"

Though he didn't show it, Hank was surprised. How could Perron know what ship he was on? He took the glass and tilted it to his mouth. The refreshing liquid further soothed his thirst. He savored it for a moment before swallowing, using that time to plan what he would say. He could lie, but obviously Perron had firsthand information, and knowing that lies were their own trap, Hank said, "Yes."

"How did you happen to fall from the ship?"

An ironic smile crossed Hank's face. He took another sip of water, then said, "I didn't fall." He could see his disclosure surprised Perron.

"You did not fall? That is not what I heard."

"The first mate and I had some words when my friends and I first came aboard the ship. He waited until he found an opportunity and, with a few of his cohorts, clubbed me and tossed me over the side."

"So you would not consider Mr. Pitts a friend?"

Hank's mind raced. Had he said too much? How did Perron know Pitts? Were they friends? He could answer the question only one way. "No, not a friend."

Perron laughed, his laughter hard and biting as he mimicked Hank. "Not a friend. You are very diplomatic Señor Henry

Remington. I would expect to meet you at an embassy party, not after you ambushed my men.

"I know much about you. I know you were originally on the schooner *Swift* and your destination was Galveston. You were traveling with three friends, and all of you, having fought for the Northern forces, had just left the Army. I also know you are a cavalry, noncommissioned officer who was severely wounded in battle. A battle for which you were awarded your country's highest medal, the Medal of Honor.

"I also know that though you are well aware Spain is a friendly nation to the United States, you elected to attack and kill my men. Now you have the effrontery to sit here demanding water from me, the comandante of this land, after what you've done!" As the man spoke, his volume increased until his last words were a shout.

Emphasizing his last words, and with a powerful swing, he knocked the glass from Hank's hand. It flew across the room, shattering beneath a window, the water and shards of glass covering the floor.

Hank slowly turned his head toward the broken glass, then back to Perron. He met the man's eyes and held them, never saying a word.

Perron glared at Hank, then swung from his waist, his big hand open, aiming for Hank's face. This slap would not be the puny strikes of his captain.

Though Hank's feet were shackled, his hands were free. He knew the smart thing to do was to take the slap, but he was tired of being used as a punching bag. He jerked to his feet and caught the man's wrist in his hand, pulling him and allowing the comandante's momentum to bring him closer. As the man's hand passed in front of him, he released it and Hank encircled his neck with his left arm. His right hand slipped the nickel-plated Colt from its polished holster.

The guard had his rifle leveled at Hank, along with his

captain, who had drawn his revolver, but the comandante shouted, "Don't shoot, you fools! You could hit me."

"That's right," Hank said. He had tried to lower himself so as much of his body as possible would be protected. "Either of you try anything and your comandante won't see the sun set. Now lay your weapons gently on the desk. Don't drop anything; I don't want anyone coming in here to check on us."

After the two men put their guns down, Hank waggled the barrel of the Colt toward the captain. "Tell your soldier to go stand in the corner and face the wall."

The captain did as he was ordered.

"Now you come over here and unlock the shackles on my legs."

The captain looked at his colonel.

"Don't look at him. This here Colt is who's giving the orders."

"Do as he says—quickly," Perron gasped, barely able to breathe with Hank's forearm across his throat.

"Don't try anything, you two. As much as I don't want to shoot, I will if I have to."

The captain knelt and, with the key rattling against the locks, it took him a few moments to get the leg irons unlocked. Once finished, Hank motioned him over to the wall with the guard, stepped back, moving the chair out of the way with one leg, and shoved Perron away from him and against the desk. The comandante caught himself with his hands on the desk and spun to face Hank.

"You will not make it out of here, Remington. Look out the window! Your safest bet is to give yourself up to me."

Hank moved over to the window while keeping the Colt trained on the three men. Glancing out, he could see an exercise area surrounded by a wide rock wall. Guards watched the enclosure from the walkway on top of the wall. He caught movement and saw Perron reaching for the revolver lying on the desk.

Hank brought the Colt to bear on the man. "Not a good idea, Señor Perron. Lead poisoning is mighty unhealthy."

The man froze, keeping his eyes on Hank.

Perron dropped back into the friendly tone he had used at the beginning. "I tell you the truth, Henry. You might make it out of here, but you will not make it out of this prison. Now get some sense into your head and give me that weapon. It is not too late for you."

Perron spread his hands, palms up. "I do not want to kill you. It will make too much trouble for me if I kill an American hero. I do not need problems with your government. Trust me, I will not kill you."

Hank knew he was boxed. He couldn't make it down the hallway alive, much less through the yard. He'd be filled full of Spanish lead before he took three steps out the door. He wasn't kidding himself. He knew another beating was in store for him, but just maybe he could find a way to escape. Making a decision, he stepped forward, spun the Colt, and offered it to Perron butt first.

The comandante smiled, took the weapon, and lowered the hammer. "Now, Señor Remington, it is your turn." Perron's voice hardened. "Move to the wall and put your face against it. Hands behind you, please."

Hank heard the hammer of the Colt being pulled back again. Moments after pressing his face against the wall, he felt the muzzle of the big .44 pressed against the base of his skull. Silence enveloped the room. Hank could hear the flag on the pole outside flapping in the wind. Faintly, in the distance, dogs were barking and the voices of two women could be heard in conversation.

He waited. Maybe now was his time. Then he felt the wrist and leg irons being fastened.

"Now," Perron said, lowering the hammer of the Colt, "you may turn around, but continue standing against the wall."

Perron moved back to the desk, motioned for his men to get

their weapons, and sat on the edge, dangling one leg off the side. His smile did not bode well for Hank. Though it exposed his teeth, nothing about his face showed humor or kindness.

"You are a problem I no longer want to deal with. It is my wish that you disappear—permanently."

When he received no reaction from Hank, Perron grew impatient. "You have thus far enjoyed the hospitality of our rebels. Now you will have the opportunity to enjoy my hospitality. You will find what it is to work. You gringos are used to an easy life, but you will find it not so easy living as a *Cubano*. I have many farms that grow sugarcane. I always need workers. Most of my workers are prisoners." At his last statement, Perron let out a laugh that sounded much like a cackling hen. "They are very cheap. I feed them a little, and they work until they die.

"How does that sound to you, Remington? Do you think you would like working in the sugarcane fields?"

Hank said nothing.

Perron's face darkened. "You will not last long. A big gringo like you will die from the heat or the fever. It makes no difference. You will be out of my hair, and should your government come looking for you, I can honestly say I did not kill you." This time he laughed. "At least not directly."

Hank remained silent.

"Have you nothing to say, gringo? Do you not understand it would be better for you if I shot you in the head right now?" Perron breathed heavily for several moments, then smiled again. "Your friends will not find you. I am sending you to the fields east of Havana."

When Hank's face remained blank, Perron went on, obviously hoping for some response. "Havana is almost all the way to the other end of the island, many days' travel. No one will know you there, and, furthermore, no one will care."

Fed up with Hank's stoic countenance, Perron turned and said something to the captain, who, in turn, barked an order to the guard. Hank watched it all play out. The guard raced over and raised the butt of his rifle. Hank's last thought was, *Not in the head again.* Blood poured from his battered head and he collapsed to the floor.

∼

DECEMBER 15, 1865

THE JOLTING of the prison wagon jarred Hank back to consciousness. Pain crashed against the inside of his skull. He winced with each jolt. Slowly he became aware of the incessant buzzing. Besides the jolting and rattling, the buzzing seemed to surround him. His ear tickled and he swatted at it with his big hand, then opened his eyes. He wasn't alone. Men sat on each side of the wagon, their legs bound with chains to steel rings in the floor.

The wagon slammed into another hole, causing his head to bounce against the floor. The buzzing continued. A distant voice spoke in English.

"Come, gringo, you must get up." A hand fastened around his arm and pulled.

Hank responded by drawing his legs up and attempting to stand, but his wobbly legs gave way and he started to fall. He thrust out an arm to catch himself and grabbed a man on the opposite side of the wagon. The man knocked his hand away and spit out something in Spanish, probably a curse.

The man who had spoken to him in English hung on to his other arm and pulled him to the bench beside him.

"Thanks," Hank said. He reached up to feel his new head injury, which was on the opposite side from the old bullet wound, and felt it moving, squirming. He grabbed at what was on his head and looked at his hand. His hand was alive with flies and white squirming maggots. He made a tight fist, killing what flies hadn't escaped and smashing the maggots in his hand. Immediately, he reached up to wipe his wound as clean as he could, and the man grabbed his hand.

"Leave them," he said. "They will eat whatever flesh is dead. The maggots are in the process of saving your life."

Hank stared at his bench mate while jerking his hand away. "Are you crazy?"

"I am a doctor. Listen to me. The maggots are all we have. There is no medicine. Even the guards have little."

Hank shuddered, but managed to keep his hand away from his head though the buzzing didn't decrease.

He was about to ask another question when both he and the alleged doctor were struck in the back with rifle butts.

"*Silencio!*" a guard yelled.

Pain coursed down into Hank's hip like he had been stabbed. He tried to whirl around, but the shackles on his hands and feet hindered his movement, and his head seemed to explode with every jerk. His companion's back was arched while, even seated, he writhed in pain.

Not wanting to again cause such a response from the guards, Hank leaned toward the man and whispered, "Is there anything I can do to help?" The man gave a tiny shake of his head.

As the pain in Hank's back and head dissipated, he worked diligently to keep his hand from his head wound. Hank knew he wasn't the most imaginative man, but he had a vivid picture in his mind concerning what was taking place in his head. He was just thankful there was a skull separating his brain from those ravenous little white worms.

The terrain had changed. While he was unconscious, they had traveled out of the mountains and were moving along a beautiful coast. The water was crystal blue, and the soft waves lapped against snow-white beaches. The inland edge of the beach was lined with palm trees that swayed in unison to the commands of the breezes that blew.

Moving on, there were coves with little kids swimming naked in the water, splashing and laughing as if they had not a care in their world. They grew silent as the prison wagon passed. There was not the usual teasing and laughing one might expect from young boys. These were serious as if they were thinking about relatives who had been taken away on such wagons. But like most young people, they watched only for a short time, then were back to laughing and swimming in the clear blue water.

Hank took the time to look around at those hapless folks who accompanied him in the wagon. The man who had helped him leaned slightly toward him and whispered, "These are all Perron's personal political prisoners, to work until they die on his farms."

Now the stench had permeated his senses. He almost gagged as he looked at each man. Everyone and everything was filthy, clothing, benches, and floor soiled from human waste. He was no exception. He closed his eyes for a moment and the gauzy, out-of-focus picture of the woman appeared in his mind. He could make out she was smiling at him. *I know those eyes,* he thought. *I've known them for a long time.* Then another voice came into his mind, almost as if whoever said it was right next to him. *"Boy, if it ain't killin' you, it's makin' you stronger."*

I know that voice, too. But from where? Who is it? Will I ever get my past back?

∽

DECEMBER 25, 1866

HANK SWUNG the long machete at the base of the cane, making a smooth cut. He moved to the next one and did the same. The doctor was behind him, catching the canes and piling them on the wagon that followed.

The sugarcane went on for what seemed like forever. At least a hundred men worked this field alone. Perron's acreage covered miles. It was harvest time and the dry season. Though it was hot, Hank much preferred the heat to the incessant rain that would start falling in May. Now there was only an occasional cloud that drifted over, but there was no quagmire to wade through, which meant less disease.

There was a shout from one of the guards, and Hank's team stopped. The water wagon pulled up and they flocked to it. Working in this heat, the body shed gallons of water per day. If a man didn't stay hydrated, he would suffer the heat sickness and die within hours. To keep the men working, the guards kept the water wagons moving.

When Hank's turn came, he shoved the dipper deep into the water barrel. As he brought the water to his mouth, he caught a quick reflection of himself. It elicited a wry grin. *Deborah wouldn't recognize me now*. He wore a wide straw hat that protected his head from the sun. His upper body was the color of coffee. The only things the men wore in the fields were hats, three-quarter-length trousers, and sandals, so that portion unprotected by the hat was continually at the mercy of the sun.

His hair fell below his shoulders. There was a wide white streak, originating at his old bullet wound, that flowed down over his right ear. When he arrived in Cuba, he must have weighed close to 200 pounds. He was sure he now weighed no more than 165, maybe 170. But the real shocker was the beard. It flowed to his chest. The long beard and hair helped protect him from the swarms of mosquitoes that moved in at sundown. They were miserable little creatures. Several of the prisoners had gone mad from battling them.

The water guard motioned them away from the wagon. "Get back to work," he shouted in Spanish. Hank smiled to himself. He could understand every word the guard spoke. Pablo, the doctor, had taught him the language over the past year. He had learned a lot even though it had been a difficult time.

He had attempted three escapes. After being captured and dragged back to the farm, each resulted in beatings. He wondered what his back looked like now, having been cut with the whip so many times.

After the third escape attempt, he was thrown into a deep pit and left there to die. That had happened during the rainy season. Although standing, moving, even sleeping in the rain was miserable, it provided him with water and abundant food sources. Besides the bananas, pineapples, and avocados that Pablo and others tossed in surreptitiously, the rain washed in bugs, lizards, and snakes, which he thankfully devoured. When the guards realized he was not dying but gaining weight, since he wasn't working in the fields, they yanked him out of the pit and put him back to hard labor.

Hank swung the machete, taking down another stalk of cane. His mind went over his new plan. He had made friends with one of the teamsters who hauled the cane to the sugar mill. His plan was to hide beneath the cane and, once he was near Havana, leave the wagon and find a United States ship in the harbor to spirit him away. Tonight was going to be the night.

Pablo had tried to talk him out of the escape attempt, for he felt sure Hank would be caught. No matter how dark his skin became, or how good his Spanish, his height would give him away.

Hank continued to cut the cane. *I've got to get back to the States and find out what happened to Mac and the boys.* He swung a vicious cut at the sugarcane, felling three stalks. *And I still need to read a few chapters of the Good Book to First Mate Pitts.*

12

February 2, 1869

HANK WAS TIRED. He was still recuperating from a case of the fever. It had hit him two weeks earlier. When a prisoner contracted this disease, it was one of the few times the guards would allow rest. With most sicknesses, a man had to work through it or die. With the fever, no one could continue to work. It was indiscriminate, striking guard and prisoner alike, and it was debilitating.

He had been working in the field when he first noticed the headache. It was centered right behind his eyes. As it grew, he became sensitive to light, and it felt as if his head would split open right down the center of his nose. He was taken to his bed, and by the time he reached it, he was vomiting up every meal he'd had for a week. Hank wished for the presence of his good friend, Dr. Pablo, but he had died of the fever a year earlier, shortly after one of Hank's failed escape attempts.

Pablo had warned him not to trust the teamster, and he was right. He hadn't even made it off the farm before the guards stripped the sugarcane from the wagon, exposing him. The teamster, his hand being filled with pesos by the camp comandante, watched as the guards tied Hank to the whipping stake and began beating him. If it hadn't been for Pablo, he would have died. It took him weeks to recover from the whipping. His back was like chopped beef, but the guards had him working the next day.

Hank rolled on his side and hung his head off the edge of the bed. He felt like he was going to vomit, but nothing happened. This was the first time in three years he had gotten sick, but this time made up for the many healthy days he had experienced. Fortunately, he was beginning to feel better. He hadn't puked all day, and the intense ache in his joints was subsiding. Many of the locals called the disease the bone-breaking fever. At its worst, it was aptly named.

Snoring filled the darkened barracks-like building he had called home for over three years. He lay still, weak, and thankful his headache was easing off. He saw the outline of a guard entering the room from the door at the far end. The man walked confidently along the center of the long room, passing between the ends of the beds. The shadowy figure slowed as he reached Hank's bed, walked to him, and leaned down into his face.

"Señor Hank, is that you?"

The man spoke in English. He sounded like Maceo, but Hank knew that was impossible. How could Maceo be here? He, with his whole family, was probably dead by now.

"Señor Hank, answer me. It is Maceo."

"Maceo? What . . . what are you doing here?"

"To rescue you, my friend." Maceo held a small bottle to his lips. "Drink this. It will make you appear dead to the guards."

Hank looked at the vial like it was a snake. If this man wasn't Maceo, it could be Perron's devious attempt to kill him. But what if it was Maceo? Could this be his ticket out of prison? Hank grasped the vial and, in one gulp, emptied it. The liquid was slimy and ill tasting—nothing happened. Then his body convulsed and he watched the dark figure of Maceo fade from sight.

HANK AWOKE to a flash of bright sunlight stabbing into his eyes. He knew he was feeling better, because if he hadn't been, his head would have exploded with pain. Still, he turned his head to escape the light, and felt a soft hand caressing his cheek. His eyes slowly came into focus. There was a lovely woman leaning over him, wiping his face with a cool cloth. He looked closer at her. It was Tasha, Maceo's wife.

"Tasha? How did you get here? You shouldn't be here." His body jerked in fear for her safety. "The guards! You must leave now!"

"No, Señor Hank," she said softly. "You are safe. You no longer are in the camp."

He raised himself up on his elbows and looked around the room. "Not in the camp? Then where am I? You must not be found. They will kill you."

Maceo stepped into the room. "I see our guest is awake. I always seem to find you sleeping, my friend. Welcome back."

Hank looked first at Tasha and then at Maceo. Realizing he was no longer in the camp, a weak grin slid across his face. "Hopefully, you won't make me leave this time, *amigo*."

Maceo threw back his head and laughed. "Ah, the gringo still has a sense of humor. He stepped forward and extended his hand to Hank. The two men clasped hands like long-lost brothers and held the grip, staring into each other's eyes.

"It appears you are always saving me," Hank said.

"I believe it is the other way around, my friend. Although I think this might go a little ways toward making us even. Though, truly, I could never repay you for saving our families."

"I will get you something to eat," Tasha said and left the room as Maceo pulled a chair next to Hank's bed.

Maceo looked Hank over from head to toe. Pausing at the hair and beard, then moving down past the narrow waist to the wiry legs.

"Because of us, you have been through much, *hermano,* brother."

"You don't have to translate for me anymore, Maceo," Hank said in Spanish.

"Very good, at least you learned something at the farm."

The two men laughed together, and Maceo continued in Spanish,

"There is a ship leaving Havana tonight for Texas. We have booked passage for you. It is time for you to leave Cuba."

Tasha returned with a bowl of stew. Hank smelled the aromatic contents before she reached him, and immediately began salivating. He pushed himself up in the bed, leaning against the bare wall, and reached out in anticipation. What little meat he had eaten over the past three years had been what he could catch, and most of it raw.

He took the bowl and saw the large pieces of beef floating among the potatoes in the thick tomato sauce. His first spoonful assaulted his taste buds with flavor he had not experienced for years.

"Slowly, my friend," Maceo said, watching Hank shovel the food into his mouth. "You have been sick with the fever. You must take it slowly."

As his friend spoke, Hank felt his stomach roll and it issued a disturbed growl. Nausea flooded over him, and what had tasted so good now rushed to get out of his body. He turned his head quickly to the floor and expelled all that he had eaten.

Tasha ran to the kitchen and in seconds was back with a wet

cloth. She pushed Maceo away and sat on the side of Hank's bed, cleaning his face with the cool cloth. Maceo returned with a bucket and large cloth, knelt, and began cleaning the floor.

"Sorry," Hank said. He looked at his two friends cleaning up the vomit and taking care of him. "You shouldn't have to clean up after me."

Tasha continued to wipe his forehead. "You rest. You have been through much. Your body needs time to heal." She looked up at her husband as he stood from cleaning the floor. "Will he be ready to leave on the ship? It is so soon."

"He must. We can't stay here any longer. We too could be recognized."

Hank looked back and forth between his friends. "I wasn't thinking. Of course, you are in danger. Leave me. I can make it to the ship. You did more than I could ever have hoped for; now it is time to protect yourselves." He looked around for the first time. They were in a solidly built home. It had doors and windows of glass.

"Where are we?"

"Calm yourself, my friend," Maceo said. "We are in the home of a childhood friend. He will never betray us. He has given all of his servants a vacation and has taken his family to Girón for a few days. We have the place to ourselves. And remember, you are dead. No one is looking for you."

Hank relaxed back into the comfortable bed and enjoyed the luxurious feel of his clean body against clean sheets. The thought came to him, *I'm clean.* He lifted the sheet and looked down at his wiry body. Besides being thin, he was naked. He looked up at Tasha.

A tiny grin played across her full lips as she first looked at Hank then across at her husband.

Maceo looked at his wife and laughed. "Even with you so thin, I couldn't handle you by myself, and you were filthy. Plus, you had the stench of death on you from lying with the corpses when we brought you out of the compound. Don't worry, brother, she didn't see anything new."

Hank looked from Maceo back to Tasha, and, though her hand was over her mouth, the grin could be seen in her eyes. She turned and ran from the room. Hank watched her go, then turned back to Maceo. "Well, it sure feels good to be clean."

Maceo laughed again. "Good. Now let's get rid of that horrible beard. We didn't have time to cut it, but Tasha gave it and your hair a good washing. You might be surprised what came out."

Tasha came walking back into the room with scissors, a straight razor, a mug, a brush, and a steaming bowl of water. She set them on the dresser and came back with a small mirror and a towel.

Hank was feeling better. Maybe a little of the food stayed down. Any nourishment was more than he had taken over the past week. He pushed himself up in bed. "I think I can get up and do that myself, if you have anything I can wear."

"Of course," Maceo replied. He walked out of the room and returned minutes later with a complete set of clothes.

Hank eyed the clothing. "That must have cost you plenty. I have nothing to repay you with."

"Don't worry, my friend, both Tasha and I have money. Perron, the dog, may have taken our land, but he hasn't been able to touch our money, and we owe you much more than a set of clothes."

Hank eyed Tasha. "If you'll leave, I'll get dressed."

Tasha laughed and dashed from the room, closing the door behind her.

Hank swung his legs over the side of the bed. They were feeling stronger. Grasping the side of the bed, he pushed up. Maceo stood nearby just in case. Hank found himself steady. The weakness might still be there, but it was dissipating rapidly. He dressed quickly and looked at the boots. His feet had felt only sandals for the past three years. Hopefully, they would readjust to boots quickly.

He slid the boots on. They were almost a perfect fit, as were the clothes.

"How?" he asked Maceo.

"Tasha has a good eye. She did all of the sizing. I take it everything fits?"

He hadn't put the shirt on yet.

"So far, everything is perfect."

"Tasha wants to see you cut that beard." Maceo walked to the door and called his wife. She came back in and stopped, looked at Hank, and clapped.

"I understand I owe you for the choice and fit of these clothes. Thank you."

She nodded and watched him move to the dresser.

His reflection peered out at him from the mirror. It was shocking. The beard hung almost to his navel, and his mouth was nearly invisible under the mustache. He watched the two of them in the mirror. "I know it looks bad, but it sure helped keep the mosquitoes off." Hank picked up the scissors and went to work.

"You might not want to cut it all off," Tasha said as he stropped the razor. "When you shave, the skin beneath the beard stands out white beside the rest of your sun-darkened skin. That could bring attention."

"Thank you," Hank said. "Hadn't thought of that." He went back to work with the scissors, carefully trimming the beard and mustache. When he had finished, his mouth was visible, the long whiskers were gone, and he had a very presentable beard.

"You look very distinguished, Señor Hank. Similar, but better looking than your late President Lincoln," Tasha said.

She helped him cut his hair to where it touched his shirt collar. Then she stood back and examined her work. "I like your hair that way, but even with a hat on, that wide white streak is visible. The only way to get rid of it is to cut your hair very short where it cannot be seen beneath your hat."

"Cut it," Hank said. "I'm gettin' hungry again."

She laughed. "Oh, good. We have plenty for you to eat. But this time we'll take it slower." She continued to look at his hair. Then she snapped her fingers, spun around, and dashed out of the room.

Hank looked at Maceo, who shrugged his shoulders. She returned quickly with a small bottle. "I got this from Olivia's dresser," she said to Maceo.

"Olivia is our friend's wife," Maceo said.

"Yes," Tasha continued, "sometimes, as we get older, it is necessary to cover up a little of the gray. This is something I used to use, but since the jungle, I find I have no desire to cover up. Olivia still uses it." Tasha poured a little of the liquid into her palm, rubbed her hands together, and then rubbed the color into Hank's hair. After a few minutes, the white had disappeared. It was almost impossible to see a difference in color. If anything, the streak was somewhat darker than the rest of his hair.

"That's amazing," Hank said. "I've kinda gotten used to my hair being longer, and I didn't really want to cut it. I like it keeping the mosquitoes off my neck." He turned, grasped Tasha by her biceps, and kissed her on the cheek. "You are truly a miracle worker."

Not noticing she was blushing, he slipped the band-collar ivory shirt on over his head and tucked it into his dark brown trousers. Over the shirt he put the matching dark brown frock coat on, picked up the wide-brimmed, ivory planter's hat and placed it on his head, taking just a moment to adjust it. The hat, along with the shirt, coat, and trousers, was a perfect fit. He turned to his audience and held his arms out from his sides.

Tasha, her eyes twinkling, clapped and said, "It is a good thing Maceo does not beat me, or I would leave him right now. You look like many of the buyers who come here from the States.

Don't look at the girls on the way to the boat or you will be kidnapped by them before you can reach the wharf."

"I guess that tells me," Maceo said, giving his wife what was supposed to be a stern look.

She dashed over, hugged him, and planted a big kiss on his cheek.

"Alright, woman, I guess I'll keep you." Turning back to Hank, Maceo grew serious. "No one will suspect you as anything other than what Tasha said. She's done a great job in outfitting you. Now let's get us something to eat. *I'm* getting hungry." He slapped his wife's ample bottom as she turned to the kitchen.

Hank removed the hat and coat and followed his friends into the kitchen.

The three of them sat at the small table in the kitchen. Tasha had brought bread and filled their bowls with stew. Hank ate slowly, hungry, but not caring to repeat his earlier performance.

He looked at Maceo. "I have many questions. How are Anton and little Liliana, your father Riel, and Rodrigo, Angelita? What is your life like now? Are you still hiding in the mountains? What do you hear about Perron, and how in this world did you find me?"

Tasha answered first, a small frown wrinkling her brow. "Ah, my sweet Angelita. She pined for you for at least a week, then found herself a man she could control with her dark eyes and long eyelashes. She is doing as well as could be expected for one so flighty."

Her furrowed brow disappeared and her lips spread wide in a smile. "Sweet Lily is no longer little. She is growing into a stunning girl, and I thank my Lord she is not like her aunt." Tasha crossed herself. "She is kind and most considerate of others. Thankfully, those years in the jungle taught her humility."

"You should see Anton," Maceo said. "Both he and Lily wanted to come with us to see you, but we thought it safest if they were not involved. He is fifteen and growing into a fine young man. As I look back, I am almost thankful for the jungle time. He learned the importance of hard work to survive, and about helping others. I am proud of both of them."

"Oh, Hank," Tasha said, leaning forward, eyes sparkling with excitement, "we no longer live in the jungle. We have moved back to our homes!"

Hearing they had returned, Hank could hardly contain himself. "Perron allowed you to go back? What about your land?"

This time Maceo responded. "Perron is dead. At his death, a more level-headed officer was placed over the region. He is still a Spaniard." This, Maceo spit out like a bad taste. "But he is a more just man, if such a thing exists in Spain. I think he realizes we Cubans cannot be ruled over as slaves. He offered us peace and our land back. It is not over, for we will not stop until the Spaniard is driven from our land, but for now we have an unsteady peace. It will not last long."

Hank, speaking around a roll he was munching on, asked, "And your father?"

Tasha reached for Maceo's hand and held it. He looked down at the table for a moment, then up at Hank. "He is dead. He was my father, and never a better man have I known. He died killing Perron."

"How did it happen?"

Maceo stood and began pacing around the kitchen. "He was too old for this, but Rodrigo and I were gone on a raid when he received word that Perron was riding into the mountains with a cavalry escort. As you know, he hated Perron. His passion was to personally kill the man for the loss of my mother.

"He took a small group of men from the camp and rode to ambush Perron. To make this story short, he did. They killed many of the soldiers while the remaining Spanish cowards escaped. But Perron was captured unhurt. Then and there, my father, the old man, challenged Perron to a duel. Of course,

Perron was delighted. He chose swords, expecting to cut my father down with the first stroke."

Maceo had stopped his pacing and leaned both hands on the long island that divided the kitchen. The wide-shouldered man stared out a window, watching the puffy-white, wind-driven clouds march by.

———————

13

Maceo took a deep breath, turned his back to the windows, and looked to Hank. "He did not know the man he would face was a master swordsman. Perron was correct, he was stronger than my father, and he could last longer, but he could not finesse a large blade like the saber as my father could. In moments Perron bled from multiple cuts. The men who were there said Perron became a wild man, desperate with the knowledge that he could lose."

Maceo shook his head. "My father no longer had the strength. He played Perron for a moment longer and made his move, driving his blade through the heart of that evil man. With my father close, they say Perron smiled, and slipped his blade into my father's side."

There was silence in the room. Hank thought of the brave little man who had saved him and stood up for him against his son, and who was now dead. He sighed and then said, "You can forever be proud of him. He was not only a brave man, but a good one. It is Cuba's loss."

"Thank you, my friend. He was, and it is. However, he did rid this country of an evil Spaniard who had caused so much pain."

Maceo walked over to a small valise sitting on the counter. He opened it, pulled something out, and walked over to Hank, dropping it on the table. "But my father sent something for you."

Hank picked it up, his eyes wide open with surprise. "It's my belt. My knife and, yes, my derringer. How did you get these?"

Maceo smiled at Hank. "Perron. Evidently, he felt it a prize worth wearing. He was very pleased he had captured you, but I think you have the last laugh. Remember my father when you have it on."

Hank leaned back in the chair. He pulled out the derringer and checked the loads. It was loaded. He slid the knife from its scabbard and checked the edge—sharp and clean. He stood and fastened it around his waist. The belt was too long. He measured a spot, sat back down, and using the point of the Bowie knife, cut out a new hole three inches tighter than the last one. Then he stood, slipped it on, and secured the buckle. It felt reassuring.

He grinned at Maceo. "Guess I lost a little weight, but it sure feels good. I would love to thank your father."

"He knows," Tasha said. "He always liked you, though he never knew what kind of hero you really were."

Hank frowned. "I don't know what you mean."

Maceo continued, "About six months after Perron was killed, the new comandante was appointed. We were allowed to go home, and our property was reinstated. On one of his trips, I had the opportunity to speak with the master of the *Swift*, Ethan Powell. He told me all about you. It is an honor to know a man such as yourself. I have never met an American soldier, so it goes to reason I have never met one who has received the highest honor of your country. I understand more now why you were willing to sacrifice your life to save us. It is in your blood. We hope you can find your family, for I am sure they are amazing people."

Hank was embarrassed. He looked down at Tasha, tears in her eyes. "I just did what anyone would do."

Maceo smiled as he moved back to his seat at the table and with a slight touch of sarcasm said, "Absolutely."

The light from the windows had started to dim. Maceo looked out. "We must prepare to go. Your ship will be leaving at seven this evening. I have a carriage arriving at six. He pulled out his pocket watch. We don't have much time."

He stood and walked to the kitchen island and picked up the valise, bringing it back to the table. "This is yours, my friend. There are three sets of clothes, ammunition for your derringer, and the Colt you took from Perron."

With the last statement Hank looked surprised again. "How did you know?"

"The guard who was in the room with you. He is a friend of one of our employees. We found out the whole story, and you needed another weapon, so we thought this might be appropriate."

Hank shook his head. "You two are wonders. This is too much."

Tasha smiled and simply said, "Never enough."

Maceo continued, "There is powder and ball for the Colt, along with a little money to get you started in the US."

Shadows had deepened in the kitchen. The sounds of horses and a carriage were heard from the street. Shortly a knock sounded on the front door. The three stood. While Maceo and Tasha readied themselves, Hank walked back into the bedroom to check if he was leaving anything. As he looked around the room, there was nothing of material worth, but he realized he was leaving something of exceptional value—experience and friendship.

The three years he had spent in the sugarcane fields had been the most miserable time he could remember in his life. But he had survived. Something had driven him to escape confinement time and again, though his punishment was brutal. Yet he pressed on. The thought that had come to him from someone in his hidden past, "Boy, if it ain't killin' you, it's making you stronger," was right. He was stronger because of everything he had been through. And though he might never see his Cuban friends again, their friendship would last a lifetime.

THE SCHOONER *VENTURE* bumped against the dock as the lines were hauled taut. Hank waited on deck, his lone valise at his feet. The deckhands were securing the schooner to the wharf in Galveston, Texas, and he was about to set foot in the United States. It had taken him over three years to reach this place. Not the short trip that Darcy, Wade, and Mac had predicted.

The past eleven days had provided him with plenty of time to think. The short ride to the wharf in Havana had been uneventful; Maceo had been right. No search was started because all of the guards thought he was dead. It had been difficult to say goodbye to his friends, but it was comforting they were back in their homes.

Initially, it was hard for him to sleep on the ship. The fever had left him, and the fresh salt air, without sugarcane dust, was welcome. But his mind wouldn't relax, as he expected the guards to rush in and grab him the moment he fell asleep. In those awake times, he thought of Deborah. Had she and Dr. James married by now? Each time he thought of her, he remembered a brown curl sneaking out from under her nurse's cap. Her soft, caring eyes gazed at him from a wide, serious face. *Of course she cared. She was a nurse. That's what nurses do.* Unconsciously he shook his head, reached for his valise, and started for the gangplank.

The master of the ship was waiting near the gangplank. "I'm very glad you were able to complete your trip with us, Mr. Remington. As we talked about earlier, your things from the *Swift* are in our office. When you disembark, go straight across the wharf and take a right; that will put you on Strand Street. You'll travel one block, and our office is on the northeast corner." The man extended his hand. "Welcome back to civilization, if you can call Texas civilized."

"Thanks, Captain. Safe sailing." They shook hands and Hank strode off the ship. He made a quick halt to allow a horse-drawn cart to roll in front of him. Once it passed, he took two more steps and stopped again. Two men were rolling barrels of sugar toward a warehouse. Once they cleared, he continued to Strand and turned right. Immediately, he could see the shipping office sign displayed in front of a two-story building.

As he took in the busy street, people were moving in all directions. Some were stopping to talk and others tipped their hats to the ladies. As Hank continued, several men nodded to him and said, "Howdy." He acknowledged them, enjoying the soft Texas drawl. Reaching the office, he pushed open the door and left the activity outside. There was only a single man in the office, bent over his desk, scribbling on a stack of papers. He looked up as Hank approached the counter dividing the office space from the room that contained several deep leather chairs, some with footstools. *Perhaps this is used as a waiting area for passengers embarking on their ships.*

"Howdy, mister. What can I do for you?" The man rose from his desk and moved to the counter.

"Well, sir, my name is Hank Remington. I understand you have some things stored here for me."

The clerk, not a small man, cast a skeptical look at him. "And how would you know that?"

"Captain Giles of the *Venture* told me," Hank said, his voice hardening.

"Do you have your ticket?"

Hank pulled the paper he had been given at boarding from his inside coat pocket and handed it to the man.

"Name's Rockland Mace," the man said as he looked at the

ticket. He still eyed Hank suspiciously, but continued to question him as he walked to a small storeroom. Reaching the door, he turned and said, "Can you tell me what some of your possessions are?" Mace entered the room and brought out two dusty bags, one larger than the other, but no Henry.

"The first thing I can tell you is that I had a fine Henry you could drive tacks with at a hundred yards, and I don't see it now."

Mace bridled slightly. "We don't steal our passenger's things, Mr. Remington." He stepped back into the room and came out with a clean and shiny Henry. "Might this be it?"

Hank broke into a grin. "Yes, sir. That is her." He reached across the counter and took the rifle and flipped it to his shoulder. His cheek rested comfortably against the stock, the front and rear sight lining up perfectly on one of the deer heads hanging in the office.

Mace's voice had lost its doubt. "Can you tell me a few items in your bags?"

"I can. There should be three Remington .44s with powder and ball. If I remember correctly, there's a couple of Union pants and several shirts with two blouses, the stripes removed. Also, there's two boxes of Henry .44s and a box of .41-caliber cartridges for a derringer."

"Yes, sir, Mr. Remington, I reckon these are yours. I'll tell you, sir, I never expected you to be picking these things up after you disappeared off the *Swift* in '65."

"Mr. Mace, there were plenty of times when I didn't expect to be here myself."

The man looked up at Hank. "Call me Rocky."

"Rocky, I'll do that, and my friends call me Hank. Now tell me how you came to have my gear."

"First, Hank, I have an inventory of your things." He handed Hank a list, then turned and moved to the open safe. He had to squat down in front of the safe and reach back into the recesses of the bottom shelf. He felt around and finally pulled out a leather bag. It was obviously heavy and clinked when he dropped it on the counter. "This was in the larger bag. The amount is on the inventory. You may feel free to count it."

Hank glanced at the amount, hefted it a couple of times, and shook his head. "Don't need to. Rocky, do you mind if I leave these things here with you until I get a horse and supplies? I'll have it out today."

Rocky moved over to the counter and leaned on it, one hand resting against the counter and one leg crossed. "Shoot, it's been here for over three years. I don't reckon a few more hours will matter. You interested in hearing the story?"

Hank had been putting the leather bag in his valise. He looked up, set the valise on the counter, and said, "There's a story? I think I'd like to hear it."

"Well," Rocky said, a smile creasing his face, "I never like to tell a story without something to smooth its tellin'. Care for a drink?"

Hank laughed and shook his head. "Rocky, I can't tell you why, but I have an aversion to spirits, but I'd sure go for some water."

"I can take care of you."

Rocky pulled two glasses out from under the counter. He walked over to a bucket sitting on a small stand. With the dipper he took from a hook on the wall, he dipped up a glassful of water. When he returned, he slid the glass of water across the counter to Hank, then pulled a bottle from beneath the counter and poured about an inch of the amber-colored liquid into his glass. He held the glass at eye level, set it down again, and grinned at Hank. "This might be a long story," and he poured another inch, corked the bottle, and returned it to the shelf beneath the counter.

Hank followed the clerk to where two chairs were angling toward each other with a footstool in the middle. "Sit," Rocky said.

They sat in the deep leather chairs and stretched their legs out on the footstool. Rocky took a sip of his drink, cleared his throat, and began his story.

"I have to admit, I couldn't believe it when Master Ethan Powell, one of the company's best captains, comes in with Pitts and three other men in tow, guarded by several of his crew." He took another sip.

"Seems Master Powell caught Pitts going through your gear after you had been lost at sea." Rocky took another sip and winked at Hank. "I'll tell you right now, I ain't never believed you fell overboard. That's what Pitts was selling, but there weren't anyone buying."

Hank shook his head. "Pitts and some of his men jumped me. Hit me in the head and I was tossed overboard. I don't know how far we were from Cuba, but I'd guess a long way, because I swam all night and into the morning, finally reaching shore."

"You must've been mighty lucky. I sailed myself for a few years, and that east coast of Cuba is treacherous, all rocky and rough."

"I was. Found a little strip of beach, but go ahead with your story."

Rocky had just slugged down half of the remaining liquor. "So Pitts and one of his men were carrying your gear. He slammed it down on the counter and turned back to Master Powell. Looked like he wanted to punch him, but the Colt in the master's hand dissuaded him mighty strong. Master Powell told Pitts and the men with him they were fired as of right then, and they would have to find their own way back to Baltimore.

"The master turned to me and said to pay them twenty days' pay. I did and he signed the receipt. Pitts looked like he was going to explode. He said, 'You can't do this.' The master just looked at him and continued to fill out the paperwork. When he finished, he turned back to Pitts and his men and, in that cold, soft voice of his, said, 'If I ever find you on a company ship or in a company office again, I'll have you keelhauled and hanged.' With that he motioned Pitts and his boys out of the office."

Rocky turned his glass up and drained it. Then he ran his index finger around the inside of the glass, licked his finger, and stood. "I'd best be gettin' back to work. I'd love to hear what happened to you, but I've got a feelin' you're not much of a talker." He turned back to the counter, walked through the gap, and lowered the counter divider. "Your stuff is fine here. Just stop by when you're ready."

"One more question," Hank said. "Have you seen Pitts around?"

Rocky glanced up at the blue eyes that appeared hard as ice. "You don't want to mess with him; he's a brawler. He'll outweigh you by forty pounds." He stopped, thought a minute then said, "But not my business. I saw him for a few days after that, but he and his bunch disappeared a few days later, probably hired on with another company."

"Thanks. Is there a stable around here and a mercantile? I need a couple of horses and some clothes."

"Yep, best livery in town is up this street." He waved his arm, indicating the street that ran into Strand. "Couple of blocks west of that is the Wilson Mercantile, mighty fine folks." Abruptly he sat back down at his desk and shuffled papers, found what he was looking for, and started writing.

"Much obliged," Hank said. He picked up his valise, went out the door, and took a left. His long stride took him quickly up the boardwalk. The northwest wind, which had the flags standing straight, chilled Hank's face. It at once felt good and also strange, tingling the skin now exposed to the wind. While on the ship he had finished shaving the remainder of his beard and mustache. He didn't know why, but now that he didn't need the protection, he no longer wanted the facial hair. There had been a barber on shipboard, and Hank had gotten the man to remove his long hair and trim the rest. The scar was almost hidden by the surrounding white hair, giving him a stripe of white several inches long. He laughed to himself. *Why do I care? I don't have to look at it.*

Reaching the corner, he turned left at the two-story building. It was the livery. The familiar smell had reached him when he had stepped out of the ship company's office. Now it was much stronger. The man's land took up all of the block. The livery doors opened at this corner and were at least two wagons wide. When he came around the corner, he could hear the voice of a man cussing and a woman talking.

14

On the east side, the livery had a gate that opened from the stable into a corral. The man was standing just inside the gate, shaking his fist at a buckskin that had the man fixed in its stare. The woman was trying to get a look at his wrist while the man shook it and cussed at the buckskin.

"Hello," Hank said as he walked into the stable.

Both the man and woman turned around to see a well-dressed tall, slim, city gentleman in a town suit and an unusual hat. The man looked down at the blood dripping from his wrist, back up at Hank, and said, "How much I need to pay you, mister, to take this buckskin devil off my hands? This is the second time he's tried to bite me. Why, he kicked my stable hand halfway across the corral the other day."

Hank studied the big horse that appeared to also be studying him. "I don't know. Why don't I take a look at him?" Hank walked up to the gate and set his valise on the straw-covered floor, continuing to look over the horse.

When the man realized Hank might be serious, he said, "Name's Les, and this here is my wife, Nellie."

Hank pulled his gaze from the buckskin and turned to the

couple. "Hello." He tipped his hat to the lady. "I'm Hank." He looked down at the man's wrist. "Looks like you need some doctoring. That looks bad. You don't want it to get infected."

Les shook his head and pulled out a rag that had seen cleaner days, and wrapped it around his wrist. "Pshaw, this ain't bad. Why, that horse only nipped me when I surprised him. He's actually pretty even tempered."

Hank nodded. "Really? I don't think that's what I was hearing a few minutes ago."

Les cleared his throat and gave Nellie a harsh look when she placed her hand over her mouth and, giggling, ran to a rocking chair on the deck in front of the office. Once seated, she moved the chair around so she could watch the two men and the horse, picked up some leather, and started working.

Hank grasped the top rail of the gate and vaulted himself over, landing lightly on the opposite side.

"Careful, mister. Don't make no sudden moves. That horse has been known to bite when a person moves too quick."

Keeping his eyes on the buckskin, Hank said, "So I noticed." He started talking in low tones to the animal, which stood at least seventeen hands. Every ounce of that horseflesh was focused on Hank, who was speaking softly to it, then started singing some lullaby that someone must have sung to him years earlier, for he had no conscience memory of it. "As Jack the jolly plowboy was plowing through his land . . . He turn'd his share and shouted to bid his horses stand." The buckskin gazed at Hank and stretched his neck out toward him.

"Look out, mister," Les yelled. "He'll nail ya!"

Hank just shook his head and reached out for the big horse. He rubbed him gently on his tan cheek, moved the black mane out of the way, and started rubbing his neck. "Then down beside his team he sat, contented as a king . . . And Jack he sang his song so sweet he made the mountains ring."

Sitting on the porch in her rocker, Nellie joined in. "'Tis said old England's sailors, when wintry tempests roar, will plow the stormy waters, and pray for them on shore. But through the angry winter, the share, the share for me, to drive a steady furrow, and pray for those at sea."

The horse had turned his head to follow what the strange man was doing, but had an ear turned to Nellie. Hank gently pulled up the front hoof and examined it. He had noticed scarring on the horse's head, in front of and between his ears. Someone had beaten him with something heavy, a club probably. There were whip cuts across the horse's withers. He let his hand slide along his back and croup, then down his hip and leg; pulling the rear leg up, he checked the hoof. He let it down carefully, all the while talking softly to the animal.

Hank slid his hand back up to the buckskin's croup and walked close behind, moving to the other side. He heard Les say to Nellie, "Can you believe that? He ain't been bit or kicked."

He now moved up the right side, still softly talking to the buckskin. After completing his exam, he patted the horse on the cheek while maintaining direct eye contact and singing the song again. He turned to step away and the horse gave a soft whinny. He looked up at Les. "You have any apples?"

"Yeah, just a second." Les trotted up the steps and into the office, quickly returning with an apple. He tossed it to Hank and said, "That was going to be my lunch."

Hank could hear Nellie snort, trying to hold back her laughter. He broke the apple in half, turned back to the buckskin, and offered the half in his hand, palm flat.

The buckskin stretched his neck, pulled his lips back, and gently picked up the apple with his teeth. He crunched the half quickly and nudged Hank, who brought out the second half and gave it to him. Once the horse was finished, Hank walked back to the gate, again placed his hands on the top bar and leaped over.

Les looked him up and down. "You're mighty spry for a man your age."

"Yes," Nellie said, "and it's a fine Irish lullaby you were a-singing. Are you an entertainer?"

Hank grinned at the lady. "No, ma'am, farthest from it. It just kinda showed up at my mouth and I let it out." He turned back to Les. "Now let's talk about that horse. He looks to be carrying quite a few scars. I'd say some lowlife treated him mighty unkind."

"Yep," Les said, "I reckon you're right. But he seems to take to you. He's big and the man I bought him from said he's a stayer, so I'm thinkin' he'd make you a fine steed."

"I'd have a lot of work to do on him." Hank looked up into the rafters of the barn and stable, as if he was calculating. Then, a studied look on his face, he said, "Tell you what. Since you can't do anything with him, and he's already bitten you at least once—"

Les held up his hand, palm toward Hank. "Now just wait, mister. That there is a fine piece of horseflesh that'll carry a man your size all day long. I think—"

"No, you wait. You have already offered to pay me to take him off your hands. I'm just trying to figure out what would be fair. I'm thinkin' I could take him for thirty dollars if you'd throw in the tack."

"I pay you *thirty dollars* and throw in the tack? Mister, are you just plain loco?"

"Now, Les, you told me you would pay me to take him off your hands. Am I right?"

"Well . . ."

"Am I?"

"I reckon I said that, but I was just funnin' you. You don't expect me to give you money to take one of my horses, do you? I make my living buying and selling horses. I've got to take care of my sweet Nellie girl."

"Humph," Hank heard from the porch.

Les's face turned pinker. His plump rosy cheeks glowed, but there was no smile on his face.

Hank looked over at Nellie, a long needle in her hand, as she sewed the leather. It got his attention and he walked over to the edge of the porch. There on the porch rail lay several holsters, at least they looked like holsters, but they were mighty skimpy looking . . . especially when compared with his regulation Army holster that fully contained his Remington and held it in place with a large flap that went over the top and fastened on the side.

"Ma'am, are those holsters for sidearms?"

She picked one up and handed it to him. "Yes, they are. Take out your revolver and slide it into this one. You'll see how easy it comes out."

Hank unfastened the top of his holster and pulled the big Remington out, the flap dragging against the weapon. Then he slid it into the smaller holster. Holding the holster in his left hand and the Remington in his right, he slipped it in and out several times.

"That's mighty slick, but how do you keep it from falling out?"

Nellie picked up a loop of leather and held it out to him. "I haven't finished these, but that loop is sewn onto the front of the holster, and then you just slip it over the revolver's hammer, locked in tight."

He checked the simplicity of the loop. "Ma'am, that's awful slick. Are you selling them?"

"I sure am. They're eight bucks a piece, but if you'll give me that Army holster you have there, I'll knock off three dollars."

"I've got another holster like this I'll give you and take two of yours, if you've a mind to."

"That'll be fine. You planning on wearing two of them hoglegs?"

"Yes, ma'am. Gives a man more firepower."

"You want both butts to the rear, forward, or one each."

Hank laughed. "Now you're gettin' way too fancy for me. Both with the butts to the rear. That way I won't get mixed up and drop one. When can I get 'em?"

"I've got to fasten the loops on. I think I've got a left-handed one in the office. If I do, I'll have 'em ready probably by the time you finish dickering with my husband."

Hank tipped his hat and said, "Thank you." He turned back to Les. "Have you thought about my offer?"

"Are you planning on buying anything else?"

"I am. I need another good horse that'll take to carrying a pack as well as a man, plus a pack saddle, something soft if you've got it. I won't be carrying a big load."

Les pointed out a small bay gelding in the back of the corral. "See that little bay? He's small, but he'll carry a pack or a man and do it all day long."

From the stable, Hank looked the horse over. "Seems a bit small."

"Like I said, don't let his size fool you. I've had that horse for three years. I wouldn't sell him, but he's a little spirited. Too much for some of these townsfolk. Maybe a fine feller like you could handle him."

"So let me see. You're trying to get rid of a biter and a bucker on a stranger who may never come back. Have I got that right?"

"Mister," Les said, stepping close enough to Hank he had to crane his head back to look him in the eye, "I ain't never cheated no man. I'm known for getting a good deal, but I ain't no cheat, and if'n you're suggesting I am, I don't care how tall you are, we're goin' to fist city."

Nellie had stopped sewing and was watching her husband with concern.

"Then, Les . . . I can call you Les?"

The shorter man gave a curt nod, still looking up at Hank.

"Then, Les, why don't you make me a deal and stop dickering. I've got miles to cover."

Les stepped back, took a deep breath, and said, "With the tack, the two horses, I reckon you want some oats or corn to take with you?"

Hank nodded.

Les pulled a small tablet and a stub of a pencil from his jacket pocket and started figuring. He worked slowly while Hank looked the stable over. It was well kept. All of the animals looked fed and brushed. Even the hay was pulled out of the way in the double stall near the entrance.

Les stopped figuring, stuffed the pencil behind his ear, and shoved the tablet back in his pocket. "I reckon I can let you have the oats, tack, including a saddle for you and a pack saddle for the bay, and you understand this is the best deal you'll get in Galveston, and the best horses, for $280." He dusted his hands off as if he was finished, crossed his arms, and looked up at Hank.

That's actually not bad. I remember the prices in Washington three years ago were much higher. He rubbed his chin as if in thought. "Les, that's a pretty good price. It's a little steep, but I reckon you've got to make money. I'll tell you what, toss in a pair of *good* saddlebags and a rifle scabbard and you've got yourself a deal."

Les stuck out his hand. "Deal. When do you need them?"

"This afternoon. I still have to get supplies. I do have a question and a request. If you don't mind my asking, would you have fought me if I'd said you were cheating me?"

Les looked up at Hank, taking off his bowler hat. "Yes, sir, I surely would've. Nobody calls me a cheater without backing it up."

Hank grinned and stuck out his hand. "At the end of the day, our good reputation is all we have. Without it, we're nothing. You're a good man."

The two men shook hands and Les looked back up at Hank. "You said you had a request?"

Hank pulled a leather bag from his inside coat pocket.

"Put it away," Les said. "You can pay me when you pick up the horses."

Hank dropped the bag back into the breast pocket of his coat. "Fine. Yes, I have a trunk and small bag over at Mason Brothers'

Shipping Company office. If you wouldn't mind sending someone with a wagon to pick those up and bring them here, that will save me some time."

"Glad to. I'll have everything ready when you get back, except saddling the buckskin. I ain't touchin' that horse."

Hank grinned, tipped his hat to Nellie, and said, "That's fine. I'll take care of him when I get back. He turned and walked from the livery.

The wind had changed while he was in the livery, and now it was blowing strong out of the northwest. He watched a huge wedge of geese fly over, coming in from the Gulf, where they had probably been sunning. The sun was gone, hidden behind scurrying clouds headed south.

The frock coat was small protection in this wind and cold. Cuba had been nothing like this. Sometimes, in the winter, it had gotten cold, but nothing in comparison. He shivered and, hanging onto his hat, strode down the street toward the mercantile sign. Stepping inside was a welcome relief from the chilly wind.

"Come in out of the cold," a female voice called from behind a row of dry goods. She stepped out from behind the clothing, a shapely full-figured blonde. A gold band glistened on her left hand.

"Welcome. Looks like y'all are just ahead of the blue norther that's blowing in." Indicating the frock coat Hank was wearing, she continued, "You'll be needing more substantial clothes than that or you'll just freeze to death. Now you come on over here, and let's see if we can fix you right up. You can call me Myrtle, and what's your name?"

"Myrtle." Hank took his hat off. "My name's Hank. I'm heading west to find my friends, then north with a cattle herd, so whatever I need, I'd appreciate your help."

"Well, Hank," she said, "you certainly picked the worst time of year to be riding out in this country. I lived in Austin until I married my Ben. In the wintertime it got colder than a banker's heart when a norther blew through. I'm mighty glad to be down here, 'ceptin' for the bodacious storms that can come through."

Hank stood there waiting for her to stop talking. He figured he must be the first person in today, and her Ben didn't do much talking.

"Whew, my Ben says sometimes I get carried away and talk too much. I'm sorry. Now let's get you fixed up. First thing, you need to get rid of that flimsy hat. It's nice, but it won't take Texas weather. You need something substantial. Last year we got some new hats by a maker up in Philadelphia. I usually wouldn't give you a plugged nickel for anything from a Yankee, but I have to admit, this is about the finest hat I've seen. It's called a Stetson."

She looked at his head, shuffled through the stack of hats, and finally handed him one. They all looked the same to Hank— made from sturdy felt, they had a tall crown and a four-inch brim, with a hatband around the base of the crown.

Hank tried the hat on. It felt good. The air trapped in the crown above his head immediately warmed his head, and it was lighter than he expected.

"The brim will keep the rain off, and I'm hearing that during the summer, the space between your head and the top of the hat keeps your head cooler."

"I'll take it."

She set it on the counter and moved over to the chaps. "You'll definitely need chaps if you're headed west. The cactus in that country will slice you up like a tender steak."

By the time his shopping was over, there was a new pair of high-heeled boots on his feet and a stack of clothes on the counter. There was a room in the back for changing clothes. First, he'd slipped on a new pair of scratchy wool long johns. Then the wool shirt, pants, socks, and boots. The boots felt similar to his cavalry boots. At least something was familiar.

Hank had made a list of supplies he needed and gave that to

Myrtle. "If you could put these together for me, and add anything you think I might need, I'd sure appreciate it. I'm going to step across the street for a bite to eat. I'll be back to pick everything up when I'm done."

Myrtle scanned the list and looked up at Hank. "It'll be ready for you."

"Thank you, Myrtle. I appreciate your help." He again took the small leather bag from his frock coat that he had slipped back on over his shirt and vest.

"No need for that now. We'll settle up when you come back."

Hank donned his new Stetson and pushed open the door. The wind tried to yank the hat from his head, but he grabbed it in time, pulled it tight over his head, and headed across the street to the Galveston Saloon and Eatery.

15

Hank was hungry for food and information. The days at sea had allowed his body to heal from the assault of the fever. He felt strong and free. The Galveston Saloon and Eatery was built with a separating wall between the café and saloon, ostensibly to keep the rowdies from disturbing the café's patrons. Unfortunately, the wall was so thin it did little to reduce the saloon side's noise. For Hank, he didn't care; it was still morning and only the most diehard drinkers were in the saloon.

He stepped through the door, holding tight to the latch to prevent the door from slamming in the wind.

"Much obliged, mister," the bartender called. "I've had more glass broken from these northers than you'd care to hear about. Shoulda built on the north side of the street. Too late now." The man went back to wiping glasses and stacking them on the back counter of the bar. "What ya drinkin'?"

"Not drinking, eating," Hank said. "Any chance of getting some breakfast?"

"Sure thing. You can light yourself in here or over there." The man pointed a glass at the entrance into the other room. "That's the café, but they'll feed you on either side."

Hank walked up to the bar, leaned, and looked around. "Who do I tell?"

"Daphne!" the bartender shouted toward the back of the other room. "You've got a customer over here."

"You don't have to yell," was yelled back at the man. Moments later a woman looking to be in her forties swung a half door open from the back of the café. Gray had taken over her hair, and eating her own food had taken over her waistline. She marched up to Hank and looked him up and down. "They grow 'em big where you're from, cowboy."

Hank grinned at the woman. "I guess they do, wherever that is."

She shot him a puzzled look. "What can I do for you?"

"How about some breakfast?"

"You eatin' in here?"

"Yes, ma'am."

She laughed. "A man with manners. Your type's hard to find on this side of the wall. You look like about six eggs, a side of beef, and some biscuits would do you good. You need to put some more meat on those bones."

"Yep, I agree with that. Sounds great. You have any milk back there?"

"Call me Daphne, and we danged shore do. I'll bring you a glass. Coffee?"

"No, thanks."

The woman nodded, spun around, and headed for the kitchen. Hank turned back to the bartender. "You know much about this country?"

The bartender nodded. "Been in Texas nigh on thirty years. I've rode over most of it, and what I haven't seen I've heard about. What do you need?"

"I need directions to Refugio. I've got some friends out that way."

"That'll be a long cold ride in this weather. You might wait a few days till this front gets on through and we start warmin' up."

Hank shook his head. "Can you tell me how to get there?"

"Why, I've been down that way so many times, I could find it with my eyes closed, but you want to be careful, that's a mighty rough town."

The kitchen door swung open, and Daphne hurried back carrying a pitcher of milk, a glass, and a big plate. She set it down on a table and said, "Here you go, cowboy."

Hank walked to the table. The aroma of the biscuits, a huge T-bone, and eggs had his mouth watering before he could sit. "Thank you, ma'am."

It had been Washington where he had eaten his last steak. He sliced a piece from the thick chunk of meat and stuck it in his mouth. Juices flowed. By the time Daphne returned with butter and jelly, which was only as long as it took her to go to the kitchen and back, half of the eggs and a good portion of the steak had disappeared.

"Goodness," she said, "you must be hungry."

Without looking up, Hank nodded and sliced another piece of steak, chasing it with fresh milk. In minutes the meat and eggs had disappeared and a good portion of the biscuits. He slathered some fresh-churned butter on a biscuit and covered it with dark purple jelly. Shoving the biscuit in his mouth, he recognized the taste of blackberries. After finishing off several more biscuits, he lifted the glass of milk to his mouth and tilted it up, draining the glass.

Two men walked into the saloon as he was drinking the milk. They stared at him, then turned to the bar. One was big, the other smaller. The smaller had scattered chin hair with tobacco juice dribbled down his chin into the hairs. Hank ignored them and refilled the glass with milk from the pitcher.

"Gimme a beer," the big man said, then turned to Hank. He let out a short bark of a laugh. "Nice mustache you got there, feller."

The saloon was empty except for a couple of drunks sleeping it off at different tables, and the man was looking directly at Hank.

He reached up and wiped his upper lip, his hand coming away with the milk residue that had been on his lip. He grinned at the guy. "The milk was worth it." He reached over and started buttering another biscuit.

Hank had immediately recognized the man's swagger when he came into the bar, probably the town bully. He didn't like the type, but didn't feel like taking it any further. He wanted to get on the trail and find his friends and partners.

The town bully guzzled his beer and slammed the mug down on the bar. "Phil, gimme another one." The bartender, Phil, poured another beer for the man and, while placing the mug on the bar, said, "Best take it easy, Harley." Without waiting for an answer, he went back to cleaning glasses.

"Phil, you know what I heard?"

Phil continued to wipe the glass while shaking his head.

"I heard some idgit bought that worthless renegade buckskin I sold to Les last year. Now is that a hoot or what? Who'd want a piece of trashy horseflesh like that?"

Keep your temper, Hank thought. *You don't know this guy and you'll be leaving shortly. Although, a man who would beat a horse like that buckskin was beaten needs to be horsewhipped himself.*

"I also heard it was some tall feller who just got off that ship what pulled in this morning." The man, still holding his partially full mug, turned to look at Hank. "Could that man be you, mister?"

Hank could feel himself starting to burn. He didn't want to hurt this thug although it would be a pleasure to give him some of what he gave to the buckskin.

"I am," Hank said in a pleasant manner. "And you must be the low-down skunk who beats good horses."

Harley's eyes bugged out, his face flushed, and he slammed the mug on the bar, beer splashing everywhere, including on the bartender. Phil reached beneath the counter and pulled out a Greener, shoved the double barrel across the bar, and poked the bully in the chest with it. "You'll not be starting anything in here, Harley. You pay up, then take Juice with you and get out. I don't want to see you back until you can act like a gentleman."

His fists balled, Harley started to say something, but Phil shoved him in the chest with the Greener again. "Harley, do you wanna make me mad?"

Juice grabbed Harley's arm. "Come . . . come on, Harley," he whined in a nasal voice. "You know what happens when Harley gets mad. We don't want someone cleaning our blood off this floor."

Harley pointed at Hank. "This ain't over, stranger. You'd best leave town or I'll break every bone in your sorry body. I'd do it now if it weren't for Phil. Nobody, and I mean nobody, calls Harley Pine a skunk."

Hank sopped up the remaining egg on his plate with a piece of biscuit, then casually looked up. "Harley, you look like a skunk, walk like a skunk, and smell like a skunk. That must mean you're a skunk. I *am* leaving town soon. I'll be going to the livery to pick up my horses, including that fine buckskin you beat, and then I'm going to the mercantile. If you want an opportunity to break my bones, you'd best act fast."

Harley the bully was seething, but the bartender and the Greener had persuaded him this was not the time. He pointed at Hank, spit on the floor, and stomped for the door, allowing the wind to take it and slam it so hard the glass rattled.

Phil shook his head. "That hothead's going to break my glass yet." He slipped the shotgun back under the bar. "The downside of running a public establishment is that you have to deal with the public." He looked over at Hank finishing his milk. "But you meet some mighty fine folks, too. Thanks for not breaking up my saloon. It's happened before, and I know it'll happen again, but thankfully not today."

Hank nodded to Phil. He turned to see Daphne standing in the kitchen doorway. She walked to his table and reached for his plate.

"Anything else?"

"Ma'am, I can truthfully say that was the best meal I've eaten in years."

She laughed and then said, "You must not get around much. I've got some pie back there; if you'd like a piece, it's on the house. You'll need your strength 'cause you're gonna have to fight Harley before you leave."

Hank took out five dollars and tossed it on the table. "Will that cover it?"

Daphne nodded. "Way more than cover it. Let me get your change."

"No change, I've enjoyed your food and your conversation. You have a fine day."

Hank rose and put on his hat. Passing Phil, he nodded to him. "Thanks, Phil. I appreciate not getting my breakfast interrupted."

"My pleasure. But you know you'll have to fight him."

Hank grinned at Phil. "I'm looking forward to it."

Hank pushed the door open and saw Phil lean over to Daphne, who had followed him over to the bar. He could just barely understand Phil when he spoke to Daphne, his voice lowered. "You know, there's something about that feller. I almost feel sorry for Harley."

Hank looked in both directions. Harley and Juice were standing at the next block. They watched him for a moment then retreated around the corner. He crossed the street and headed toward the stable. Walking in, he saw a wagon still hitched with his bags in the back. Les had both horses tied in stalls. The packs were sitting open on the ground next to the bay while the buckskin stood placidly eating corn from the bin.

"I don't know what's going on, but he let me lead him in and tie him in the stall, never once tried to bite me. Oh, the office manager gave me this letter when I picked up your bags." Les handed him the envelope.

Hank opened it and was thrilled to see it was from Darcy. They had arrived all right. And after seeing Pitts run off, they'd left his things and headed for Refugio.

He continued to read, and in his letter, Darcy had left directions. He also said they had taken $600 from his savings, knowing he wanted to buy cattle. When he got there, they would return the money or his part of the herd, whichever he wanted. The note also said they knew he would come.

Good. I'm glad they took the money. With what they left and the money Maceo and Tasha put in the bag, I have no money worries. He looked at the second page of the letter, and it was a map to go along with the directions. He'd continue west down the island to San Luis Pass. There, a family by the name of Follett ran a ferry that would take him across the narrow pass to the mainland. That would save him a lot of time. Riding north off the island and then turning west would add almost two days.

He dropped the gate of the wagon, pulled the trunk toward him, picked it up, and moved it beside the packs. He patted the bay for a moment, then moved over to the buckskin, rubbing his back and talking to him. Then he moved up in front of him, petting the big horse and making sure the animal knew he meant him no harm. The scars on the horse's head infuriated him. Hank massaged a couple of the scars. The buckskin's eyes drifted half shut.

Finally, deciding it was time, Hank moved back to the saddle blanket. He picked it up, showed the horse, then brushed his hand over its back, making sure there was no debris there. He laid the blanket across and smoothed it, no reaction. He picked up the saddle and lifted it gently onto the animal's back, reached under, and tightened both cinches. Then he turned and walked off. He'd let the buckskin think about the saddle.

He reached down to open the trunk.

Les, a warning tone in his voice, said softly, "Hank."

He rose and turned around. There stood Harley and Juice with two more hangers-on, each looking just as scruffy as Juice.

Les reached for the revolver resting on his hip in one of Nellie's holsters.

Hank stuck out his hand and said, "No, Les, I've got this."

"Hank, there's four of them."

"There's four bodies," Hank said, "not fighters. This won't take long."

Hank remembered the fights he'd had at the farm when he first arrived. They were brutal. It wasn't about just winning; it was about surviving. The comandante wanted him dead, and if he couldn't have him shot, he'd have him beaten to death by the other workers.

The first encounter was with one big Cuban. Hank didn't know where he had learned his moves, but they came automatically, and he beat the man down within ten minutes. The next time, three jumped him. That took longer, and he had a broken rib from that encounter. It continued for months. He never lost. He couldn't. If he had lost, he would be dead. But occasionally he was hurt, and the guards still made him work. They finally tapered off. The last year, there was no fighting. But maybe that was because Perron was dead.

He had learned much from the many fights, and now these skunks had an idea they'd take him down. He took off his frock coat and hat, handing them to Les.

Then he walked out to the four who stood in the street just outside the doors to the stable. He knew men like Harley and his crew liked to talk, to build up their courage while creating fear in their victim. He didn't slow down.

Harley was standing in the center with the two new men standing on his right side and Juice standing to his left. They had unconsciously formed an arc, placing the two closer than Harley and Juice. Hank was walking a straight line toward Harley. When he was almost even with the one nearest Harley, he spun, driving the heel of his boot deep into the soft belly of Harley's cohort. The wind leaving the man's lungs sounded like an explosion, and he doubled over for a moment, then, still curled, fell to the ground.

The remaining three men stood with their mouths hanging open, watching their partner squirm on the ground, trying to coax air into his deflated lungs. Hank swung back from the kick and drove a smashing left into the jaw of the man nearest Harley. The few spectators who were out in the cold heard the jawbone snap as the man let out a gurgling scream. Holding his jaw, he tried to stagger away, but with his focus only on his broken jaw, he didn't see the wagon tongue lying in front of him. He tripped, falling on his face, and, still holding his jaw, lay moaning.

Hank reached Harley, who took a step back, his face reflecting his concern that he might have picked on the wrong man. He was the big dog in Galveston. Folks in town gave him a wide berth. When he stepped back, unfortunately for Juice, he was left as the nearest target. He looked around, saw he was in danger of being hurt like his friends, spun around, and ran as hard as he could, leaving little puffs of dust in the street to blow away quickly in the wind.

Panic in his eyes, Harley drew back his right fist in preparation to smash it into Hank. But Hank continued his steady walk toward him. The long arms of the stranger reached out and clamped on the wrist of the bully. Hank stepped a little past Harley, taking his wrist with him. Now Harley's arm was stretched slightly behind him. As Hank's shoulder was going under Harley's arm, he straightened up fast and pulled the back of Harley's elbow past his shoulder. With minimal effort, he pulled down, placing strain on the tendons that held the arm in the shoulder socket. It made an audible pop simultaneous with Harley's scream. Hank dropped the arm, which now hung limp at Harley's side.

Harley was bellowing with pain. Hank, his face cold and placid, moved to where his face was inches away from Harley's. "How does it feel, Harley? This isn't because you insulted me today, this is because you beat the buckskin. Are you ever going to beat a horse again, Harley?"

The bully shook his head and moaned a long drawn-out no.

Hank leaned close again. "You're lucky. That shoulder will heal. I could've broken your elbow. You might think twice before you try to bully someone else."

The crowd was silent as he spun around and returned to the stable.

His eyes still glued to the men on the ground, Les handed Hank his hat and coat. "Reckon I'm just as glad I didn't fight you."

16

The temperature was steadily dropping. Hank put his hat on, folded his frock coat, and put it in the pack. He opened the trunk and pulled out his blue, heavy wool Army overcoat. After shaking it out to dislodge anything that had taken up residence, he tugged it on over his red and black checked shirt.

From the open trunk, Hank pulled out a flap holster that contained another Remington. He slipped the .44 from the holster and turned to take it to Nellie. Les and Nellie were staring at him. He realized with his Southern drawl, they assumed he must have fought for the South.

"I guess the drawl fooled you. I hope there's no hard feelings."

Nellie looked at Les and then back at Hank. "Son, we're just surprised. You seem like a mighty good man." She looked out into the street where Juice was helping the wounded men, with the help of several of the townspeople, to the doctor. "At least until you're riled."

Les chuckled. "Looks like he was mighty good at that, too. Harley's had that coming for a long time. He's lucky someone ain't shot him before now."

Hank stuck the Remington he was holding into a pocket in his coat; the butt remained outside the pocket. He unfastened the belt holding his knife, and slid the other holster off. After removing the other Remington, he handed both holsters to Nellie.

She took them and looked them over. "Good leather. With the amount of leather in these two, I'll be able to make three more holsters." She handed the right-hand holster to Hank, and he slid it on his belt. Next the knife was pushed on before the left-hand holster so it would be behind it on the belt. He swung the rig around his waist and buckled it. The revolvers were dropped into their respective holsters. He drew each one out several times, looking down at the revolvers.

"How do they feel?" Nellie asked.

"Heavy, but I'll get used to it. They slide in and out mighty easy."

"You want to practice drawing them guns," Les said. "Your life might depend on it."

Hank nodded. "Makes sense." He paid Nellie and went back to packing. First his saddlebags, where he put extra powder, balls, and the two loaded cylinders for the Remingtons. Then he pulled out the fancy Colt with the gold inlaid engraving that had belonged to Perron.

When Les saw it, he whistled. "That is some fancy work on that there Colt. What you figuring to do with it?"

Hank looked at it in his hand, then said, "I hadn't really thought of doing anything with it. Why?"

"I'll tell you why. I'd like to buy it. What you want for it?"

Hank shook his head and handed the revolver to Les. "It's loaded."

The man gave him a disgusted look. "I 'spect so. No sane man would walk around with one of these unloaded. So, you got a price?"

Hank slid his hat back and rubbed his scar. "Les, I don't

rightly know. I've been out of the States for over three years. I don't know what they're selling for."

"Selling for fourteen or fifteen dollars, that's what. But wait," Les said as Hank reached for the Colt. "Just wait, Hank. I weren't finished." He handled the weapon lovingly. "This is right perty and I've a hankerin' to have it. How about if I knock fifty dollars off what you owe me for the horses and gear?"

"Les," Nellie said, "it's just a gun. Fifty dollars?"

"Shush, woman. I like it." He looked back at Hank. "Where'd it come from?"

"A friend of mine in Cuba gave it to me. It came off a mutual enemy, a colonel in the Spanish Army, a comandante."

Les's eyes glinted with eagerness. "Well, what do you say, Hank? Is it a deal?"

Hank thought about the weapon and Perron. He didn't need to be reminded of the evil the man represented. He flexed his shoulders, the scars on his back long healed, but still tight. "Sure, Les. Fifty dollars."

The older man grinned and fondled the weapon. He looked up at Hank like he could feel the pain the gun represented, and his face sobered. Then he stuck out his hand. "Thanks, son, and thanks for telling me the story behind this gun. I'll be getting lots of offers for it."

Hank shook the man's hand, glad to be relieved of the weapon, then turned and went back to packing. It took some time to load the packs. He still had the food, bedding, and clothing items at the mercantile.

He lifted the packs into the soft frame and closed them up. His Henry was leaning against the wall of the stable. He slid it into the scabbard and checked it was secure. With Darcy's letter and map in his inside vest pocket, he turned back to settle with Les. "How much I owe you, Les?"

The man handed him the receipt and the bill of sale for the two horses. He counted out the money and placed the paperwork in an oversized waterproof folding wallet. Then he dropped it into his saddlebags.

"Thanks, folks, I appreciate your help." He slipped on his gloves, turned, patted the buckskin's neck, and stepped into the stirrup.

Sure that he knew what would happen, Les went over to the bay and was holding it by its bridle, keeping the animal in the stall and between him and the buckskin.

Hank swung up into the saddle. He could feel the buckskin quiver, and waited for the coming jolt, but nothing happened. The animal stood calmly, waiting for direction.

"I swear," Les said, "that ain't the same horse."

Hank patted him on the neck again. "Les, I've got two questions for you. First, my directions tell me to go west to the end of the island and take the Follett Ferry. Does that sound right to you?"

"Yes, sir. Right as rain. You just go up here and turn left, and it'll take you straight out of town. What's the next one?"

"Do you know if Harley had a name for this buckskin?"

"Nothin' you'd want to repeat. I never heard him say anything to the horse when he wasn't cussin'. Somebody owned him afore Harley, but I didn't know them."

Hank saw Nellie get up from her rocker and go to the back of the stable. "Well, he's a buckskin and I'm a simple man. I think I'll call him Buck."

At the mention of his name, Buck cocked an ear toward Hank; then both ears turned forward to outside, where it had started to rain. With the strong wind, the big drops were driven sideways.

Les looked out the door at the rain. "Bad time to be starting out. It's about twenty-five miles to San Luis Pass. That's where you'll find Follett. In this weather, he probably won't even be running the ferry." He turned and looked up at the mounted man. "Might want to stay the night."

"No. We're ready and we're going. Got to stop by the mercantile; then we'll be on our way."

"Wait," Nellie said, walking up to him and Buck. When he saw what she was carrying, Les shot a questioning look at his wife. She nodded to him, then turned back to Hank. "In this weather, you'll need this."

Hank saw she was carrying a slicker.

Nellie continued, "It belonged to our son. He left it when he went off to war. Said the recruiter told him he wouldn't need it, that they'd provide him regulation clothing." She looked down at the slicker in her hands. "His first letter said he wished he'd taken it. It was so much better than what they gave him." The sadness left her face as she handed it up to Hank. "He was about your size, a fine strapping young man."

Hank looked over at Les, who nodded, and reached down to take the slicker. He slid one arm in and then the other. It fit like it had been made for him. He looked back down at the sweet face. "Nellie, you know I fought for the North."

"I know, but our son wouldn't be holding any grudges, and neither are we. You use that to stay dry, and once in a while, think of the boy it first belonged to. Godspeed, Hank."

Hank pulled the slicker tight around him and took the bay's lead from Les. He nodded to both of them and bumped Buck with his heels. Once outside, he turned up the street for the mercantile. The buildings protected him from the driving force of the rain, but he knew when he cleared town, this was going to be a miserable ride. Glad he was bundled in warm clothes and straddled upon a fine horse, he figured it wouldn't be near as miserable as some rides he'd been on before over the past three years.

HANK WAS RIDING out of Galveston within the hour, with most of the afternoon ahead of him. The rain slanted down from his right front. Both Buck and Red, that was what he'd decided to call the bay, were slogging along on the sandy road. Fortunately, the rain slipped through the sand quickly, leaving no puddles to splash through. That would change as the ground became waterlogged, but for now the ground made for easy riding.

Out of town, he ducked his head, thankful he had bought a new hat along with additional clothes. He guessed the temperature had dropped into the low fifties. His overcoat and slicker helped protect him. Once in a while, he'd look up to see the bay to his right and the surf crashing to the left. He was surprised there was any surf with the northwest wind, but it continued to roll in. Thousands of ducks and geese bobbed in the saltwater ponds and in the bay. Their honking and quacking added to the cacophony of the wind and rain.

It would be almost impossible to try to shoot just one for supper. There were so many, a single shot could kill seven or eight, maybe more. He laughed to himself; there wouldn't be any cooking tonight, anyway. Hopefully they'd make San Luis, where they might find shelter and food for the night if they couldn't get across on the ferry. The salt grass, growing six and seven feet tall, was blown over, whipping in the fierce wind. It lay near the surface of the water, or land, depending on where it was growing.

They continued their slogging, wet ride. Hours passed and light from the cloudy sky began to fade. He braved raising his head and spotted a few buildings several miles ahead. "Come on, boys. Just a little bit longer and maybe we'll find you a nice dry stall."

Lights were on in the seven or eight buildings that made up San Luis Pass. He spotted a false-front, two-story building that looked promising. Pulling up, he stepped down and looped the reins and lead over the hitching rail. He stomped up the steps and opened the door. Smoke and heat slammed him in the face.

"Close that danged door!" someone yelled. He rapidly pushed it shut.

The place was part saloon. A doorway was just to the right. Before reaching the door, a bar with a brass foot rail ran from the edge of the doorway about twenty feet. There were seven or eight men bellied up to the bar. The left side of the room was made up of tables. Most of the men at the tables were drinking and card playing. At the back of the room was a small stage, with room for only three or four dancers. Sitting just in front of the stage was an upright piano with a piano man, wearing a bowler hat, banging away.

"Can I help you?" the bartender yelled over the noise.

Hank walked up to the edge of the bar. "Looking to stable my horses and find a room, if one's available. Maybe get a meal, if that's to be had around here."

"Two out of three ain't bad," the bartender said. "No rooms available. We got a bunch of folks stuck because Follett ain't running his ferry in this weather. Stable's that way, across the street." He pointed in the direction Hank was going. "Just next door, I mean right there." This time he pointed to the open doorway. "That's Suzy's Slop Chute. Best food in town." He chuckled at that comment, then said, "'Cause it's the only food in town. Not the best. The place is called Suzy's, we added the rest, but the food's fillin'."

"Much obliged," Hank said.

"Drink?"

"Horses first."

The bartender nodded.

He opened the door to leave to the same yells about closing it, and stepped back into the rain. The fresh air was welcome after the smoky interior of the saloon. He untied Red and Buck, swung back into the saddle, and rode the horses diagonally across the street.

The lights were out and the door was closed. He swung down

to the ground. There was a hitching rail slightly behind a watering trough. He tied both horses with enough slack for the two of them to get a drink, and they both promptly took advantage of the opportunity. He walked around behind them to where the latch should be. It was taken in. He banged on the door.

He was about to hammer on it again, when it swung open.

"Get in here!"

Hank stepped inside the open door, which closed quickly behind him.

An average-sized, older man with a potbelly was holding a lamp over his head so he could see Hank's face.

"Whatcha want?"

"Need to board my horses until the ferry starts running."

"You need feed?"

"If you've got it."

"I got it. Can you pay for it?"

Hank was beginning to dislike this fella's attitude.

"How much?"

"How many horses?"

"Two."

The man thought for a second. "That'll be two dollars, a buck apiece. If you stay tomorrow night, same thing."

Hank slid his hat back. "I'm not trying to buy your place; I just need to put up a couple of animals and feed them."

The man pulled his shirt up, a shirt that at one time could've been white but was hard to identify through all the dirt, and scratched his ample belly. He scratched for a few seconds, then squinted up at Hank, and said, "Mister, I ain't the one looking for a place to stay. If'n that's too rich for your blood, then you're welcome to leave, and don't let the door hit you in the rear."

Now Hank was getting mad, but this was the only chance for his horses. He looked down at the man for a moment. "Alright. Open the door and I'll bring 'em in."

"No, you won't. I ain't openin' this front door. We'd all get soaked." The man looked over Hank's dripping slicker and chuckled maliciously. "Guess that train's already left where you're concerned. Bring 'em around to the back. Wind won't blow in from back there."

Hank started to go out the door.

"Wait! Wait! You ain't bringin' no horses in here 'til they get paid fer." He put both hands on his hips.

Immediately Hank regretted not putting some coins in his vest pocket. He had been in such a hurry to get out of town his money was still in his pouch inside his coat. He reached in and pulled out the pouch. It clinked with the heavy sound of gold that always attracted attention. The man's eyes grew bigger. Hank dug around in the pouch until he found two dollars, pulled the drawstrings on the pouch, and slid it back into his coat pocket. He dropped the money into the man's hand.

Pulling his slicker tight, he placed his hand on the door and turned to the man. "You own this place?"

"I don't see where that's any of your business, but no, I don't. I sometimes work nights."

Hank nodded. "Go open the back door. I'm bringing them around."

Without waiting for the man's response, he pushed open the door, to be greeted by sheets of rain stinging his face. He pulled his hat down to keep from losing it and released the door. It slammed closed in the high wind. Angered by the insolent bearing of the liveryman, he stomped through the mud to his horses, untied them, and led them around the building.

By the time he reached the back of the building, the door was open, the man holding it with his body, trying to stay out of the rain.

"You took long enough. Get in here. I'm gettin' wet."

Hank gritted his teeth and led the horses into the stable, putting them in adjoining stalls. The man closed the door, latched it, and walked over to him.

He had hung an additional lantern near the buckskin's stall and was still holding one. In the additional light, Hank could see him better. He had a scraggly two days' growth of beard covering his face under a beat-up old bowler hat pushed to the back of his bald head. The plug of tobacco in the side of his mouth had his cheek pushed out so far he looked like a squirrel carrying pecans. He constantly wiped his runny nose on the sleeve of his filthy shirt.

"That buckskin's a big horse. He'll be eatin' a lot. I need another ten cents for him."

Hank looked at the man like he was crazy, but kept his mouth shut. He pulled the pouch out again and dug through it, looking for a dime.

"Where you gonna be staying?"

"I'll sleep here with my horses and gear." He hadn't planned it, but with the hungry gaze his pouch received from the man, he wasn't going to leave anything here by itself.

"Then that'll be another fifty cents."

Hank looked up from his pouch, staring at the guy.

"If'n you stayed over at the saloon, where the only rooms are, you'd pay a buck and sleep four to a bed. Here you're by yourself on fresh straw. Come to think of it, I oughta charge you more."

At the look Hank gave him, he said, "But for you, I'll make it four bits."

Hank dug out fifty cents along with the dime and dropped them into the man's hand. "Anything else?"

"Nope, that'll do it." He turned around and started walking away.

"Wait," Hank said, "aren't you going to help with the horses?"

The man turned slowly around, a disgusted look on his face as if he were dealing with a dimwitted child. "Mister, you paid for a roof and feed for your horses. If you want help to take care of 'em, it'll cost you more."

Hank shook his head and turned back to Red. "Forget it. Just get the feed for them."

Hank had stripped the packs from Red and the tack from both horses before the man came back with the corn. Hank watched to make sure each horse received a fair portion. Satisfied, he went back to drying them off with handfuls of hay while keeping a sharp watch on the greedy-eyed little man.

17

The man had gone into the tack room, which was on the opposite side of the barn, and closed the door. When he entered the room, Hank could see past him. In the dim light he could make out another door that opened to the outside. He shook his head when, just before he closed the door, he saw the man pull a bottle from an overhead shelf and take a long drink from it.

I can't be choosy, not in this weather. The stable looked to be in good shape, well maintained. Whoever owned it certainly had more pride in his work than the man working here tonight. He finished wiping the horses down, rummaged around in the barn, and found two blankets. He put one over each of his horses. It would be cold tonight.

Buck was in the larger stall. There was room in the stall for him to also bed down. He shook out his bedroll and spread it over the straw, his saddle at his head. From his saddlebags, he took a dry rag and unwrapped it. Inside was a small can of gun oil, a rod, and a brush. Taking his time, he broke down each Remington, removing the cylinders and carefully removing the caps, checking each one. Then, with his knife, he checked the powder. The powder in every chamber was wet.

He took out another rag and emptied the powder, removing the balls and setting them aside. It had been a long day and he was tired, but not so tired to leave his weapons wet. He sure didn't need them rusting, and he wanted to make sure that, when the hammer fell, the gun fired. After cleaning and reloading each Remington, he checked the extra cylinders in his saddlebags. They were dry. He then cleaned and oiled the knife, the derringer, and his Henry.

Sleep was threatening to overtake him, but he had learned, probably from the Army, to take care of his horses and weapons first. Then worry about himself. He took the rag full of loose powder, carefully lifted it from his bed, walked to the door, cracked it, and dumped the powder in the mud. Once the powder was gone, he washed the rag clean in the rain. The wind pushed the door against his forearm, still blowing hard. Once satisfied, he pulled it back inside and latched the door. He wrung it out and hung it to dry on a peg in the wall.

Hank sat down on his bed, pulled his boots off, and wiggled his toes. It felt good to have his feet free. He didn't know if he would ever get used to being confined in boots again, after Cuba. He had dried his holsters, but left them lying open, his Remingtons resting on the edge of his bedroll. He also had his knife in easy reach. He leaned his head back on his saddle and pulled his heavy coat up over him, the slicker over the coat. With the insulation of the straw beneath his bed and the heavy wool coat and slicker on top, he was almost toasty. Within moments, he was asleep, his right hand relaxed around the Remington.

Hank hadn't survived all of his years before the war, during the war, and his time in Cuba by being a heavy sleeper. He had been asleep for several hours when he came wide awake, his grip tightening on the Remington. He glanced up at Buck. In the dim light of the barn, he could see the big horse, nostrils flared, his head turned to watch something. Hank could see three shadows moving toward his packs.

He waited. Were there more? He watched the thieves reach the packs. He waited. No one else showed themselves. The three were all bunched around the packs, occasionally looking over at him to make sure he was still sleeping. He let them rifle through his packs a bit longer, then pulled the hammer of the Remington to full cock.

The norther had passed. The wind and rain no longer pounded the stable, so the sound of the big Remington hammer going to full cock reverberated throughout the open space of the building. The three men froze.

"You boys lookin' for something?" Hank asked softly.

Silence.

He waited, then said, "I'm not askin' again. If one of you doesn't speak up, I'll have to decide which one to ventilate first."

The man who let him into the stable spoke. "We . . . uh, wuz just lookin' fer somethin'. Thought it might be out here."

"Did you think that something was in my packs?"

"Oh, we wasn't in your packs, mister. We wuz just lookin' around them."

By now Hank had stood and towered over the three men. He reached down and pulled the bag of coins from his coat. "Could this be what you were looking for?"

"No, sir. That sure weren't. I needed to find a bridle and thought I might've left it over here."

"Light a lantern. I didn't get your name when I came in."

"It's Jethro, Jethro Jenks. It's my brother-in-law what owns this here stable."

"Well, don't stand there, Jethro. Light the lantern."

"Yes, sir. I sure will." The man moved cautiously to the lantern and lit it. Light flooded the stable. The other two men were still frozen, their hands stretched high in the air.

"Where does your brother live, Jethro?"

The bald-headed man, his forehead covered with sweat even in the cold barn, swung his thumb behind him. "Right next door."

"Good. Why don't you run next door and get your brother?"

The man's eyes got big. "No, sir. I sure don't want to do that. He'll be mighty unhappy, what with me waking him up in the middle of the night."

Hank swung the Remington to where it covered the man's big belly. "You think he'd be happier if I just put a .44 slug in your belly? I don't think anybody could blame me."

Instantly, the man swung around and ran for the door. The other two men, their arms still stretched high, twisted their necks, watching him leave.

Only minutes passed before splashing could be heard from running feet. Then two men charged through the door. The first was Jethro, and right behind him was a trim-looking man of about sixty years old. Clutched in his left hand was a huge old Colt Walker, but just because it was old didn't mean it wasn't deadly. Hank swung the Remington to cover the new entry.

"I'd take it kindly if you'd drop that hogleg where you stand," Hank said.

The man took in the two men standing around the open packs. He looked at Jethro, who now was showing a hangdog expression, and turned to Hank.

"Mister, I'd be obliged if you'd allow me to lay this revolver down. It's been with me since it was new and I'd not like to damage it."

Hank nodded.

The man leaned over and gently laid his Walker on the straw-covered floor, straightened to his full height, reared back, and slapped his brother-in-law with a roundhouse open hand. The crack of the blow sounded like a teamster had popped his whip. Jethro was hit so hard he was knocked to the floor.

Lying on the floor, his hand on his cheek, he looked up at his sister's husband and whined, "Now why'd you go and do some-thin' like that?"

"Get up," the older man said, and turned to Hank. "Mister, my name is George Braun. You may call me George if you like. I can see what was happening here, and I must apologize. The sheriff is in town. He couldn't get across the pass with the high wind blow-ing. If you like, I'll get him while you hold this vermin. He'll take them into custody. Of course, you'll have to stay for the trial, but if you decide to, I'll pay for your stay."

Having already decided to let the men go, Hank shook his head. "I'm Hank Remington. I'll not be pressing charges, although I think something should be done with these men, including your brother-in-law, so this doesn't happen again."

"Yes, you're right. I'll take care of that. I'm sure you haven't paid for your stay yet, so there will be no charge, and I'd be obliged if you'd take breakfast with my wife, Martha, and me. It isn't that far to daylight."

"I appreciate the breakfast offer. A home-cooked meal would be mighty fine. As far as not paying, your brother-in-law had me pay before he would let me bring the horses into the stable."

George spun on Jethro, who had gotten to his feet and was still rubbing his cheek. The older man stared at Jethro for a long moment, then shook his head and said, "Jethro, you're fired." He motioned toward Hank. "Give him back his money."

Jethro looked down at his feet and moved the straw around with one foot. He mumbled something unintelligible to Hank.

George leaned forward. "Speak up, blast you! Be a man."

Jethro looked up and said, "I cain't give it back. I already spent most of it."

Puzzled, the brother-in-law said, "You spent it? All the stores are closed." Then realization hit him. "You spent it on liquor at the saloon, didn't you?"

Jethro slowly nodded.

"Well, then, how much?"

Jethro refused to answer.

George turned to Hank, who said, "Two dollars and sixty cents."

George's face blanched with shock. "Two dollars and sixty cents? Are you staying several days?"

"Nope, just tonight. I bought corn for both horses."

George paid Hank. As he walked by Jethro's two accomplices, arms still stretched high above their heads, he looked at them with disgust. "Put your hands down and get out. Don't let me ever see you in here again."

The two men stood looking at him, unable to believe their good luck.

"I said get out!"

They spun around and dashed for the front door, blocking each other for a moment as they wrestled their way out the door.

George looked over at Jethro. "Go to the tack room and get your things, then follow your friends."

Jethro looked up at his brother-in-law and whined, "But I ain't got nowhere to stay and it's cold outside."

"You should have thought about that before you tried to rob an honest man. Now get out."

Jethro started to walk to the tack room.

"And, Jethro?" George said. "It would be better for both of us if you left town."

Dismissing the thief, the gray-haired George looked back to Hank, who had slid his revolver back into its holster. "May I pick up mine?"

"Sure," Hank said.

"Mr. Remington, I am sorry for the thieving and exorbitant prices you were charged. Jethro did not used to be like this, although his parents spoiled him horribly. But that is not your concern. I thank you for not shooting them. You would have been completely justified." George bent, picked up his Walker Colt, looked at it for a moment, and said, "This has been a fine weapon. Heavy though it is, it shoots quite well."

"Yes, sir, I imagine it does."

"Yes, well, we'll see you for breakfast when you're ready. Your gear will be safe here."

Hank nodded. "I imagine it will."

HANK PULLED up Buck on the outskirts of Refugio. He had lived an interesting and wet five days, and now it hadn't rained since stepping onto the ferry across San Luis Pass.

His breakfast with the Brauns had been delicious and interesting. Martha was a gracious hostess and superb cook. She seemed to hold no animosity toward Hank because of her brother-in-law. He had quickly forgotten his unpleasant encounter with Jethro.

Crossing on the ferry was an exciting experience. The sky was deep blue, washed by the heavy rains. He saw untold numbers of ducks and geese that were so thick, at times the sky was darkened with them, and several alligators watched them dock. Neither horse seemed to like the ferry, so they were happy when they reached land. One of the travelers, a drummer from New York, was headed for Wharton and offered to show him the way.

He had thought of Texas as a dry land, dusty, with little water. Wrong. Several creeks presented themselves. There were no bridges, so it was necessary to ford them, and they were just the beginnings. The larger rivers, Brazos, Colorado, Lavaca, had ferries, but the smaller creeks and streams, which there were plenty of, required fording. A few were shallow, but with the recent rain, many were high, requiring him to search for a shallow place. If he wasn't concerned about the few things in the packs that needed to stay dry, including his powder, it wouldn't have been a problem. He could have swum across anywhere.

And there was something else this part of Texas had plenty of —mosquitos. Multitudes of the sucking little demons were everywhere, and they were especially bad around sunset. His goal was to find a dry camp, close enough to water to take the horses, but a sufficient distance to reduce the number of the miserable little fiends.

He had also taken to stopping a couple of times a day to practice shooting. He found that accurate firing came naturally to him. His past must have included a great deal of shooting. Hank had been concentrating on getting the Remingtons out of their holsters fast. He still could be faster, but he knew, no matter what you were shooting, speed didn't count for much if you missed what you were shooting at.

With his Southern accent, he had found that people were friendly unless he was wearing his US Army overcoat. Then every person he met on the road either frowned at him or spit as he passed.

Today, he was dry. He'd forded only one shallow creek this morning. Now, with the rising sun, he found himself outside Refugio. He had to admit to feeling a little excitement. It would be good to see his old friends again. From Darcy's letter, he knew they believed he was alive. He would find them and couldn't help but believe they would be surprised.

Hank clucked Buck into a walk, and they entered the east side of Refugio. It wasn't a big town. Several people he had talked to on the road told him it had a reputation for being a rough and dangerous town, but after Cuba, he felt anything would be tame.

He pulled up at a general store that was also marked post office. Whoever was running it should know where his friends were. After tying his horses to the hitching rail, he stepped up on the boardwalk and opened the door. A little bell rang announcing his arrival. He looked around inside, then stepped over to the counter, where a clerk stood wearing an apron and a green visor.

"Howdy," the clerk said, "what can I do for you?"

Hank pointed at the jar of lemon drops. He'd found, since being back in the States, he had a penchant for sweets. "I'd like a nickel's worth of that hard candy."

"You bet," the man said. He grabbed a small bag, filled it with the lemon drops, and handed the bag to him.

Hank fished a nickel from his vest and gave it to the man. He popped one into his mouth, sucked on it for a moment, then moved it to the side of his mouth. "Might you tell me how to get to the Dillon or Smith place?"

"Sure, I can tell you how to find the Dillons, but the Smiths have been dead for nigh on six years. They was hit with the fever right after their son Darcy went to fight for the Yankees."

Hank shook his head. "Sorry to hear that. So how do I find the Dillons?"

"Well, sir, you just ride straight through town. On the outskirts you'll see a road kick off to the left, kind of a dogleg. Take that. 'Bout two miles you'll see a ranch house on the left. That'll be the Dillons' place."

"Thanks." Hank turned and went out the door. *So the boys must be operating out of the Dillon place. It'll be good to see 'em.* He twisted the top of the hard candy bag and dropped it into his saddlebag. After untying his horses, he swung up on Buck and headed out of town. Finding the turnoff, he bumped Buck into a trot. The two miles quickly fell away, and there the house sat.

It wasn't much to look at. In fact, it looked like the boys must be really busy with cattle because they sure weren't taking care of the home place. If the house had ever been painted, it was impossible to tell. The boards were splintered and cracking. One windowpane was so badly cracked, he was amazed it managed to hang together in the frame. Several of the posts on the low fence around the house were broken and leaning. There was a gate in the fence, but it hung on the remaining hinge, with a single piece of wire through the gate and fence holding it closed.

Still in the saddle, he was looking at the dilapidated barn when the door opened and a man stepped out with a shotgun.

"Howdy," Hank said, "I'm looking for Wade."

The white-haired man spit onto the porch. "You another Yankee like him?"

"I fought for the North, if that's what you're asking."

"That's what I'm askin'. You can just turn them cayuses around and head on out of here. I don't allow no Yankees on my land."

"Are you Mr. Dillon?"

"I am." Dillon said. His pants were worn and his boots runover. "And that's about all the conversation I'm hankerin' for. Now git!"

"Mr. Dillon, if you could just tell me where Wade has gone, that would help."

"Wade ain't no Dillon as far as I'm concerned, and I ain't got no idea where that boy is." The man eared both hammers back on the shotgun. "Now I said git, and I mean git. You hang around here much longer and you'll be pushin' up stingin' nettle come spring."

Hank eyed the man for a moment, then turned Buck around and rode away from the ramshackle place. With what Dillon had said, Wade must be long gone, but where? Did his friends stick together? Did Wade or Darcy know of another part of Texas where they could find cattle? Were they even alive? All the waiting, the planning he had done in the prison farm, all of it could be for nothing. Maybe he should have gone to the Tennessee area and searched for family. Buck and Red walked slowly back to town as if echoing Hank's disappointment.

18

Arriving back in town, Hank rode to a watering trough a few yards down from the post office. He dismounted, let the horses drink, then led them to the post office and looped the reins and lead rope over the hitching rail.

The bell jingled again when he entered. He turned and headed for the counter, where the clerk was stuffing a few letters in alphabetically marked cubbyholes behind the counter.

Turning, the clerk said, "You're back mighty soon. What else you need?"

"Supplies, and more information if you have it."

"I've got plenty of supplies. That's what I do, but I don't know if I can help you on the information. Why don't you spit it out, and we'll both know?"

"I'm looking for three men. They're all friends. I was supposed to come back from the war with them, but I got delayed. Two of them are from here, Wade Dillon and Darcy Smith. They should have been with a third man, goes by the name of Mac."

The clerk straightened, slid the visor back from his eyes, and scrutinized Hank closely. "What's your name, mister?"

"Hank Remington."

The man shook his head. "Well, I'll be double-dipped and taken for a horned toad. You are him. Hold on." The clerk turned his back on Hank, pulled out a shallow, narrow drawer, and rummaged through it. It didn't take long, for there were only four envelopes in the drawer. He picked one up, blew the dust off, and stood, holding the letter.

"Name's Moore, Josias Moore. They told me what happened to you. I never expected you to show up, but they sure did. They said you was tougher than a trapped badger—said you'd never quit, no matter how far you had to swim." Josias squinted his eyes as he examined Hank. "You ain't swam all the way from Cuba, have you?"

Hank laughed. "No, I reckon not. I took a ship."

The man still had a look of disbelief. "Must've been a slow ship."

"No. I got tied up in Cuba." Hank looked at the letter. "If that's for me, can I have it?"

"What?" Josias said, looking down at the envelope in his hands. "Sure, it's for you. Here." He handed to Hank.

Hank pulled the big Bowie knife from its scabbard, slid the razor-sharp blade under a loose corner of the envelope and cut straight across; then he shoved the knife back in its resting place, flipped the loop over it, and pulled out the two-page letter. Like the first, this one had a map and written directions on the back of the map.

As Hank read the letter, Josias said, "The boys weren't happy. They had some fool idea of rounding up all the unclaimed cattle and drivin' them up north. I thought they was crazy.

"But it tore Darcy up something fierce that his folks and his sister were dead from the fever. Then old man Dillon ran Wade off." Josias shook his head. "Lordy, Lordy, that war sure hurt a lot of people." Then he went back to his explanation. "They said they was headed up to Dog Town. Darcy said there was so many cattle west of there, you could walk all the way to the Rio Grande on their backs and never touch the ground." Josias chuckled and grinned at Hank. "That boy always had a way with words."

Hank went over Darcy's letter. It was much like the first, short and direct. Once he reached Oakville, to the northwest, he'd follow the Frio River all the way to Dog Town. He was anxious to be on his way, but he needed to replenish his supplies. Without another word, he turned and walked up one aisle and picked up three big cans of peaches. He never got tired of canned peaches. He could just imagine what they must taste like picked ripe, directly from the tree.

He set the peaches on the counter and took out his little notebook, where, last night before going to sleep, he had jotted down the things he needed for the rest of his trip. He tore the page out and gave it to Josias. "Thanks for the information. You think you could help me with this? I'd like to be on my way."

Josias looked at the list and nodded. "Got it all. I'll have you fixed up in no time."

Hank paid for the supplies, took the first load outside, and began loading Red's packs. Once finished, he walked back inside and picked up the two additional boxes of .44s for the Henry. "Mr. Moore, I thank you for your help."

"You take care, Hank. Tell them boys howdy for me. I always liked Wade and Darcy. They was respectful boys, even though they chose the wrong side."

Hank was about to pull the door latch when an excited, well-dressed man burst into the store. "The Tiel boys have old Carlos down at the saloon, and they're hurrahing the old man awful bad! Someone best do something about it 'fore the old feller gets hurt."

Josias threw off his apron and ran around the end of the counter. Hank had already dashed out the door, pausing only long enough to yank the Henry from its scabbard. The small town had three saloons. He was debating on waiting for Josias and the other man to come out the door and show him, or just start checking saloons, when three shots rang out from inside the Redfish Saloon. He took off for the establishment, Josias and the other man well behind him.

His boots made little noise in the now dusty street. Jumping onto the boardwalk in front of the saloon, he slid to a halt before crashing through the swinging doors. Since he towered over the top of the doors, he could not only hear but see what was going on. Three young men, their backs facing the door, stood in front of the bar with guns smoking. An old Mexican man was between them and the bar. The floor around where the man stood had three bullet holes in it, near his feet.

One of the men, a swarthy slim gent with his holster riding low on his hip, said, "I invited you to have a drink with me, Carlos. Whatsa matter, you too good to drink with us?"

"Señor Tiel, you know Carlos does not drink."

Several townspeople stood around watching; a couple of them were laughing. The bartender, a heavy man, was at one end of the bar, his arms crossed, sending the message he was doing nothing to help the old man.

One cowboy was at the back of the room. He obviously wasn't enjoying the spectacle and had slipped the thong from his revolver.

The speaker Carlos had addressed laughed a hard, brutal laugh. "You're never too old to learn, compadre." He slid his revolver back into its holster and took a step toward the old man, who stared evenly at him.

Hank pushed through the doors just ahead of Josias and his companion.

"Hold it!" His statement was emphasized by the Henry's hammer cocking. "The man said he doesn't drink. I don't drink either, Talky; you want to make me drink with you?"

The speaker and his companions spun around. Two of them had their guns drawn and started to bring them to bear on Hank.

That was a terminal mistake. He pulled the trigger of the Henry. The lead slug slammed into the young man's chest, driving through the edge of his tobacco plug before plowing through his heart. A stunned look momentarily reflected his surprise, then disappeared as he crumpled to the dirty floor.

But Hank's rifle wasn't the only thing that fired. Another gun erupted from the back of the room. The two explosions caused the spectators to dive for cover. The second partner of the man Hank had dubbed Talky dropped his gun and fell to his knees, blood coming out of a belly wound.

During the shooting, Carlos had never moved. Now he stepped over to Tiel and looked at the young man who was staring at the men on the floor, his six-gun forgotten. "You got your brothers killed, Señor. The fault is yours. Your kind mother would be very disappointed in you." Carlos made the sign of the cross, turned, and walked toward the door, stopping before passing Hank. "*Gracias, Señor*. You have saved me from disgrace, but you have become a marked man." With that he turned and walked from the saloon.

Hank kept his eyes on the man still standing. "Drop your gun belt. Be smart."

The man tore his gaze from the dying man on the floor and focused on Hank. Tears had welled up in his eyes and he slowly went into a crouch, his right hand just above his Colt. "You just shot my brothers, mister, and now I'm gonna kill you."

Hank had worked the lever on the Henry right after he fired. Resting in the rifle's chamber was a fresh live round. "I wouldn't do that, boy. Your folks don't want to lose three sons in one day."

Hank watched him. He had time now to get a good look at him. The man couldn't be more than twenty-five. He felt sadness wash over him. The two boys lying on the floor were someone's sons. There would be a great loss to a family today. He didn't want to kill this young man standing in front of him, but it wasn't his choice. He hardened himself.

"Drop the gun belt, boy. You can't beat a cocked rifle, no matter how fast you are."

Josias, off to Hank's side, spoke up. "Listen to him, Ray. Don't fight this man. I know about him, and I can tell you he's deadly. And he's right. All he has to do is pull the trigger on that Henry. No matter how fast you think you are, you can't beat him."

Using his left hand, Ray wiped his eyes and started to straighten up. Then the brother on the floor moaned and whispered, "Kill him, Ray. He done kilt us. He deserves killin'."

Josias yelled, "Don't do it, Ray!"

Hank watched in cold horror as the boy's hand streaked for his gun. *He is fast. But how can anybody be fool enough to draw against a drawn weapon?* He didn't know where in his memory it came from, but he knew never to try to hit a hand or gun that was moving. The thing to do was to aim for the heart and keep shooting until there was no more fight in the man. But he broke his own rule. He couldn't hit the gun or hand, but he could hit the shoulder. He threw the rifle to his own shoulder.

The boy's revolver was starting to come level. He settled the ball of the shoulder in his sight, waiting one more moment in hopes the kid would change his mind, even though he knew he wouldn't. At the very last second, he squeezed the trigger.

The bullet traveled straight and true, slamming into Ray's shoulder and blowing flesh and bone out his back. The gun fell harmless to the floor, never fired, for the nerves that carried the commands through his shoulder and down to his trigger were forever severed. He would never pull a gun, or anything else, with his right hand.

Ray crashed back against a table, glanced off it, and struck the bar. He held on to the bar with his left arm, then slowly lowered himself to the floor, and crawled over to his dying brother.

"I tried, Roger," he whispered to his brother. "I really tried." Then pain covered his face; he produced a guttural moan and, thankfully, passed out.

With the last shot, the doctor rushed into the room. He looked at the three boys on the floor, then looked at Hank. "You do this?"

"Yep."

Josias spoke up. "They were hurrahing Carlos. They could've killed him. Those boys turned on this feller. He had no choice."

"Makes no never mind," Doc said. "When Big John hears about what's happened, he'll have a mad on and be loaded for bear." He looked back at Hank. "Mister, you'd better hightail it out of here. Right, wrong, or indifferent, you've just killed or shot all of Tiel's sons. He won't stop until you're dead." After saying his piece, he checked Randall and Roger. Roger was still alive, but only barely. Then he went on to Ray.

Speaking to no one in particular, he said, "If he lives, drawing that gun is the last thing he'll ever do with that arm." Then he could barely be heard when he mumbled, "Might be a blessing."

Hank turned and walked to the cowhand sitting in the back of the room. The man was busy reloading the empty chamber on his Colt. He had just seated the ball and capped the chamber when Hank walked up.

"Mind if I sit?"

The man looked up, then nodded toward a chair. "Suit yourself."

After Hank sat, he pulled two cartridges from his pocket, placed the Henry on the floor, and twisted the magazine release located beneath the muzzle. Then he dropped the two rounds into the magazine, twisted it closed, and laid it on the table. During that time, neither man spoke.

"Thanks," Hank said.

The man looked up. "Don't like people picking on those who can't take care of themselves. Mind you, I don't meddle. Figure a man should saddle his own bronc, but that ole boy was outnumbered."

While he'd been talking, Hank examined the man. He had

pale blue eyes, kinda icy. He'd seen thirty a while back. His gear was well taken care of, though much of it was old and worn. Boots were run over and thin at the sides. The man's hat had four holes in it and was long ago the worse for wear.

"Where you headed?"

"I was planning on movin' yonder." The man thumbed in the direction of north. "But I heard what the doc was saying. I'm not real good at runnin'. Thought I might stay a spell."

"I look at it a little differently," Hank said. "I don't much care what people think, and I'm headin' up to Dog Town. I don't see why I should let this Big John interfere with my plans."

"Interesting way to look at it."

The two men sat silently around the table.

Josias walked up. "Thank you, Hank, mister." He nodded at the cowhand. "Carlos has been in this country longer than I have. I've been told that years ago he owned most of this land, but through hook or crook it was taken away from him. Now he has a small spread west of town. He's always been friendly with the Tiels. Don't know what got into the boys other than too much liquor."

He turned to leave, then turned back. "Those boys are Big John's night and day. He'll be comin' for you whether you stay or go, but thanks again for stepping in. Carlos could've been bad hurt."

"Thanks for the warning, Josias," Hank said. "I'll be headin' out to find my friends."

Josias waved and headed out of the saloon, waiting for a moment outside while the dead and wounded were removed.

Hank and the other man watched, waiting for the last body to be taken out. Then Hank said, "You lookin' for a job?"

"If it's punchin' cows, yes; anything else, no."

"It'll be punchin' cows, maybe. Got some friends up Dog Town way that maybe have a ranch and cattle, and maybe could use another hand."

"Lot of maybes."

"Long story. But if they do, I own part of it, and I'll start you right now. I've got to admit one thing, though, I don't know what the pay is. Maybe you could tell me."

The man looked at him, a slight grin breaking his face for the first time. "Mister, that's the funniest way of hirin' someone I've ever heard." Then he went on. "Pay for a cowhand normally is thirty and found, but times been tough since the war. Lot of people pay less, all the way down to twenty. I've been known to work for less, punchin' cows, of course."

Hank reached into his vest pocket, pulled out a Liberty Head, ten-dollar gold piece, and tossed it to the man. "That's an advance on this month's thirty dollars, if you want the job."

The man caught the small Liberty Head and looked at it, put it to his mouth and bit on it, and looked at it again. "Don't see many of these nowadays. Much obliged. I'll take the job. Name's Bart Porter."

Hank noticed the look Bart gave him, as if wondering if his name would be recognized. "Hank Remington. You ready to hit the trail?"

Bart nodded and stood. He was about three inches shorter than Hank with a slim waist and wide shoulders. "Everything I own's in the stable. Let me git it and I'll be set."

"I'll walk out with you."

The two men headed for the door. They passed one table where three of the spectators were drinking. As they passed, one of the men laughed, then said, "Guess you boys are running. Looks like you know what's good for you."

The words froze Hank. He spun and grabbed the loose-mouthed drunk by the front of his shirt, twisted, and dragged him erect to his tiptoes where the man could look him in the eyes. His sudden move had surprised everyone. There was silence in the saloon.

"Any of you other folks want to echo this *gentleman's* sentiments?"

Continued silence.

By now the man was choking, unable to breathe past the big hand twisting his shirt collar.

Hank looked around the room, then eyed the remaining men at the table. They held their hands in front of them and shook their heads. The drunk's lips were starting to turn blue when Hank threw him back into his chair so hard the man almost fell over backwards.

Turning, Hank strode out of the saloon with Bart following.

"You're a mighty sudden man," Bart said.

Hank pointed to his horses. "I'll mount up and meet you at the stable." He turned toward the horses and could hear Bart's boots on the boardwalk as he clumped off in the opposite direction.

Hank untied his horses and mounted Buck, his mind going over the days since he had stepped off the ship. *I've beaten three men, killed one, and shot another. I was sure hoping to have some peace. I swear, I think Texas might be as bad as Cuba.*

At the sound of racing horses, he looked west and saw seven or eight men beating their horses to keep up with the huge man in front.

19

O ne of the riders was pointing at Hank. They rode straight for him. He only had time to flip the thongs from his Remingtons and pull the Henry from the scabbard. He turned Buck to face the men, where they were slightly to his left, and waited.

They brought their horses to a sliding stop in a cloud of dust, the streets already dried in the hot sun. The big man in the lead stared at Hank, his eyes burning with hate as he guided his horse inches from Hank.

"I'm John Tiel. You shot my sons?"

"I did."

"That's all I need to know." He turned to a cowhand to his right. "Throw your rope over this man's neck. We'll hang him from the big oak west of town."

The man reached for his lasso, but stopped at the sound of Hank's voice. "Mister, I ain't going to be hanged. You touch that rope and you're a dead man. You'll get my second slug. Tiel, since you're starting this dance, the first is yours."

Several of the cowhands started reaching for their guns.

"I don't think I'd do that, were I you."

The voice came from behind them. It wasn't loud, but cold and soft, and every cowhand in the group heard it. Hank looked behind the men. Bart sat a little mustang roan, his revolver trained on the crew.

Josias stepped out of his store onto the boardwalk, carrying a big ten-gauge shotgun that he had trained on the cowhands. "John, you're barking up the wrong tree. Your boys were hurrahing Carlos, heaven knows why, but they'd already fired into the floor around him. They were drinking, and they drew on this man. He had to shoot in self-defense. Why, he even shot Ray in the shoulder. He could've killed him."

Tiel's voice was loud and shaking with emotion. "Josias, I'm going to tell you one time. Take that shotgun and yourself back inside your store right now, or you'll never make another dime in this town."

Josias never moved. "John, when you're wrong, you're wrong. You know me, I wouldn't lie to you. What I'm telling you is the truth. Be glad you have one son left. This man could have killed him, but he didn't. Mourn your boys, and take care of Ray."

Tiel glared at Josias in rage. He was wild. It was obvious all he had in his mind was killing Hank. "I can't leave! This man killed my boys. My future. It's all gone. I have only one son left and him a cripple. Damn it, man, what would you do?"

Josias shook his head. "John, I'd go home and be thankful I had one son left."

"No!" he shouted, then turned back to Hank.

Hank knew there was no turning back for Tiel. He understood the rage the father felt. Hank had wanted to kill Perron and would never have listened to anyone's reasoned argument if he had a chance. Now this man would have to make his move.

One last try. "Mr. Tiel, I didn't want to have to shoot your boys, but they left me no choice. Let this be over. You still have one son. Don't forget him."

The rancher's eyes were wild. He looked left and right at his men.

No matter how much they might want to help him, they weren't overcome with rage. They knew they were between three guns, one of which was a shotgun. They might kill the two men, but before it was over, there would be a lot of cowhands on the ground.

Hank saw the decision in the man's eyes. He was going to draw. Just like his son, he was going to try to draw his gun against a rifle that was cocked and pointed at him.

"Don't do it," Hank shouted at the man. But even as the words passed his lips, Tiel went for his gun.

Unlike his son, he was slow. He was a rancher, not a gunfighter or a wannabe gunfighter. He had to pause to cock the weapon; then he was bringing it up, slowly, up and up, almost on him. Time to pull the trigger. He started to squeeze.

The blast of the shotgun ripped the big man from his saddle. The whole load of the ten gauge tore into the man's left side. His arm had been back to balance himself as he drew with his right. Since the shot string had to travel such a short distance, for Josias was standing less than eight feet from Tiel, the shot had spread very little. In fact, it made only about a three-inch hole and devastated the man's upper body.

It seemed the ground almost shook when the huge body crashed into the ground. Hank sat looking at the man, not even watching the cowhands. The rifle had drifted down to rest on his legs, and all he could think of was he had killed a whole family. It was his fault. If he hadn't gone to the saloon to help the old man, this family would be alive. Was it a fair trade? One for four?

No one else went for his gun. A soft voice spoke up from behind the cowhands. "Alright, boys, pick up your boss. It's all over."

It looked like the whole town had gathered at the commotion, but everyone was silent. It took four of the cowhands to load and tie their boss on the saddle. Then a dejected group rode west, out of town.

Hank looked over at the white-faced Josias. "You gonna be all right?"

Two well-dressed men stepped up beside Josias, one carrying a Spencer, the other a Henry. One of them spoke up. "He'll be fine. It's about time this town got cleaned up. We've put up with Tiel and the rest of these troublemakers for too long. If they don't leave town, *we'll* be stretching some necks on the old oak west of town."

Three drifters who had been watching the fracas from in front of the nearest saloon walked over to their horses and high-tailed it out of town.

Josias nodded to Hank. "Yes, sir, I'll be fine. I ain't killed a man since the war. But I ain't forgot how bad it feels. John believed he was above the law for a long time." Josias looked at the other two men now being joined by others. He gestured toward them. "These are Refugio business owners. I think I can speak for them when I say thank you. We've been needing to sweep out the riffraff for some time. You pushed us over the edge."

The other men nodded and several tossed a thanks to Hank.

By this time, Bart had joined Hank and sat the little mustang, hands resting on the horn.

Josias continued, "Hank, I, along with several of these men, noticed how fast you responded to the call for help. We need a man like you. We'd like to hire you as marshal, if you've a mind."

Surprised, Hank shook his head. "Sorry, I've got some friends waiting on me at Dog Town. I'd best move on."

"Understand," Josias said, "but the offer's open. You get up there, and if it's not what you thought, come on back."

Hank swatted at a mosquito. "Don't think I could handle these mosquitos."

The other men laughed. Hank turned to Bart. "You ready?"

Bart answered by turning the mustang up the street. Hank touched his hat to the men and rode out of Refugio.

"Marshal," Bart said. "Interesting." He looked at Hank as they rode, then nodded his head. "Yep, that might fit?"

Hank looked over at his companion. "What's that mean?"

"You got the look of a lawman. I ain't one with the words to describe it, but you do."

"No, thanks."

The two men rode in silence for a while. Hank reached around to his saddlebags, opened one, and dragged out the sack of lemon drops. He opened the bag and offered it to Bart. The man looked in, said, "Don't mind if I do," and popped one into his mouth. Hank followed suit and secured the bag back in his saddlebag.

Bart pointed northwest and, around the hard candy, said, "I know Dog Town. Been there several times. We can cut off a little northwest of here. It'll save time."

"Sounds good."

Bart motioned to the right and the two men turned off the road and headed cross-country.

They rode on for a while; then Bart spoke up again. "Did you see those three boys take to their horses just before we left?"

Hank nodded. "Looked like they were in a hurry."

"Yep. They took off right after the feller with the shotgun said what he did about cleaning up the town. I've seen places like Refugio, with a reputation for being a tough town. You can push folks for only so long. These towns ain't made up of milksops. Most of those men fought in the war. They know which end the lead comes out of. By tomorrow morning, those who didn't take the hint are gonna find themselves dangling from that oak tree the shotgun man was talkin' about."

A big jackrabbit raced across in front of them, followed by a coyote that was right on its tail. The two men watched the life-and-death drama playing out in front of them. One animal dies so the other can live. *It can also be like that for humans,* Hank thought. *If I hadn't fired today, I'd be the one dead or wounded, maybe Carlos too, and it only took an instant. A decision had to be made to live or die. Those boys and their father had the option, but they chose wrong. Maybe that's the difference. I'm willing to make that decision and not leave it up to someone else to make it for me.* He still felt bad for the killings, but he no longer felt responsible.

At the edge of a line of live oaks, dust boiled up from behind the bunchgrass and tall prickly pears. It lasted for almost thirty seconds and then stopped. The two men caught a glimpse of the coyote, its head twisted to keep from stepping on the big jackrabbit clamped in its jaws.

"Looks like there's a coyote that's gonna eat well today, if you can call eatin' one of them bony jackrabbits eatin' well," Bart said.

"How long you think it'll take us to get to Dog Town?" Hank asked.

"If you want to push, we can make it in two days. I'd recommend three, easier on the horses."

"Three it is."

It had turned into a beautiful late winter day in South Texas. The sun was out and glistened on the patches of oak trees that broke up the grassland. Cattle seemed to be everywhere. In fact, they had seen more cows than deer, but no people. Of course, that was probably because they weren't following any roads.

Hank marveled at the big longhorns. When they were spotted, they would stand for a short time, then dash into the oak and mesquite thickets. Their horns were massive. When they took off, nimbler than he would have expected, the clattering sound of horns striking one another rang across the brush country. *This is going to be a lot easier than I thought.* He voiced his thought to Bart, which elicited a laugh from the man.

"It's obvious you ain't never worked with longhorns. They're about the orneriest beast what's ever walked this earth. A bear thinks twice before jumping one, and then he makes sure it's a young one. These here critters can be pure mean. You find an old mama cow back in the brush and she'd just as soon kill you as let you draw her young'un out." He laughed again. "Easy." He shook his head.

Hank realized he had a lot to learn about cattle, people too. Here he was in his thirties and still having to work to learn things about people he probably already knew. Sometimes it was downright frustrating, but on other occasions things would just pop into his mind from nowhere. Maybe one of these days his memories would return, but if they didn't, he'd continue to do like Deborah had told him: "Make new memories."

He wondered where she was now. Probably married to Dr. James. It'd been so long, she probably had at least one child. He had never been able to get those deep, dark brown eyes out of his memory along with her wide, soft mouth. A smile crossed his face when he thought about that soft mouth becoming tight and firm when someone didn't follow directions, probably cultivated from her nurse's training. He hoped Deborah and Dr. James were doing well.

THE TWO MEN pulled up at the edge of a patch of live oaks. Less than a mile from them was a town, if it could be called that. It was made up of a few clapboard houses, a hotel, general store, two saloons, and a small livery. All of the buildings had the same gray color of dry, unpainted cedar. Nothing in the town appeared welcoming.

"Not much to look at," Bart said as he pointed to a house on the west side of town. "Good food. Widow woman cooks it herself and has a couple of rooms to let. Heck of a lot cleaner than the hotel or saloons."

"Let's stop at the store first," Hank said. "I'd like to find out if my partners are anywhere about. Then we'll eat."

Bart nodded.

The two men pulled up at the Frio General Store. After tying their horses, they walked in. The only person inside was a lady doing the clerking.

"How are you two gentlemen? May I help you?"

Both took off their hats and smiled.

"We're fine, ma'am," Hank said. "My name's Hank Remington, and I'm—"

"Oh, my goodness! You're that friend of Mr. Smith and Mr. MacGregor. I would have recognized you even without your name." She paused to look him over. "But I must say, you aren't as heavy as I expected, but I just can't believe you're here. They told us all about you mysteriously falling overboard. However, Mr. MacGregor said it didn't matter how long it took, you'd be here. Why, it's been almost three years since they arrived in Dog Town. You must have had quite an adventure."

Behind a wry grin, Hank said, "Yes, ma'am, I'd say it's been *quite* an adventure. Would you be able to tell me where I could find them?"

"Oh, yes, I certainly can. Come with me." She took the two men to the steps of her establishment and pointed to the road going west, out of town. "You just follow that road for about six miles. Then it forks. Take the right fork, and you can't miss it. Mr. Remington, sir, they will be so happy to see you." She left them with a smile, turned, and walked back into the store.

"Well, six miles, I don't think it'll be going anywhere if we stop to eat," Hank said. "How you feel about that?"

Bart grinned. "Like it. I was afeared you'd want to hightail it on out there."

"I'm hungry, too. Let's get these horses over to the stable. I imagine they'd like a drink and a go at the feedbag."

The two men rode the horses to the stable, took care of them, and walked back to the house Bart had indicated. When they came to the door, there was a sign, "Come In," so they did.

The room had been made into a dining room with three tables having four chairs around each. Beneath the front window, a couch had been placed facing the dining area. Two men sat at one table, finishing off a bowl of peach cobbler.

Bart gestured at the cobbler. One of the men saw him. "'Bout the finest food you'll find this side of San Antone."

His partner looked up and nodded, busy chewing the last mouthful.

"Looks mighty good," Hank said.

The two of them sat at the table next to the two cowpokes. They had just pulled their chairs up to the table when a lovely woman, carrying a few extra pounds, came in from the back.

She exclaimed, "Bart Porter, as I live and breathe," then dashed over and gave him a big hug.

Hank noticed at the mention of Bart's name, both men at the adjoining table jerked their heads up and stared. Then they put their money on the table and quietly walked out.

Bart was occupied and didn't notice.

"Molly Flynn, why, you look younger every time I see you." He stepped back and grasped the lady by one hand and held it up so she could pirouette. When she had completed her turn, he said, "Like I said, looking younger and better looking every time."

With her free hand she slapped his arm. "Bart, you old cad, you're just looking for a free meal."

This time he laughed and, still holding her hand, turned her toward Hank. "Molly, this is my boss, Hank Remington."

She stuck out her hand. Hank promptly stood and accepted the small hand in his. He felt a firm handshake from her warm hand. "Pleased to meet you, ma'am."

She took her hand back and tossed her head, moving the blond curls around under the loose net. "There are no ma'ams here, Hank. If she were still around, you could call my mother ma'am, but not me. Now what can I get you?"

"Food, Molly, and plenty of it," Bart said.

"Do you men like chicken? I'm frying up a batch right now."
She gestured toward the other table. "Those boys wanted steak,
which I have, but I was frying up some for me and the kids for
later today. Would you like fried chicken?"

"Well, Molly," Hank said, "I wouldn't want to take fried
chicken away from any kiddos, but if you've got some extra, I'll
sure take it."

Bart nodded. "Me too."

The two men sat back down as Molly went back to the
kitchen.

Glancing over, Bart saw Hank's questioning look.

"I knew her in San Antone a few years ago. She had a
successful restaurant there. She fed me a few times when I was
down and out. Her husband was killed in the war, and shortly
after, her place burned down. So she moved here. She's quite a
woman."

Hank nodded. "A woman who likes you."

Bart squinted and looked out the window. "She doesn't want
to tie herself to me. I have too much baggage."

"I noticed something else. When Molly mentioned your
name, the two men at that table looked like they knew the name,
and they got out real quick."

Bart said nothing.

Hank continued, "I also noticed in Refugio, one of Tiel's
riders recognized you and spread it around the cowhands. I'm
thinking that's why none of them were too anxious to open the
ball."

Bart stared at the table.

20

"Look," Hank said, "normally I wouldn't pry into a man's past. But if that past is going to get me included in something, I want to know what it is."

Bart still didn't look up, but he nodded. "I reckon you deserve to know, 'specially if I'm workin' for you." With that he tossed a questioning look at Hank.

"You've still got a job unless there's something heinous in your past."

"I've killed several men. After the war, there was a squabble over some land. Carpetbaggers said it was theirs; my brother said it was his. In the fight, my brother and his family were murdered. I tracked the murderers down and killed 'em." He looked defiantly at Hank. "I'd do it again." Then he looked down at the table. "Somehow I got the reputation of being a fast gun. They sent the state police, but finally stopped looking for me. I ain't never killed no lawman. Only folks who deserved killin'."

"All right, then let's enjoy our meal."

At that moment, Molly came walking in with two big plates loaded with fried chicken, potato salad, and creamed corn.

Bart looked at it for a moment. "Molly, where'd you get potatoes this time of year?"

She put her hands on her hips. "If you must know, Mr. Porter, I have a cellar that still has potatoes stored there. That's one of the things that makes my food so good."

Just before taking a careful bite of the steaming fried chicken, Hank said, "Smart woman." He gingerly bit into a chicken leg, sweet and juicy. The taste brought a picture to his mind, much like one of those tintypes he had seen in Washington. He could see himself seated at a big table surrounded by kids his own age and younger. It was still foggy, he couldn't make out faces clearly, but he could see a man and a woman. The woman was the same one he had seen before. He strained to make the picture clearer, but nothing happened. Then it slowly faded until it was gone.

Returning to the present, he was holding the chicken in front of his face, staring out the front window. Bart, a concerned look on his face, was watching him.

Hank shook his head. "It's nothing. You know, I told you I lost my memory. Sometimes when I do something, a picture or sound pops into my mind. That's what happened when I took a bite of chicken, but I couldn't hold on to it."

"Maybe the more it happens, the sooner you'll get your memory back," Bart suggested.

"Maybe."

The two men finished their meal, including the peach cobbler Molly had made from canned peaches. They paid for their meals, and, with a handshake for Hank and another big hug for Bart, Molly bid them good day.

The horses were fed and watered, lolling lazily in the corral. They appeared to be somewhat resentful at having to go back to work, but stood resigned as they were saddled. It wasn't long until Hank and Bart, with full bellies, headed west for the ranch. Time passed quickly in the late afternoon sun. It was warm and relaxing after having eaten.

Dozing in their saddles, they almost missed the turnoff, but the horses made the slight turn without being bidden. Not far up ahead they saw a sign. Pulling up to it, Hank let out a laugh. "Well, I'll be dipped. They named it the Remington Ranch. Those boys just never stop surprising me."

A mile down the road, they came to a modest house. To one side sat a bunkhouse, and across the yard was a barn with an attached corral. Outside the corral where it connected to the barn was a watering trough. The men rode their horses up to the trough and dismounted.

Bart was nearest the open barn door and Hank was loosening the cinch when a voice from inside the barn said, "Help yerself to the water. 'Tis a sweet and precious thing available here to any man who rides in friendly."

Hank rose and leaned across Buck's back. "Is that the worthless Scottish sergeant who still hasn't learned to speak good American?"

There was silence from the barn. Then the sound of a heavy body moving quickly toward the barn door. Mac slid to a stop when he stepped from the barn and saw Hank. He stood still, staring; then a huge grin split his face.

"Oh, Lordy, 'tis a wondrous day."

He walked around the horses and closed on Hank until he was close enough to grasp him by the arms. "'Tis a bad thing, to go a-swimming in the night and leave your mates."

"Hello, Mac."

The two men grasped hands and held the grip. Finally releasing the handshake, they stepped back. Hank looked Mac over, determining that he looked no different except maybe some of the belly was gone. He looked harder, tougher, if that was possible.

"Laddie, it's dying I am to hear your story. I'll get the coffee started while you're taking care of your horses." He turned to Bart. "I'm Liam MacGregor. My friends call me Mac."

Bart extended his hand. "Pleased to meet you. Bart Porter."

The only indication that Mac had recognized the name was a slight tilt of his eyebrow, but Hank caught it and figured it hadn't gone unnoticed by Bart.

"We'll see you inside, Mac," Hank said.

It wasn't long before all three men were seated at the kitchen table, where a scruffy but clean man was working around the stove, mumbling to himself.

"The grouchy-sounding feller is Juan O'Riley. 'Tis a sad thing, but his ma liked the name Juan and hung it on him. He goes by Skeeter, but don't be asking me why. All I know is that it's a magician he is in the kitchen or camp. Skeeter, be saying hello to Bart and your new boss, Hank."

The man turned and mumbled something, then went back to fussing at the stove.

"Sit, boys, sit. It'll be a surprising time when Darcy gets back, I'll tell you that."

Hank couldn't stop grinning. It was great to hear his friend's Scottish accent. He looked around the kitchen. It wasn't fancy, but was well equipped. Mac had mentioned Darcy. "Where's Wade?" Hank asked.

At the mention of Wade, the big Scotsman's face fell. "He be gone, Hank. Killed by those heathens desirin' to cut our first herd in Kansas. In fact, the leader of the gang was an old friend of yours."

Hank shot Mac a questioning look.

"You'll be rememberin' the fine gentleman First Mate Langston Pitts?" Mac went on without waiting for a reply from Hank. "Well, it was an angry Ethan Powell, captain of the *Swift*, who found Pitts opening your things after you disappeared. He had no proof of the skullduggery of the man, but he did catch him thieving. Once arrived in Galveston, he fired the blackguard. I'm wishin' he had waited until getting back to Baltimore."

Skeeter arrived with the coffee. Hank shook his head and

asked for water. Skeeter looked at him like he was crazy, poured the cups for Mac and Bart, and mumbling to himself, got Hank some water.

Hank's eyebrows had pulled down and his jaw muscles were tensed. Through tight lips, he asked Mac, "How did the man get to Kansas?"

"I'll not be knowing the answer to that question, he just was. We got out here the winter of '65, and it was a cold one. In '66, we started putting a herd together, but with just the three of us, it wasn't until '67, last year, that we finally started the drive, but I'll let Darcy be telling you that story. Shortly after passing into Kansas from the Indian Territory, up and rides the devil himself. Here and thankfully I had forgotten him. But now, accompanied by a bunch of bandits, Pitts rides up big as you please." Mac stopped long enough to take a cautious sip from his steaming cup.

"He claimed we had picked up some of his cattle, and they'd need to cut the herd to find them. Pitts had an ugly fellow with him carrying a Henry, casual like. The vermin had timed it just right. The cattle were restless, and all the men except me, Skeeter, and Wade were driving cattle. You remember how hotheaded Wade was?"

Hank nodded, thinking Mac was always the man with the temper, although Wade wasn't far behind.

Mac continued, "That boy told 'em they weren't cutting any herd, and went for his gun. The feller with the rifle just moved the muzzle a tiny bit and shot Wade straight through the heart. He was dead before he hit the ground. That started the music. Skeeter here stepped out from behind the wagon and, with that old shotgun of his, emptied two of their saddles. At the first blast of the shotgun, Pitts and his crony what shot Wade wheeled out of there. I winged one, but he hung to his saddle. Within minutes, the men were back at camp. After losing his family, Wade dying really tore Darcy up. He wanted to chase after Pitts and hang him.

But that's just what the blackguard wanted. Whilst we was chasing him, he'd double back and cut our herd."

It was quiet in the kitchen. Skeeter, who had gotten himself a cup of coffee and joined them at the table, broke the silence. "He was a good boy. A real cowman."

Hank asked, "Did you ever see Pitts again?"

Mac shook his head. "Not once did I lay these peepers on him. Told the marshal in Abilene. Course, it wasn't his job to go after him. Said he'd never heard of the man."

The sound of a horse riding up broke the cloud of gloom that lay over the kitchen.

"That'll be Darcy," Mac said.

Sure enough, the younger man's boots clumping and spurs jingling announced his arrival on the porch. The door opened and he came to a sudden halt. Shocked at first, then a big grin spread across his face. "I'll be double-dipped! We knew you'd be along. Didn't know how long, but we knew you would." Like Mac had done, Darcy raced across the room to shake Hank's hand. Only he was jerking it like he was trying to prime a stubborn pump.

"Good to see you, Darcy," Hank said. He, too, was grinning. He finally regained his hand and waved around the house. "Looks like everything has gone well for you."

Darkness chased Darcy's grin away. "Not everything, Hank."

Mac stepped in. "Aye, not all. But, Darcy, me lad, I have already shared the sad news with Hank. Let's be happy he's back."

Darcy nodded. "Yes, you're right, Mac." For the first time Darcy noticed a stranger in the room.

Hank, watching his friend, said, "Darcy, this here is Bart Porter. He pulled my bacon out of the fire in Refugio. He was looking for a cow job, so I hired him on."

The name obviously rang a bell for Darcy, as it did with others. He listened to Hank, then extended his hand to Bart. "Welcome to the Remington Ranch. Any man who Hank speaks for is fine with me. We've got a lot of work to do to get ready for the upcoming drive. We'll push off the first of April."

"Thanks," Bart said. "I could tell you both recognized my name. I ain't never killed a man who didn't need killin', and I know cattle. You'll get an honest day's work out of me." He picked up his cup and drained it. "Good coffee," he said to Skeeter, nodded to Mac and Darcy, and looked at Hank. "Thanks for the chance. Now I'll go take care of our horses and toss my stuff in the bunkhouse." He headed out the door.

After watching Bart leave, both Mac and Darcy immediately turned back to Hank and said, "How . . ."

Hank held up his hands. "He's just part of the story." He sat back down in his chair and leaned on the table, his friends joining him. "I want to know how you went from nothing to this ranch in just three years, but first, I'm going to tell you everything. Pitts, with several of his crew, jumped me right after we entered the Windward Passage . . ."

THE COWHANDS HAD BEEN FED and, though they desired to hear more of the story, respected their bosses and left soon after supper. Cattle guards had ridden out to be replaced later in the night. Lamps were lit in the bunkhouse and the house. Skeeter was the only man other than his bosses to have heard the complete story. Several times he would stop and just shake his head.

". . . and that is how I ended up hiring Bart. The rest is just the ride from Refugio to Dog Town to here." Hank leaned back and relaxed in his chair. Mac and Darcy took a deep breath and released it.

Mac joined Skeeter in shaking his head. "Boyo, you have been through it. It's the Lord you need be thankin' for those Cuban folks and their feeling of indebtedness. If not for them, you'd still be cutting sugarcane in Cuba."

"Believe me, Mac. I do every day. Now tell me how you two are so prosperous."

Mac laughed. "Prosperous it is. Well, yes, compared to the ragged trio who showed up here in '65, that we be. But lad, for all your bad luck, we have had good, exceptin', of course, the loss of Wade.

"By the by, it was your six hundred dollars that kept us going. Without it, we would've had to go to work for someone else and make the attempt to save enough to start out on our own. You, laddie, you're why we, and I mean all three of us, have this. But let me tell you about it.

"Thanks to Wade and Darcy here, we knew where to go. There are still plenty of the wild cattle around, but you should've seen it three years ago."

Hank laughed. "I would've liked to, believe me."

"Yes, I'm thinkin' you would. But Darcy here and Wade took on the monumental task of teaching me how to herd those wild critters out of the thickets. It almost got us all killed several times, but we survived. In '66, we didn't have the size herd we was lookin' for, so we kept roundin' them up.

"Last year, we had 'em built up to about three thousand head, and early in the year there was a rider come through tellin' us about Abilene, Kansas, and a feller there by the name of Joseph D. McCoy. Those boys were saying he would buy every single critter we could get there, and at a premium. Well, we needed more riders to drive 'em, and thanks to your money, we were able to do it. So we had the three of us, Skeeter, a horse wrangler, and eight more riders."

Hank interrupted. "How many riders do you have now?"

Darcy answered, "We kept Skeeter and three of the best. With Bart, that means we have four cowhands, not counting us."

"Well, right now, you sure can't count on me. I can ride a horse, but I know nothing about cattle."

Mac and Darcy laughed. Darcy said, "You'll learn quick, you have to, or there's the alternative, which we ain't going to think about."

"That's fine with me."

Mac went on. "So the rider from McCoy told us the best route was up past San Antonio, Austin, and Fort Worth. He even had a map for us, called it the Chisholm Trail. So we took out. Made about eight to ten miles a day, and those stubborn critters put on weight, if you can believe it. But I've never seen so many problems in all my born days. Storms, floods, stampedes, thieves, Indians, especially through the Territory, and dust. You'll find out."

Mac's eyes were gleaming when he continued, "We only lost about fifty head, and, Hank, McCoy paid us thirty dollars a head. Can you believe that? Here in Texas when we left, a man couldn't sell one of those longhorns for more than two dollars, and that was for the hide."

Mac looked over at Darcy, who was grinning so wide it looked like his face would split. Mac leaned toward Hank and said, almost in a whisper, "Hank, after we paid all the bills, we made eighty-two thousand dollars."

Hank's eyes were wide. "Mac, are you kidding me?"

"No, laddie, most of that money is sitting in the bank, but we kept some in cash. And your part is over twenty-five thousand dollars."

Hank sat at the table, shaking his head. Finally, he said, "Who would've thought those folks in Washington wanted steaks so bad?"

At his statement all three men broke out laughing.

"You boys have done an amazing job. I'm just sorry I wasn't here to help. It doesn't seem fair I take a third. Maybe we should take less and send Wade's share home to his folks."

Darcy shook his head violently. "No! They disowned him.

They don't deserve a thing. It broke his heart that his pa talked to him like he did. That man will not benefit from the death of a son he didn't want."

Hank laid his arm on Darcy's shoulder. "You're right, Darcy. I want to thank you boys for your hard work. So how many head we taking this year?"

Darcy spoke up. "I think we should stick with three thousand. That's a big handful. Though it would bring us more money, more would be a major headache, and we could lose them all. I vote to keep it at last year's number."

Mac nodded. "It's all in I am. If that's what Darcy's a-thinking, he's the man who knows cattle."

Hank also nodded. "Good enough for me." He pushed back from the table and stood. "It's been a long day. I'm going to head for the bunkhouse and catch some shut-eye."

Hank's two partners shook their heads. "Nope," Darcy said. "We built this house so each of us would have a room. Yours is the room in the corner, gives you two windows. Bart unloaded your horses and brought in your gear."

Hank stood and stretched. "Well, show me the way before I pass out on my feet."

21

The days raced by. Hank rode primarily with Darcy for the first two weeks and caught on faster than he had expected. Maybe in his unremembered past he had used a rope, because it seemed he knew the basics. He wasn't anywhere near as good as Darcy or Bart, or any of the other cowhands, but in a short time he was better at handling the lariat than Mac.

Hank fit right in with the other hands, and they all worked as a team. There was only one knucklehead. Seems there was always at least one in a bunch. All the men knew that he, Mac, and Darcy had fought for the North, but if they found that repulsive, they never indicated it. But occasionally, a young cowhand named Tandy would say something that was almost over the line, but not quite.

Tandy Jacobs was a big, loud, rawboned blond. He was also pushy with several of the other hands, men smaller than him. What he couldn't get through his mind was that Mr. Colt was a huge equalizer and every cowhand carried one. Tandy hadn't been in the war. He had been old enough, at eighteen, but instead, had been appointed to the contemptible Home Guard, a group that later became known as the Heel-Flies, named after pests that every cattleman was all too familiar with. Tandy had been made a captain and placed over a group of warriors ranging in age from eight to sixteen. With their newfound authority, they immediately began terrorizing anyone who might have the misfortune to come into range.

Hank worked with each and every man, never thinking himself better than any of the men. Unfortunately, Tandy, with his youth and lack of experience, determined that this was a sign of weakness and gradually became more pointed with his comments. One late afternoon after the work was over, and only a few days before they started moving cattle north, Mac and Darcy decided to join the men in the river. It had been a hot day in the choking dust. The clear water looked inviting.

Hank had sat his horse, watching the men cavort in the cold water. *Who cares if my back is cut up with whip marks? It doesn't change who I am.* He made up his mind to join the men and was just about to step down when Tandy spoke up.

"Hey, Hank."

The boy never called him boss like the other men did, but Hank didn't mind. The kid was young, and Hank never needed a title to make him feel good. He looked over to Tandy.

"Come on in. The water feels good."

He waved to the boy, and several of the other men echoed the youth's sentiments. Hank waited for a moment more and started to swing his leg over the saddle.

The boy yelled from the water, "Whatsa matter, you don't want all the men to see that big yeller stripe down your back?"

The splashing stopped, all except for Tandy, who looked like he was having a great time. The other men stood in the water, looking at Hank and then at Tandy. Bart, who was in the water, stood shaking his head. Hank sat still in the saddle.

Tandy glanced around and saw the serious faces staring at him. He looked at Hank and grinned, obviously believing his size, well over Hank's six feet and two inches, had him intimidated.

Slowly Hank swung his leg over the saddle and stepped to the ground. He unfastened his gun belt and hung it on his saddle horn, followed by his hat.

Tandy watched, no concern on his face.

Hank turned around to face Tandy, who was still in the water, grinning.

"Come on out, Tandy, and take your medicine."

The young man's face gradually turned to a frown. "You gonna fight me, old man?"

Mac rolled his eyes and looked at Darcy, who was having a tough time holding back the laughter threatening to burst out.

"I'm going to teach you a lesson, Tandy Jacobs, that should have been taught to you a long time ago."

Now Tandy was grinning again as he made his way out of the Rio Frio. "I dealt with a lot of you Yankee lovers when I was in the Home Guard; it's time I taught *you* a lesson."

Tandy stepped up on the bank as Mac yelled to Hank, "Don't be killin' the lad. He only needs a wee little straightenin' out."

Tandy looked around at Mac, then Darcy, then the other cowhands. They all were either grinning or shaking their heads. From the look on his face, he was beginning to realize he might be in trouble.

Once Tandy was out of the water, Hank said, "You have a choice—take your lickin' or apologize."

"Humph," Tandy said, "it'll be a cold day in h—"

Hank hit him. It was a short jab with his right hand, but it carried the might and leverage of an experienced fighter. A shocked Tandy was knocked to the ground. He sat there shaking his head.

"Boy, here's where you learn to respect your elders."

Tandy jumped to his feet, concentrating as he moved in on Hank. He had his right fist cocked up by his head, moving it in small circles. Evidently, when he was in charge of eight- to sixteen-year-olds, this maneuver had impressed them. Hank stood waiting, his arms to his sides. Finally, Tandy swung, a long looping right that if it hit anything, would definitely drive it to the ground. Unfortunately for him, everyone, especially Hank, knew it was coming long before it was thrown, and all the fist struck was air.

Hank stepped inside the roundhouse right and threw the same short jab, but this time with his left. Tandy wound up back in the same position, sitting on the ground.

"I'll still take an apology, boy, if you're smart enough to give it."

This time Tandy jumped to his feet and charged Hank, his arms spread like a huge ungainly bird. Hank grabbed the boy's big wrist, turned with it, and went under the boy's arm as the momentum carried the young man past. He put his boot on Tandy's rear and shoved. Tandy's rush had taken him toward the lake, and, with Hank's help, his upper body was faster than his feet. He plowed a furrow into the bank with his chin, ending face-down in the river.

I've got to end this, Hank thought. *I want him to learn, not harbor anger because he's been humiliated.*

"Tandy," Hank said, "an apology is all it takes."

The boy came off the ground in a rush, spinning on the edge of the bank. When he closed within range, Hank let loose with a powerful right, hitting him directly on the jaw. Tandy's arms dropped to his sides. He spun around and collapsed face-first into the river, out cold.

Hank walked over, grabbed the boy by the collar, and dragged him out of the water. He then stripped down, hanging his clothes on his saddle. With his back to the hands, everyone was able to see the livid scars left by multiple whippings at the sugarcane farm.

Hank walked by and into the water as Tandy returned to consciousness. The young man stared at the mutilated back.

Darcy watched as Tandy's mouth dropped open. "There's no yellow in that back, boy." Then he turned to Hank. "Does he leave or stay?"

Hank had sunk into the clear water. He came out, blew a stream of water, and said, "It's up to him."

Tandy looked from Darcy to Hank. "Uh . . . Mr. Remington, sir, jobs are hard to find these days, especially for the likes of me. I'd like to stay, if I could."

Hank nodded. "Good. Why don't you get back in this water? The cold will help that jaw."

"Mr. Remington, *boss*, I'm sorry."

"Thanks, Tandy. Now get on back in here. And call me Hank."

"No, sir, boss. Reckon I haven't earned the right."

MARCH 5, 1869

Longhorns were strung out for almost a mile. Hank, his bandanna pulled up over his nose, rode drag along with Tandy and a cowhand the new trail boss had hired, by the name of Potsy Blinker.

Potsy's first name was actually Alexander, but he had earned the name Potsy from his severe dislike for snakes, not because he was fat.

The young man had a brother who felt the call of nature when they had been squirrel hunting on Cibolo Creek. The two brothers had killed four squirrels and were about to walk back home in Gonzales. But Potsy's brother had to go. He had quickly gathered up some leaves and found a place where he could lean against the trunk of a fallen oak. No sooner had he pulled his homespun pants down than he let out a yelp and tried to jerk them back up.

Potsy ran to his brother's aid to find a five-foot rattlesnake trapped against his brother's buttocks by the pants. Only about two feet—including the rattles, which were now buzzing with vigor—hung outside the pants. Without thinking, Potsy had run up, grabbed the exposed end of the rattler, and yanked. His brother gave another yelp and took off running for home, leaving the rattlesnake dangling in Potsy's hand. With all of the strength his ten-year-old body could muster, he swung the snake until the swing ended with the snake's head splattering against the massive trunk of a pecan tree. He threw the snake down, grabbed the squirrels, and raced toward home, never catching his older brother.

Their ma had his brother on the bed, face-first, with his pants pulled down around his ankles and his shiny white bottom blemished with four pairs of red spots where the snake had bitten him twice. All he and his family could do was try to comfort his older brother until the boy died.

At that precise moment, young Potsy had declared he would never squat in the woods. From that day, he carried a white, glistening slop jar, and when he was old enough to ride, he could always be identified by that pot bouncing on his slicker and tied tight with a cantle string. Potsy got teased about his slop jar until the hands heard his story. He still received the name Potsy for his concern, but usually the cowhands would look at each other as if Potsy wasn't that crazy after all.

Potsy, who was riding drag between Hank and Tandy, said, "Good start."

Hank glanced over at Potsy. "You been up to Abilene before?"

"Yes, sir, I surely have. Last year. That wuz my first time."

Tandy spoke up. "Well, I guess I need to listen to you so's I won't be too stupid."

Hank looked past Potsy at Tandy. The boy had made a complete turnaround since the scuffle. Hank wasn't sure, but, just maybe, he might turn out to be a good man.

Darcy had been laughing last week. All of the hands were either sleeping in the bunkhouse or riding night herd. He, Hank, Mac, and the new trail boss, Carson Bond, were sitting around the table, talking about the upcoming drive. Carson was outlining assignments he would be making the next day. Darcy, half in jest and half serious, told Carson he could save himself a lot of trouble if he assigned Tandy with Hank. He told Carson about the fight and mentioned that since then, Tandy had stuck to Hank like a tick on a coonhound. Carson thought it was a good idea. Hank agreed to it, and ultimately Tandy and Hank were assigned together. The more time he spent with him, Hank was finding that the boy was hungry for attention from a male figure.

Hank had no idea there was so much work to getting a herd trail-ready. Two-thirds of the longhorns had come from the brush country; the others had been purchased from neighboring ranchers.

Several of the cowhands, as experienced as they were, had close calls with death. Those five-, six-, and seven-foot horns could be deadly, and to hear the experienced men tell it, they'd rather tangle with a grizzly than a mad longhorn in the mesquites. In the tight thickets, there was almost no room to maneuver, and just because you got a rope on one weighing 1,500 or 2,000 pounds, didn't mean you were going to control him. In his short time of longhorn education, Hank had already developed a strong sense of respect for the breed.

Two weeks before they pulled out, backed up by Hank and Mac, Darcy had officially introduced the trail boss, Carson Bond.

Darcy had said, "Some of you boys are new here at the Remington Ranch. It looks like everyone is fitting in mighty good. All of you know we're the owners." He indicated Mac and Hank as well as himself. "You may know Carson Bond, our trail boss. I want everyone to understand he's the boss. The three of us will be working alongside you, just like we've always done, but if you have a problem, this is the man you come to." He indicated Bond, and the man stepped forward. He took off his hat, wiped off the sweatband with his hand, and settled it back on his head.

"Howdy, boys, just so you know, I've been up the trail more than once. Some of you know me; some don't. That don't make any difference to any of us. I'll be treating everyone the same. You'll have poor pay, good grub, little sleep, and more work than you think you bargained for. You've worked with me for a couple of days now, and we'll have another week or so before we hit the trail. Hopefully, by then, you'll have gotten to know me, because here's the rub.

"Once we start north, we're all committed. I'm committed to the owners and you, and you're committed to me. I ain't gonna quit till we get to Abilene, and you ain't neither. Now that don't mean you can't quit, because you can. What it means is you won't get paid if you don't finish the drive. I ain't saying if you get hurt or sick or have a death in the family, you won't get paid. What I'm saying is I'll brook no quitters. I'd like to know that we understand each other."

There were a few "yes, sirs," and all the men nodded.

"Good, just a little more and you can get back to work. A few of you fellers have been up the trail before; this is for you as well as the newcomers. Our jobs are to let these cattle lead us to Abilene, at their pace, grazing all the way. Over this drive, I'm hopin' those animals put on an average of a hundred pounds apiece. So, to do that, we let 'em get up, start grazing, and the chuck wagon will head on out, followed by the point riders. When we get to Abilene, I want those longhorns to think they had a wonderful idea coming up to Kansas."

Several of the men nodded, and there were a few chuckles.

"I want to talk to you about your horses. The owners here have purchased some fine stock. Some finer than others."

That comment brought some out-and-out laughs.

"You men have been allotted ten apiece. You've picked your own, and I hope you've been taking care of 'em because they're going to be working hard for you. We're going just shy of a thousand miles. That's a lot of riding. For every mile one of those cows travels, you'll be making between two and three, what with chasing strays, night herding when you're circling the herds, and keeping joiners from coming in. So take care of those horses. Make sure you clean those blankets and keep 'em dry and smooth on that horse's back. Some are going to be killed, but don't let it be your fault." The boss looked around his men. "Any questions?"

No one said a word.

He looked at them one more time. "I don't usually repeat myself, but take me at my word. If you think you might quit on the way, do it now." He looked each man in the eyes. No one responded. He nodded. "Alright, let's get back to work."

Hank had observed the way the point men had watched the cattle graze and then moseyed in front of them and slowly turned north. Nothing had happened at first, then a tan and white cow stepped off after them, then another. Before long, the whole herd was heading north.

Fortunately, their crossing of the Rio Frio had been simple. Where they crossed, chosen by Darcy, was no deeper than four or five inches all the way across, with sloping banks on each side. The cattle didn't hesitate, but walked straight in. It looked like the only problem they'd have would be the cattle bunching to drink, but then the leads, after drinking, moved on through the water.

Hank leaned back in the saddle to stretch his back. Fortunately, with all of the riding he had done, from Galveston and around the ranch, his body had adjusted to being in the saddle for long periods of time. He still got a stiff back occasionally, but nothing serious. Though he liked Buck, there was a black in his string that was like riding in a rocking chair. The horse was also extremely quick.

In one instance, when Hank was trying to get a rope on a yearling, the animal changed direction and dashed on the opposite side of a big mesquite. The black was charging past the mesquite, but threw on the brakes, spinning on a dime, and cut off the longhorn. It would have worked out extremely well if Hank had still been in the saddle. When the horse cut back, Hank kept going. Fortunately, the longhorn didn't feel the need to make it worse by attacking him. As it was, only Hank's pride had been damaged, along with a sore shoulder.

Tandy had seen it all. He raced over until he saw Hank getting up and dusting himself off; then he slowed to a walk and tried to hold in his laughter, unsuccessfully.

While Hank was dusting himself off, Tandy grabbed the black and led him over to him. A wry grin on his face, Hank said, "It ain't polite to laugh at your elders." He took the black and stepped into the saddle, turning toward the longhorn. The young bull had stopped to watch the show.

Tandy laughed out loud and grinned at Hank. "Yes, sir. I'll remember that. Just try to keep your saddle, 'cause long like you are, you look mighty funny slappin' at the air."

"I'll try not to make it a habit. Now let's get that bull."

The yearling, head high, trotted proudly out of the brush and straight to the herd like that had been his plan all along.

22

The herd had been moving for forty-two days, according to the trail boss. All of the men not riding night herd were bedded down, either having just come off of or waiting for their shift. Hank and Tandy, who were on duty from midnight to two thirty, had just been roused out. They saddled up and headed out with Darcy and Mac, the two pair riding in opposite directions around the herd.

Hank had tried singing, but gave that up after so many complaints had been registered with Bond that he finally asked Hank to try whistling. They were lucky, Tandy had a fine baritone voice. Even the cowhands liked to listen to him sing, although Tandy leaned toward the sad songs, like "The Dying Ranger" and "The Dying Cowboy." Tonight, Tandy was tuning up for "The Dying Cowboy."

"Don't you know something that's a little happier?" Hank asked.

The boy stopped singing, looked at Hank in the moonlight, and with a serious voice said, "The cattle like these better," and continued singing.

Hank grinned, thinking the boy was joking. He looked over at him and saw he was completely serious. Shrugging, Hank decided to enjoy the young man's singing and not comment.

Tandy had settled in to being a good cowhand. He never shirked any job and every morning was one of the first to help Skeeter clean up, load up, and get the chuck wagon on the way. Hank knew he wasn't the only one who had noticed the change in Tandy. Mac and Darcy had commented on the fact that Hank should have beaten the daylights out of that boy as soon as they had hired him. Darcy, having been the one who hired Tandy, claimed he always knew the boy would come around, causing Mac to roll his eyes and go for another cup of coffee.

Hank looked over the cattle. It was a beautiful night. They rode about twenty-five to thirty yards away from the bedded cattle. Looking across the cattle, from south to north, the Red River could be seen. The big white moon sent glimmering beams across the cattle, bringing out a pale color and glistening off the thousands of horns. Past the herd, the moon, shining on the big Red, cast a wide white ribbon across the brushy countryside.

Hank enjoyed the solitude of night herding. It gave him time to think. The drive had been perfect so far. About to cross over into the Territory, there was still plenty of fresh-growth grasses. That had been one of Carson Bond's biggest concerns. Since they had started the drive early in the season, he worried the new grass would play out the farther north they traveled. With the amount of early rain, the grasses were up and fattening the cattle. The downside to the rain was the rivers.

Darcy had said river crossings were always dangerous. Unless there was a shallow, hard rocky bottom, the fear of loss or injury was always present. Though the cowhands never let their concerns show, except for morbid tales of past injuries or death, tensions rose as they neared the next river. So far, Hank thought back, they had crossed the Colorado, Brazos, Clear, and Elm Fork of the Trinity, though he'd lost count of the number of creeks. In the morning, their next juncture was the Red River, the border between Texas and the Territory. Carson had a crossing he normally used, but the river changed almost daily.

It was a high-banked monster, appropriately named because the water that ran between the banks was a rusty red color. Here the approach had been cleaned by the cowhands, though they complained mightily, except for Tandy, that they were hired to punch cattle, not do farmer's work. The mighty banks had been tapered sufficiently to get the cattle down to the river, three hundred head at a time. Though at this point the Red River was at least a hundred yards wide, the ribbon of water made up only about fifty feet. Deeper than usual, but just barely deep enough to require the animals to swim, the river was less of a problem than the approaches. The riverbed was notorious for quicksand. The quaking sand could swallow up a horse and rider, leaving only the man's hat floating on top. For that reason and the approaches, it had taken Darcy quite a time to find an appropriate area to cross.

On Hank and Tandy's northern limit of their circles, they pulled up and gazed across the river. The soft gurgling of the running water was enticing to the dust-laden cowmen.

Tandy stopped his singing and said, "I could sure go for a swim, but I reckon we'll get one tomorrow."

"I imagine," Hank said. Because of Hank and Tandy's demonstrated ability in crossing the previous rivers, Carson Bond had selected them to lead the cattle across. Since they had three thousand head, the two men would be crossing the river all day. They swung back around and Tandy started singing again.

Passing on the south side, they could hear the occasional horn clank well behind them along the trail they had just traveled. It looked like they were the first herd up for the year, which, if nothing happened, would mean a good price, but they were followed closely by a herd almost twice their size. Hank understood there was another herd behind them. They were lucky they started when they did.

Their shift went quickly by. The two men were joined by Mac and Darcy at the rope corral, where they unsaddled their horses, gave them a quick rubdown, and headed for their bedrolls.

"TAKE 'EM THROUGH EASY, boys. Just like you've done in the past. Darcy found a good crossing, and I suspect we'll have this herd well across before dark." Bond nodded to them and rode to the side.

Hank and Tandy, about thirty feet apart, led the first three hundred toward the steep bank. The boys had worked hard and broken down the edges, but this herd would take care of sloping it out. The leaders hesitated, but the big horns coming up behind them prodded them into moving, and they followed the two men over the edge. The job of lead wasn't bad as long as you stayed with your horse. If for any reason a man found himself in the river in front of those cows when they made their mind up to cross, he could be a goner.

Two cowhands followed on each side of the small herd, one set upriver and one downriver. They had the job of keeping stragglers from swimming off on their own and subsequently leading the herd away from the crossing.

The first group hesitated again at the water's edge. Hank and Tandy kept riding until their horses were swimming. The lead cow watched and then stepped into the river, followed by the others. Before long they were all entering the water. Once out on the opposite side, the cattle scrambled up the embankment and immediately went to grazing.

By the time Hank and the others got back, there was already another group starting down the southern slope. The crossing was tiring on the horses. Hank changed to Buck about halfway through the job. The others followed suit, alternating the switch so there remained a sufficient number of men to herd the cattle.

By two in the afternoon, the last bunch was moving down the slope, headed for the water. Hank entered the water a little ahead of Tandy. He was glad this part of the drive was coming to a close. He was tired and couldn't wait to sit down to some beans, biscuits, and whatever Skeeter had dreamed up. Mac was right. Skeeter was magic when it came to food.

He glanced back over his right shoulder to see Tandy entering the water. Concern drifted across Hank's face when he saw how close behind him Tandy had allowed the cows. He watched him for another minute or so. It looked like Tandy was pulling ahead. He turned his attention back to where he was going.

Buck had just started swimming when Hank heard Tandy croak. He looked back and the boy's horse had balked, then reared upon reaching the deeper water, and Tandy's hat was floating down the river. The lead cow was no more than ten feet behind where the boy disappeared under the water. Hank reined Buck around and saw the towheaded boy pop to the surface. The herd bore down on him. If they reached him first, Tandy would be ground into the mud of the Red River by a thousand hooves.

Hank went for his six-gun to kill the lead cow that was almost on top of Tandy, but remembered all of the weapons were in Skeeter's wagon for the crossing. Then he yanked his rope loose, shook out a loop, and tossed it over the boy. Tandy grabbed it and held on tight. Hank took a loop around the saddle horn and pointed Buck toward the far shore. The cattle were almost on top of Tandy. All of the other cowhands were too far to play any part in the little drama taking place on the river.

Desperate, Hank slammed his spurs into Buck. The big buckskin sprang forward, and with every jump he came out of the water like a leaping fish, but carried Hank and Tandy farther ahead of the approaching cattle. Hank dragged Tandy to the far bank. The boy jumped up, coughing and wheezing, and staggered to Hank's side. Hank had kicked his boot out of the stirrup, and Tandy swung up behind him. The cattle were just starting to walk out of the northern edge of the Red River.

Tandy's horse had tried to turn back, but the sight of the approaching cattle scared it worse than the water, and it turned and swam across to the opposite side. Once out, he galloped up the bank and stopped, looking back and quivering.

Hank rode next to the animal and Tandy grabbed the reins. So far, neither man had said a word. They rode to the side of the herd and Hank let Tandy down.

The young man looked up at Hank.

"Thanks, I owe you."

Hank laughed. "I couldn't let anything happen to you and let all my work go to waste."

Tandy, though still shaken, grinned back. "Yeah, I see what you mean." He swung back up on his horse, and the two men watched as the last of the herd scrambled up the embankment.

Across the river, longhorns were massing as far as the eye could see. Carson Bond rode up and looked at Tandy. "You alright, boy?"

"Yes, sir. I don't know what happened to my horse. I've used him to cross time and time again. He ain't never give me no trouble."

"That's a horse for you," Carson said. "He'll do something over and over until one day he gets a notion. Maybe he seen a stick in the water and thought it was a snake; maybe a cloud drifted over he didn't like, no telling. But I'm glad you're safe." Carson looked back at the herd moving away from the river. "Let's get back to work. We need to get these cattle moving so the next herds can get up here."

"Yes, sir," Tandy said.

"Hey, Tandy," Potsy called as he came riding up. "Thought you might need this to keep what few brains you have from boilin' away." He tossed Tandy his hat.

"Thanks, Potsy. You're right. I need to keep all I have."

Potsy nodded and looked over at Hank. "Reckon I need to go fishing with you. You pulled in a mighty big fish." He broke into laughter as he pulled his bandanna up over his nose and positioned himself at drag.

Both Hank and Tandy followed suit. The cattle slowly drifted north and the dust drifted over the wet cowboys. Hank grinned as he thought, *That water really felt good, but it didn't last long. I guess if you're not dirty, you're not a cowhand.*

HANK WAS SOLD on the fact that Carson Bond knew what he was doing. They only lost twelve head, and not a single hand, going through the Territory. They'd been stopped by Indians several times, and after bargaining, Carson gave them bacon, tobacco, and two or three cows. It was usually Hank and Tandy who cut the cows from the herd and turned them over to the Indians. They would cut out the weaker ones that had little chance of making it to Abilene.

The trail Carson was taking bore west of the Flint Hills. Hank was thankful for that, since the country they were crossing was rough enough. He felt for Skeeter driving the chuck wagon. They'd had to replace one wheel already, and he wouldn't be surprised if another one broke before they reached Abilene. One thing that everyone appreciated now—the grass. Big bluestem covered the land as far as the eye could see. He wasn't sure he had believed the trail boss when he said the cattle would fatten up, but he did now. Hank had no idea how much weight the cattle had put on, but they were definitely beefier.

He could see Tandy riding ahead of him and grinned at the thought. Potsy had called Tandy the big fish a few times, but Tandy had taken it well, so it didn't stick. Now, all of the hands, even Potsy, were back to calling him by his name. He had become quite a different lad from the one Hank had knocked into the

Frio. *Speaking of changing, I guess I've changed quite a bit.* He didn't know how much weight he had put back on, but his shirts and coat had grown tight across the shoulders. His trousers still fit well except around his thighs; they were a little tight there.

Hank didn't mind work done on his feet, like the cowhands did. Therefore, he was constantly being assigned hard labor jobs even though he was one of the owners. Carson Bond was no respecter of persons, but Hank didn't mind. In fact, he enjoyed the feeling of his muscles working, the tension in his back and arms. He always slept better after a hard day of working. Not that he didn't sleep well after a long day of riding—every day was hard.

It felt good to be around a group of men where everyone carried their own load. One thing about it, on a trail drive, a man had plenty of time to think. "How you feelin', Blacky?" The horse perked up his ears as if he was listening.

"Aye, and he's started talkin' to horseflesh," came from behind him.

"Howdy, Mac. Don't you know you're not supposed to slip up on a man?"

"Wonderin', I am, my boy, if you're goin' daft with the prairie sickness."

The Scotsman rode up beside Hank.

"I may be. I sure like this country. Gives a man peace of mind."

"Aye, it does, but I'm preferring a place where the company of the fair sex can be enjoyed."

Hank laughed. "I don't think you're alone. I've heard some of the boys talking. Since we're in Kansas, they've started talking about a visit to Wichita when we go by."

"Aye, I'm thinking our trail boss might be agreeable to a short repast, though Abilene is not too many miles up the trail. Carson was saying another two weeks will see us at the trail's end."

"These boys are liable to explode with serious disappointment if we pass up Wichita," Hank said.

"There be truth in that, and I'm thinkin' that's what the boss is thinkin'. We'll just have to see."

The two men rode along without speaking for several miles. The days had started warming, and the heat from the herd could bring a man to a sweat just riding alongside.

Mac spoke up. "We've been fortunate."

"How's that?"

"Besides the dunkin' your Tandy boy took, we've lost no one. It's too bad about the horses, but losing only two, and them from gopher holes, ain't bad."

"You're right there," Hank said. "No one's tried to cut the herd, and we've had no stampedes. Can't get much luckier than that."

"Aye, but we haven't gotten into the Territory where it happened before. Pitts hit us after we passed Wichita."

"I don't want to wish us any bad luck," Hank said, "but I've got some settling I'd like to do with Mr. Pitts."

"After finding out what he did, I'm agreeing with you, but it'd be too bad if any of the boys got hurt because of it."

Hank nodded. "You're right. I'm just thinking out loud."

Mac waved and headed forward, continuing his check of the outriders. Hank watched him stop alongside Tandy. The thought of the boy and his nickname brought another grin to his face. Then he grew serious as his mind, unbidden, brought a clear picture of Deborah to the front. *I wonder where she is now. Did she go to the Colorado Territory like she talked about? Are she and Dr. James happy?* He pushed that thought out of his mind. It didn't matter whether or not they were happy; he wasn't a home-wrecker, especially to the man who saved his life.

What will I do after we get to Abilene? Do I really want to go back to the ranch in Texas? What about my family? Where are they? Who are they?

23

Six days later Carson Bond stopped the herd outside Wichita. They were going to rest for two days, pushing on for Abilene the third day. He had named Darcy as *segundo* and paid each man twenty dollars as an advance on the pay they had coming in Abilene.

Skeeter wanted to pick up a few supplies, so Mac and Carson would go in with him and the first group of cowhands. The trail boss and Skeeter were going to be back early. The other men were told to be back for their shift, starting at six the next morning. Mac was going to stay to make sure everyone made it back. Tandy was in the first group.

"Hank," Tandy said, "I'd just as soon wait for you. It's just another day."

"Nope. You heard what the boss said. You today, me tomorrow. You can go in and scout it out for me. As much as I like Skeeter's cooking, I'm gettin' a mite tired of beans. You find a good place to eat and let me know. Now, go ahead, and have fun."

Tandy grinned. "I aim to. I don't think I've ever been to a town as big as Wichita." The boy ran with the others to their horses. He leaped into the saddle, pulled his hat off, swung it around a couple of times, and took off for town.

Skeeter looked over at Hank and shook his head. "Glad I ain't that young no more." To the rest of the cowhands standing around, he said, "Don't you girls worry, I'll be back 'fore suppertime." He popped the reins and the two mules started off.

Mac waved and he and the trail boss rode out with the wagon.

Hank looked over at Darcy, who was nursing a cup of coffee, and motioned with his head. Darcy tossed the coffee and walked over. "Let's go for a ride," Hank said.

Their horses were saddled with the cinches loose. They tightened them and swung aboard. The herd was quietly munching the abundant bluestem.

"I've been thinking," Hank said.

Darcy rode on, letting his friend talk.

"We'll be getting into Abilene in a few more days. I don't think I'll be going back to Texas with you."

Stunned, Darcy pulled his horse up. "Why not?"

"Darcy, I've got to find my family. It's going on four years now. If I have any kinfolks out there, they've got to be thinking I'm dead. They can't go on like that. I've got to figure out how to locate them. Dang it, I've got to find out who I am!"

The two men continued around the peaceful herd, with the cattle lowing and chewing their cuds. Finally, Darcy spoke up. "Hank, you're part of this ranch. There wouldn't be one if not for you. Heck, Mac, me, or Wade wouldn't have made it back to Texas if not for you."

"Darcy, I appreciate what you're telling me, and you have no idea how much you boys helped me in the hospital, but I've got to try to find my family."

Darcy slid his hat from his head, pulled off his bandanna, and wiped his face. The days, now in the middle of June, were hot. He wiped the sweatband of his hat, put it back on, and while retying his bandanna around his neck, said, "You'll always have a third of the ranch."

"That's something else I wanted to talk to you and Mac about. I don't deserve a piece of the ranch. You boys made the first drive. You survived all your troubles with the cattle, the weather, and the Indians. You deserve what you earn."

Now Darcy was getting mad. "Dang it, Hank. Are you even listenin' to me? I already told you we wouldn't be here if not for you. It was your money that kept us going when we had none. Without you there just flat wouldn't be a Remington Ranch. I don't know how I can say it any plainer!"

Again, silence fell on the two men. They nodded to Potsy as he and his sidekick made the circle in the opposite direction. Hank gazed out across the open plains to the west. The bluestem grass was reaching four feet tall and still growing. There was a slight southeast wind. It glided across the tops of the pale green grass, causing it to gently bow. In the distance the bluestem looked like waves of the sea, only occasionally broken by lines of cottonwood, cedar, box elder, and elm as they followed the streams that cut south. *I'd sure like to head west and see those mountains I've heard talk about.*

He turned to Darcy. "I've got to be going back East. That's where I'm from. It's time. I've never felt I had a wife or kids, but I feel, deep in my soul, that I have a family. I keep seeing this vague outline of a woman, a strong but kind-faced woman. I'm thinking she may be my ma. She doesn't deserve not knowing what happened to her son."

The two men felt the light breeze freshen and looked at each other. Darcy spoke up. "All right, we can talk about this more when we get to Abilene. Mac needs to be involved."

Hank nodded. "True, but I'm not changing my mind. Now, what's with the wind? This time of day, it should be dying down." He looked across the cattle. The lowing had stopped and most of the big heads were up, testing the wind. It had swung to the east and was getting stronger.

Both men looked west. Far across the prairie, there was the beginning of a faint line of clouds that painted the edge of the horizon as far south and north as they could see.

Darcy said, "That's not good. We need to be getting the boys back from town. It looks like we're going to have a major blow tonight."

They rode back to camp. The hands had already put out the fire. The coffeepot sat to the side, still steaming. "Skeeter left us some biscuits and beans, boys. Let's eat up. We got trouble coming."

As Potsy rode by, Darcy called him over. "Potsy, get to town and tell them boys to hightail it back. We need everyone here tonight."

Potsy waved, simultaneously leaned forward, and kicked the bay in the flanks. The horse leaped forward and raced toward town. Hank led the horse he was riding to the remuda. Buck was standing against the rope, looking at him.

"Hi, Buck." He scratched the big horse between the ears. Removing the saddle and tack from the horse he'd been riding, he smoothed the blanket on Buck's back and fastened the saddle. He dropped the reins, ground hitching Buck, and looked around. All of the men who had not gone to town were saddling up. He walked back to Darcy.

"What's the plan?" he said as his eyes were drawn to a faint flash in the west. Darcy was also watching.

"That's what I was afraid of. We've got a storm comin', and the way this wind is freshening from the east, it could be big. We've been lucky we haven't had a stampede. I was starting to think we'd make it all the way to Abilene." There were several flashes up and down the line of clouds, which had moved closer. "I sure hope Carson and the boys get back before that thing hits."

The cows were lowing again, but not the soft contented sound from earlier. They were more strident. They had begun to move, not in any direction, but milling around, as if they weren't happy but didn't know what to do about it.

"Mount up, boys!" Darcy called. "Circle the cows. Sing, whistle, do anything you can to try to keep 'em calm."

One of the cowhands said, "Where's Tandy when you need him? I'll bet he's got a song for this."

As the hands separated, going to their usual spots, hoofbeats of running horses could be heard. Within moments, all the hands who had been in town came racing up. Except for Mac and Carson Bond, all the men headed for the remuda to get fresh horses.

Carson and Mac rode straight for Hank and Darcy and dismounted. "We've got big trouble," Carson said. To emphasize his statement, a distant rumble sounded in the west. "That's a bad storm coming. Notice this east wind is already getting stronger. That monster to the west is sucking everything into it."

While Carson was talking, two fresh horses were led up for him and Mac. The two men nodded their appreciation.

Carson waved to gather all the hands who weren't already circling the cattle. "Boys, this is gonna be tough. I know most of you have had the pleasure of a stampede before, and you're very likely to have it again tonight."

The cowhands were listening, but the thunder kept drawing their eyes to the west as the storm rushed toward them.

"If they take off, don't try to stop 'em. The last thing we want is to have to tell your folks you were killed in a stampede this close to Abilene. Just let them run the steam out. Hopefully the storm ain't thick, so as fast as it's movin', it should be out of here pretty soon. When them cattle start slowing, then you can think about turning 'em."

Hank looked at the men. They were solid. Concerned, yes. But every man was ready to do his job. He had a flash of himself wearing his uniform, talking to a group of men such as this. He could remember the young, serious faces staring back, some afraid, but all determined. Then the picture disappeared.

"If they go south," Carson continued, "we've got big trouble. With all the herds coming up behind us, there must be ten or fifteen thousand head back there. It'll be a mess sorting. The big thing to remember, if you're headed south and you see longhorns coming toward you, forget trying to do anything except get out of the way. Let's just pray that if they stampede, they'll head anywhere but south. Any questions?"

Out of the group one of the men spoke up. "I guess going to town tomorrow is out of the question?"

All of the cowhands broke out in laughter.

Carson grinned and shook his head, then said, "Get on them cayuses and go earn your money!" Then he turned to Hank, Darcy, and Mac. "You're going to lose some cattle tonight. There's nothing that can be done about it. Like I told the boys, just protect yourselves. I want to see all of you alive in the morning."

The three of them nodded and mounted their horses. Tandy had been waiting. As soon as Hank mounted, he was up at his side.

"How was town?" Hank asked as they rode out to position themselves at their outrider position to the west of the herd.

Tandy grinned. "What I saw of it was mighty fine. But we didn't have time enough." Tandy stopped as the sun grew dim from the tall clouds racing in front of it. Then he started again. "We weren't hardly in town no time when the boss came runnin' up, yellin' for us to get mounted and head back to the drive. We almost ran over Potsy racin' into town, with his white slop jar bouncin' away."

Tandy had no more than finished when there was a flash to the west and shortly a loud clap of thunder. The longhorns, already nervous, jumped at the clap, but didn't run.

Leading the line of tall thunderheads was a low black cloud that looked like it was being churned horizontally. It reminded

Hank of the bow wave he had fallen into. The cloud was as dark and ominous as the water had been.

"Whew," Tandy said, "I think this is gonna be a tough one. I been in one other stampede, and there weren't this many cows, maybe six, seven hundred. I'm here to tell you, that was scary."

Darkness came on quickly, but the lightning was so thick it was almost like continuous daylight. The men had donned their slickers when they rode out to the herd, knowing they were going to get a gully washer, and now they did. It was like someone had a huge pitcher in the clouds and was pouring it out on top of them. Even with hats pulled down tight, it was difficult to see more than ten feet in front of them.

The cattle were now bawling, letting the cowhands know they didn't like what was happening and wanted to be somewhere else.

Tandy leaned over to Hank so he could be heard above the rain and continuous thunder. "Stick with me, boss. We'll make it."

The herd had managed to hold their position through all of the previous lightning and thunder, but suddenly a huge bolt raced out of the clouds and struck directly at the rear of the herd. The explosion was louder than any gun he could remember. Hank felt the hair on his arms and neck stand out straight, and swore he must be in Hell, for he smelled the brimstone.

The cattle jerked as one and leaped forward.

Hank could faintly hear Tandy yell, "There they go!"

And so they did. Balls of lightning rolled across the long-horns, only increasing their speed. They raced desperately and futilely to get away from the flashes and what sounded like explosions.

Hank held on to Buck. He trusted the horse more than he did himself in this roaring, blasting, flashing caldron. Light, darkness, darkness, light. Flash after flash. Brilliant light to see by and then pitch blackness, and racing headlong adjacent to tons of pounding hooves.

Buck stretched his long legs and raced with the frightened cattle, tall grass whipping around him. Hank watched the cattle drop down into a wash ahead.

Cattle piled up on the opposite side and were run over by those behind them. Most continued up and out of the wash, but many turned and thundered either up or down the draw, depending on their location. In the flashes he could see the wash directly ahead, full of cattle and horns. It was at least twenty feet wide. If they dropped into it, they would be crushed by the cattle and stomped into the mud.

He yelled at the big buckskin, never knowing if the animal heard him, "Come on, boy," and kicked him in the flanks.

At the edge, the big horse lifted and sailed over the slashing mass of cattle beneath them, landing well on the other side and keeping pace with the stampede. Hank breathed a sigh of relief and then thought, *Tandy!* He looked back over his shoulder, to his left, to his right. Tandy was nowhere in sight. Had he plowed into the wash?

Hank's heart sank. There was no way the boy could survive. He would be gored, trampled to death. Hank started to turn Buck, but there was no possible way. The only option in all of this bedlam was to keep on racing with the cattle.

Another bolt of lightning crashed ahead of the herd, and they surged toward the northwest. In that flash, he could see riders ahead of him, desperately trying to turn their horses out of the way of the maddened animals. He saw one of the riders go down, the horse and man disappearing in the midst of the herd.

They rode on. The storm finally started weakening. Lightning flashes became fewer and farther away, but the cattle kept running.

Hank's heart was heavy. Tandy had made it almost all the way to Abilene. Then he could feel the change in Buck's gait. The horse had slowed, though only a little. He looked over at the longhorns to his right, no more than thirty feet away, and saw their tongues hanging out.

What was it Carson said? Running is not natural for the longhorn. He'll do it when he's scared or mad, but he prefers walking. Sure enough, the animals started slowing. Hank heard some gunshots. The boys on point were trying to turn the stampede. More gunshots, and now that the rain had let up to a fine sprinkle, he could see the lead start swinging to the right. More turned. When he neared where they were turning, he pulled his Remington from under his slicker and let off a couple of shots in the air. Sure enough, his section was following the others.

It took time, but once the cattle turned, they were able to get them to turn again and they fell into a trot, then a walk, and they were milling. Three thousand head that had only a short time earlier raced through the night like crazed animals.

The rain had stopped. Hank pulled off his slicker, shook it out, and rolled it up. He watched the cows. They were still edgy, but tired. He had just tied his slicker behind his saddle when he heard a horse coming up behind him.

"Howdy, boss."

Hank whipped around to see Tandy riding nonchalantly toward him, his slicker already tied. In the occasional flash of distant lightning, he saw the young man grinning at him.

"Don't look so surprised, boss. I ain't no ghost."

Hank grinned at him. "You dumb ox, I thought you were killed in that draw."

"You mean the one you and your horse sprouted wings and flew over? I swear from where he left to where he touched ground had to be at least thirty feet. If there were a horse jumpin' contest, which would be the stupidest thing I ever heard of, you and that horse would win, hands down, every time."

Hank just shook his head. "So what'd you do?"

"You was ahead of me, and I saw you jump, so I just turned

that horse and rode down to where I found a crossing, simple as that. Wait 'til I tell the boys. They ain't gonna believe that crazy jump."

Shortly, Carson Bond rode up. "You fellers all right?"

"Yes, sir," Hank said. "How about everyone else?" He dreaded this question, because he was sure he had seen a rider go down.

"I'm sorry to say it looks like Jonesy went down when the herd cut west after that big lightning strike. I try to tell riders you've got to widen the space from these here longhorns when you've got a stampede. He was just too close and they caught him by surprise." He shook his head. "Danged shame, Al's taking it mighty hard. They've been friends since they were kids." Carson sighed and got back to business. "I'm having everybody stay on guard tonight. We'll eat in shifts once it breaks daylight. I know they're tired, but I want to get these hardheads moving on to Abilene as soon after daylight as possible." He waved and continued his rounds.

24

They'd buried what little they could find of Jonesy that morning before the herd was started. Hank looked around the men. *Men,* he thought, *boys really. All experienced cowhands, but not a one over twenty-five, living a hard, dangerous life they love.* The faces were hard-set, sadness in their eyes, but determination to keep on to Abilene. Not a quitter in the bunch.

That had been ten days ago, and the herd was now gathered in the holding pens adjacent to the railroad tracks in Abilene. Joseph D. McCoy, Abilene cattle buyer, had been at the gate of the pens as the cattle were driven in, along with the three owners and the trail boss.

"Well, Mr. Bond, congratulations on bringing through a fine-looking herd. You are the first of the season. Although I understand there are several herds behind you."

"Yes, there are, Mr. McCoy. I thank you for your assessment of this herd, and remind you that though others are behind us, we are here."

McCoy smiled at Bond. "Yes, Mr. Bond, so you are. What's your count?"

The two men had both been counting as the cattle passed through the gate.

"I make it 2,980."

"My count was 2,985. Shall we split the difference?"

Carson nodded.

"Fine, we'll make the final count 2,983."

The Remington ranch owners and the trail boss waited for McCoy to continue. He looked back over the herd and at the cowhands, still mounted, circled around the men.

"I think you'll be happy with the price this year. It seems those folks in Chicago, and farther east, are craving good Texas beef something terrible. Would thirty-two dollars a head be satisfactory to you?"

Carson looked at the owners, who, in unison, gave him an emphatic nod. He looked around at the men seated on their horses, took a deep breath, and said, "That would be fine."

The two men were unable to say anything for a few moments because of the raucous hooting and shouting of the cowhands. Finally, Carson Bond turned around and stared at them. They settled down immediately. He turned back to McCoy and extended his hand. "It's a pleasure doing business with you, sir."

McCoy shook Bond's hand. "And you, sir. I always expect good stock when you bring them through." He turned and shook hands with the three owners. "Would all of you gentlemen"—he also looked to Carson Bond—"be my guest at dinner tonight? I think we'll be having something else instead of beans."

Everyone grinned, acknowledging his humor.

"Now, if you gentlemen would care to follow me to my office, I will pay you for your trouble."

Bond hung back and Hank turned to him. "Mr. Bond, you have done a yeoman's work in getting our herd here in excellent shape. Would you be so kind as to tell the men to take care of their horses, get themselves a room in the Drover's Hotel, and run a tab for drinks and food on us? Also, would you please join us?

Then you can pay the men." Darcy and Mac nodded, agreeing with Hank's request.

The trail boss turned to the men. "The owners said for you to take care of your horses, get rooms at the Drover's Hotel, and eat and drink, on them."

The cowboys again started whooping and hollering. Bond held up his hands until they calmed down. "Meet me in the lobby in an hour and I'll have your pay." He turned to join the group while he was sent along with shouting and cheering.

"They love you now," Hank said as they walked toward McCoy's office in the hotel.

Carson grinned. "They'd love their old schoolteacher, if they had one, if he said they had free drinks."

Everyone laughed and walked up the steps to the hotel and into the cattle buyer's office.

Once all were seated, McCoy pulled out a log and made the first entry in it for the year. "Gentlemen, I calculate that your herd of 2,983, at $32 a head, comes to a total of $95,456."

Hank stared at the man like he was crazy. Could there be that much money in the world? Mac and Darcy looked at him and grinned. Then Darcy nodded. "Mr. McCoy, that is a mighty fine number as far as we're concerned."

"Fine, would you like cash or a note? I know you must pay your men. Oh, wait, like I said, this is the first herd of the year, I forgot. What are you going to do about your horses?"

They looked to Carson. "Most of the men brought their own horses. I'd recommend those who didn't be given a horse. A few of them will go to the eastern cities, but most will head back to Texas, like me. So we'll probably ride together. I'd suggest you at least give them their favorite."

Hank looked around at Mac and Darcy. "What do you want to do?"

Mac said, "It's my thinkin' we'll be hiring several of the lads to stay on with us, permanent like. The horses will be going with us."

McCoy nodded. "That's settled. Now, how would you like to get paid?"

Mac looked to Carson Bond. "Carson, do you have the figures?"

"I do, Mr. MacGregor. We pulled out on the fifth of April, and this is July the fourteenth. By my figuring, this is what we owe the men." He handed a slip to Mac, who looked it over and passed it to Darcy and Hank.

Darcy spoke up. "These numbers look good to me. However, we'd like to give the men a hundred-dollar bonus and allow them to take two horses out of their string."

"That's mighty generous," Carson said.

Hank stepped in. "We're not finished. We'd like for Skeeter to have a three-hundred-dollar bonus and for you, Mr. Bond, a thousand-dollar bonus."

Bond's eyes grew big. These numbers were unheard of on the trail. "Gentlemen," he said, "I'm much obliged, but I should tell you, word will get out, and the other ranch owners will not like this."

"That's not our concern," Hank replied. "Though this is my first drive, Mac and Darcy have confirmed it to me, these cattle were handled exceptionally well. For that, we are grateful. Now, we would like to hire five men to work full-time. They'll return with Mac and Darcy and the remuda. Here are the names."

Bond looked at the list. "These are good men. I will tell you I don't think Potsy will hire on. The boy sticks with me pretty close. I know his family well. As far as the rest, they'll ride for the brand." Bond turned to Hank. "I've heard the rumor you'll not be returning. In case you haven't noticed, Tandy has adopted you. If you don't go back, he won't."

Hank frowned. "I don't know where I'll end up. I'm sure he'll want to go back to Texas."

Bond shrugged. "Maybe so."

Mac figured quickly and handed a slip of paper to McCoy. "The cattle buyer nodded, stood, and walked out the door, returning momentarily. "Your money will be here in just a moment. I assumed you wanted this in gold and the rest in a note."

"Exactly right," Mac said.

Within minutes a man wearing a white shirt, garters on his sleeves, and a green visor came in laden with six leather draw-string pouches and set them on the desk. Mac stood and felt each one. First, he picked up two bags and handed them to Carson, who stood when Mac turned to him. "This one is for you, and it's a job well done. Hopefully you'll be available next year."

Carson grinned at the three owners as he hefted the gold. "If the Lord sees fit to leave me in good health, I'll be ready."

"Good," Mac continued. "The second bag is for Skeeter, he's earned it, and tell him we leave in three days." He picked up the larger pouch, also handing it to Carson. "This, of course, is for the boys." He took the trail boss's hand. "I'm thankin' you again."

Everyone shook Carson's hand, and he said, "Reckon I'd better go pay those boys 'fore they come looking for me." He nodded and left the room.

While Mac was up, he picked up the other three pouches and handed one each to Darcy and Hank.

"Gentlemen, I thank you for your business. I've got to get out to the yards. We should have another herd coming in behind you. Don't forget, supper at six o'clock here at the Drover's Restaurant."

McCoy walked them into the lobby, and they walked over to register while he headed out the door.

Once they had signed in, Mac said, "It's talking we need to do now."

Hank shook his head. "I'm not talking to a soul until I get this trail dust washed off. How about we meet in the restaurant in, say, an hour?"

Mac and Darcy concurred and the three men headed up to their rooms.

~

McCOY HAD BEEN unable to make dinner. Another herd had arrived, and the trail boss was a friend of Carson Bond's, so he had accompanied McCoy to the corrals.

"Mac," Hank said, "my mind's made up. The Remington Ranch is yours and Darcy's. You can pay me back the six hundred dollars I loaned you and we'll call it even."

The three men were sitting around the table in the Drover's Hotel, having big thick steaks. Most folks who had never been on a cattle drive assumed the cowhands always had steak, which was far from the truth. Only if a cow broke a leg did they eat beef, for each animal represented an investment.

Darcy and Mac had been trying to talk Hank out of leaving, but he had his mind made up, and as much as he admired Mac and Darcy's work in building the ranch, he didn't feel he was entitled to any part of it.

Mac shook his head and looked at Darcy. "Can you be explaining why this man is so stubborn, when it's for his own good?"

Darcy had obviously conceded the fight. He just shrugged.

"Hank, me boy, I'm knowing you must search, and that is all well and good. But you are going to either get your memory back or not, and the odds are slim of you ever finding your family without your memory. So search, and when you get tired, come home, come back to Texas. For the Remington Ranch is going to be one of the biggest and best in Texas. Don't you want to be part of that?"

Hank leaned forward and smiled at his friends, for they were his true friends. "Mac, what you are offering me would tempt any man, but I can't take what the two of you have worked so hard to develop. I can't and I won't."

Hank sliced a big bite of steak and shoved it into his mouth, savoring the taste of the meat and watching his friends as he ate. He saw Mac sigh and shake his head again.

"Alright, boyo, but we are not cutting you out entirely. After expenses, we'll have about ninety thousand dollars left. We're taking one-third, thirty thousand dollars, and putting it in the bank here in your name."

Hank finished chewing, swallowed the meat, and started to respond.

Mac held his hand up. "No, laddie! We are not arguing or changing our minds. It will be there. So you do what you will with it. It is no longer ours to worry about." Mac made a swishing motion with his hands as if he were washing the problem away.

It was Hank's turn to shake his head. "Don't you two ever talk about me being stubborn. You're both more stubborn than any Army mule I've ever seen, but I know when I'm licked. Thank you. I imagine that's the best interest anyone has ever been paid on six hundred dollars."

They all laughed. Hank was glad it was settled, and he was sure his friends were, too. He was just about to say something when Tandy staggered up and dropped into the extra chair at the table.

The boy pushed his hat back and grinned at each of the men. "I think I'm a little drunk."

Hank looked out the window. It couldn't be any later than midafternoon. "You sure didn't waste any time."

"The boys helped me. I ain't never really been drunk before. It feels funny. My head feels all wobbly. You wanna have a drink with me, boss?"

"Tandy, you completed this drive like a man. You survived that stampede. You helped me learn how to handle cows. You've treated the other men fair. I think you've earned the right to call me Hank."

The three partners watched the young man ponder what Hank had said. It was obvious he was having a problem focusing on their faces. When he finally focused on Hank, he said, "You're right," and slammed his big hand down on the table. "I have." Now his drunken grin got bigger. "You wanna have a drink with me ... Hank?"

"I think you've had enough. Why don't you head up to your room and sleep it off? I'll have a sarsaparilla with you later."

Tandy slowly processed what his friend had said, then stood, pressing one hand on the table to reduce his swaying. "You're right, Hank. I'm gonna go sleep it off." He turned and headed through the entrance of the restaurant, into the hotel, not quite navigating through as he slammed against the wall.

Hank jumped to his feet. "I'll see you boys later. I'm not leaving for the East until tomorrow." He managed to get to Tandy, who was now leaning against the wall for stability. He put his arm around the big fella's shoulders, grasping him under the arm and lifting.

Tandy turned his head, looking like an owl, examining Hank. "Hello, Hank. You wanna have a drink?"

"Maybe later," he said, turning his head as the full brunt of Tandy's drunken breath hit him. As they staggered up the stairs, Tandy burst into song, choosing one of his favorites, "The Dying Ranger." His loud voice carried throughout the hotel lobby and restaurant, but he couldn't manage more than the first two verses. He started crying and turned his owl-like head toward Hank. "That's almighty sad, Hank."

They had just made it to the top of the stairs. "What's your room number?"

Tandy, who was still looking at Hank and blinking, said, "I dunno."

"You got anyone in the room with you?"

"Just me and Potsy, my good ole friend."

Hank turned to see Potsy looking up at them and called, "Potsy, what's your room number?"

"Lucky seven, Hank. You need some help?"

Hank shook his head and guided Tandy down the hallway. The boy was starting to snore, and his legs were getting looser. "Come on, Tandy. Just a little farther. You can make it."

They reached number seven and Hank pulled the latch, the door swinging open. He guided Tandy to the nearest bed, turned him around, and eased him down into a sitting position. When he turned him loose, Tandy fell over, crushing his beat-up, dirty hat. Hank went ahead and pulled the boy's boots off and turned his head when the smell hit him. Someone else needed a bath. He lifted the boy's legs up onto the bed and noticed Tandy had his same problem. The boy's feet stuck out over the edge. He walked to the head of the bed, grabbed the passed-out drunk under his armpits, and dragged him as far as he could toward the pillows. The hat had rolled under the heavy body as it slid across the covers. Hank yanked it out from under the deadweight and punched it back into shape, hanging it on the bedpost. He repositioned Tandy's gun belt, which was lying in the chair. Surveying his handiwork, he shook his head and slipped out the door.

HANK HAD DROPPED off to sleep quickly after taking a stroll down the single main street in town. The Long Branch had been jumping with cowhands and a few riffraff, but it looked like the marshal had things under control. He'd heard of the man who wore the badge in Abilene. When he'd hired on as marshal, he established a rule: No handguns worn inside the city limits. After breaking a couple of heads, Marshal Tom "Bear River" Smith had little trouble. He was equally at ease with his fists or guns.

It looked like the boys were having a fine time, not counting the two or three drunken fights that had gotten started, but lost steam on their own. After a few misguided fists flew, the cowhands threw their arms around each other and headed back into the saloon.

He thought about the future of these young men. Most would pass their time punching cattle until one day they got off their horse and died. Which, he thought, wasn't a bad way to live, out in the open spaces, doing something you loved, not bad.

As he walked past the Long Branch, he caught sight of a big man crossing in front of the door of the saloon. He thought he recognized him, but after a moment realized it couldn't be Pitts. He started to walk over and take a better look, but the exhaustion of the trip was weighing on him, so he headed for the hotel and sleep.

It felt like he had just lain down when someone was shaking him. He woke, the fog of sleep blown away by the expression on Potsy's face. "You've got to come quick, Hank. Tandy's been in a fight and he's hurt bad. If Bart hadn't pulled a hideout gun, I think Tandy would be dead, but now Bart's in jail, and I think Tandy's dying."

Hank slammed his feet into his boots, his mind digesting the information Potsy had just told him. He reached for his gun belt, then remembered the law and let it lie. "Where's Tandy?"

"At the doc's." The two men rushed out of the hotel, Hank following Potsy. They banged up the steps that ran along the side of the mercantile to the doctor's office on the second floor. Bursting in, Hank saw the doctor standing over a bloody body surrounded by cowhands. When they saw Hank, they made a path so he could get to Tandy. He rushed forward and his eyes fell on the bloody boy.

25

When Hank's eyes fell on the boy, his heart sank. There was no way Tandy could survive what Hank saw. He turned to the doctor. "Doc?"

The doctor, who had been sewing a tear in the boy's flesh over his belly, finished, leaned back to stretch his tight muscles, and said, "He might live. I've seen men hurt worse than this, and they survived." He looked the boy up and down. "But . . . he'll not be the man he was. His face will heal, but his own ma won't be able to recognize him. The man who did this knew what he was doing. The boy is passing a lot of blood, which means his kidneys are damaged. But you don't need the blood to know that. Look at this."

The doctor turned Tandy on his side, who elicited an unconscious groan. His back was black around his kidneys, indicating that whoever did this had evil intentions.

Hank tore his eyes away from Tandy's back. The doctor had cut away most of his clothing, leaving only what was necessary for the man's modesty, for all his friends were here. His chest was blue and purple from multiple heavy blows, but the darkest part was over his heart. Hank's eyes traveled farther up and came to rest on the boy's throat. He had taken several heavy blows to his throat. His breathing was heavy and forced, as if the air had a tough time making it in and out of his lungs.

Finally, Hank looked at his face. He had been worked over by a ham-handed professional. Both eyes were swollen shut and bleeding from cheeks and brows. His shredded lips were swollen three times their normal size, exposing his broken and shattered teeth. His nose was twisted and swollen to twice its normal size.

A smashed hand reached out for Hank, and he took it in his, gently, then leaned close to Tandy to understand him.

"He . . . put on . . . my . . . hat."

It was all the boy could manage to say between gasps.

"Don't talk," Hank replied. "All your friends are here, and the doctor is taking good care of you. You'll be back on a horse before you know it."

The boy tried to raise his head and look around, then whispered, "Howdy . . . fellas."

All the men responded in their own way, with a nod or howdy or "you'll be riding soon."

Tandy nodded at the last statement and squeezed Hank's hand, looking up at him through bloody slits. He gripped Hank's hand for a moment longer and relaxed.

"Let me through!" the doc thundered.

He placed the stethoscope against the boy's chest, listened, and then pulled it out of his ears. "All right, everybody out. You can leave one man here to keep watch. The rest of you, clear out." Then his voice softened. "Look, fellas, I'm not gonna lie to you. He probably won't make it through the night, but he needs quiet so he can sleep. Rest is the medicine he needs right now."

"Cain't we do something, Doc?" one of the cowhands asked.

He nodded. "You sure can. You can pray. The good Lord is the only one who has the power to help him now. All I can do is make him as comfortable as possible."

Hank turned to the cowhands. "Let's go, men. The doctor needs his space, and Tandy needs his rest."

The men filed out and down the stairs. Potsy hung back. "I'd like to sit with him, Hank, if I could."

Hank put his hand on the cowhand's shoulder. "Sure, Potsy, he likes you."

"We were . . . are friends."

A whisper came across the room. "Hank?"

He jumped back to Tandy's side. "I'm right here, Tandy."

"Thanks."

Hank, after his past three years, believed himself a hard man. He'd seen brutal death and torture more than any man should, and it usually took something huge to bring him to tears, but now his eyes filled. This boy had changed so much. He had become a good man. He leaned forward so his mouth was close to Tandy's ear. "Thank you, son."

Tandy's body relaxed, and he was in a deep sleep.

Hank nodded to the doc and turned to Potsy. "I'm going to the jail to talk to Bart. If he changes, come and get me."

"It was awful, Hank," Potsy said. "Tandy had just put his hat on the bar, and that big man came up and slapped it on his head. Everybody knows you don't put another man's hat on. Then he said, in a high-pitched voice, 'Look at me, I'm a cowgirl.'

"Tandy was drunk. I know you put him to bed, but not long after, he came downstairs and said, 'Let's go to the Long Branch.' Then it all happened. I'm tellin' you, Hank. That feller knew what he was doing. He took Tandy apart, and big as he is, if it hadn't been for Bart, he'da killed him right there."

"What did Bart do?"

"He wasn't there when it started. I guess the ruckus attracted him. One of the big feller's friends was holdin' a gun on everybody, so we couldn't do nothin'. But Bart walks in, pulls a hideout gun, and shoots that feller dead. Then, as this big feller was about to stomp Tandy, Bart said, 'Drop that foot and you're a dead man.'

The beating stopped and the big man backed off. That's when the marshal showed up and coldcocked Bart with his pistol."

"Thanks, Potsy."

Hank turned and rushed down the stairs. All of the cowhands were gathered at the bottom of the steps. "You boys might as well get some sleep. It could be a long night."

"We'll wait, Hank," one of the men said, and everyone nodded.

"Suit yourself. I'll be at the marshal's office."

When he went through the door, Bart was sitting behind bars, and Mac, Darcy, and Carson were standing in front of the marshal's desk. They were all talking, and the marshal was sitting, listening, leaned back in his chair with his feet propped on the desk.

The Remington crew turned as soon as he walked in.

"It was Pitts," Mac said. His face was livid with rage. "If yon lad, Bart, hadn't shot the other feller, Pitts would've stomped Tandy to death, if he hasn't already."

"Marshal Smith," Hank said, "it's my understanding from Mr. McCoy that you are a fair man. We have a young man lying near death in the doctor's office. He was beaten unmercifully by Langston Pitts." Hank pointed to Bart now standing behind and holding onto the bars of the jail. "If it hadn't been for Bart Porter, the boy would be dead now, not fighting for his life."

The marshal looked Hank over. "And who might you be?"

Both Mac and Darcy spoke at the same time. "Our partner."

Hank said, "I'm Hank Remington."

"So you're the one with the jumpin' buckskin. That was quite a feat."

Hank let out a sigh of frustration. "Marshal—"

Marshal Smith held his hand up. "Relax, fellers. The onliest reason I've got your cowhand in the hoosegow is because he was carryin' a gun. I already got the lowdown on what went on in the Long Branch, and I've run Pitts out of town."

Hank's thick black eyebrows snapped together and his jaw muscles flexed. He could barely get out, "He's gone?"

Smith eyed Hank. He'd been around a long time and he knew trouble when he saw it. His feet dropped from the desk as he leaned forward, eyes locked with Hank's. "You calm yourself, mister. Technically, Pitts did nothing wrong."

The marshal held up his hand again as all three men started to respond. "I said technically. There weren't nothin' I could hold him on. The boy threw the first punch. I'm right sorry about your cowhand, but it was cut and dried."

He motioned a thumb toward Bart. "As far as this one. He should consider himself lucky. All the witnesses said if he hadn't shot the man holdin' the gun, your cowboy'd be dead. He owes a twenty-dollar fine for carryin' a gun, and he'll sit in jail the night. He can pick up his rig when he leaves town."

All three men reached into their vest pocket, but Mac was the first to yank out a twenty-dollar gold piece and toss it on the marshal's desk.

Marshal Smith picked it up, opened a drawer, and took out a tin box. He lifted the lid, dropped the gold piece into the box, returned it to the drawer, and closed the drawer, nodding. "Good. That's done. He'll be fed breakfast in the morning, and I'll release him then." He gave an ominous look to everyone in the room, including Bart. "But I'm telling you, the next man carrying a gun, whether it's one of you or your hands, is gonna fare a lot worse. I want no short guns carried in my town!"

"There won't be, Marshal. Now, do you have any notion where Pitts headed?"

"He and his crew, there's five besides Pitts, took out along the railroad tracks headed west. The bartender at the Long Branch said he heard something about Denver City, or Denver as they're calling it now."

Hank worked to calm himself down. After a few moments, he said, "Doesn't the train run out that way?"

The marshal nodded his head. "Yep. Don't go all the way, but it does go a far piece. I imagine they'll flag the train down, load up their horses, and ride the cushions as far as they can."

Hank turned to Bart. "In the morning, if you have a desire to ride with me, find me. I'll either be at Doc's or at the hotel."

Bart gave a hard, short nod. "I'll be going with you."

Hank turned back to the lawman and, by way of explanation, said, "I kinda took that boy under my wing."

The marshal nodded. "I'm knowin' how you feel. Good luck."

The four men walked out of the marshal's office.

Mac was the first to speak. "Hank, isn't it east you'll be heading?"

Hank shook his head. "Not a chance. I'm going to settle this with Pitts once and for all. If the law can't take care of him, I will."

Carson Bond spoke up. "Hank, you're going after a dangerous man with a gang. You'd best be careful."

Mac started to speak again, when Potsy came running up. "Hank, Tandy's asking for you."

The two of them took off, their boots slamming on the boardwalk.

Hank burst into the office. Tandy was breathing hard, his head turned toward the door. When he saw Hank, he reached out his hand. "Hank, I don't know how long I'll be on this earth. I'd be obliged if'n you would hang around, 'cause you're my pard."

The effort to speak through his battered throat took whatever strength the boy had remaining. Hank could feel the weakness in his hand. Mac, Darcy, and Carson had followed him into the room. He looked at them, seeing they had heard what Tandy had said.

He leaned back over the boy. "I'll be here, pard. Don't you worry."

The young man's lips retracted into an attempt at a smile. Then he relaxed and fell into a fitful sleep.

The doc watched the conversation. "Just before you came in,

he was agitated. I gave him some laudanum. He'll rest. You folks go on. I'll call you if there's any change."

Mac pulled Hank over into a corner. "Pitts will be having to wait."

"You're right, Mac, but I'll find him. A bad penny always turns up. Why don't you boys head on, and get some rest? I'll hang around up here."

HANK WAS HAGGARD, his beard growing again. The doctor had run him out twice to shave and get a bath, promising he would call if Tandy changed. It was a miracle Tandy was still alive, but the boy was actually getting better. The swelling in his throat had gone down to the point his breathing was normal. Doc explained the improvement was because he was big and strong. His thick neck muscles had protected him from the vicious blows.

Tandy continued to pass blood for a week, but nowadays the blood had ceased and the pain in his back had dissipated. When Doc talked about the boy, he just shook his head. He said over and over again that he should have died the first night.

Hank sat near his bed, looking Tandy over. The boy's face would never be the same. Fortunately, the swelling had gone down quite a bit and the doc had been able to straighten his nose. But he had a livid scar that ran across his nose and into his left cheek. Both of his eyebrows had scars through them that left obvious spaces, and he had several broken teeth.

Hank leaned over the sleeping boy and looked at his eyes. It was a miracle his vision was still good, probably thanks to his eyes being so deep set, and thanks to him being so hardheaded. *We've got something in common,* Hank thought. While he was leaning over examining Tandy's face, the boy's eyes popped open. They were still bloodshot, but nowhere near as bad as they had been.

"Ain't I perty?"

Hank leaned back. "Not much. Although, I'd say you're a mite better looking than before the fight."

Through his healed lips, Tandy grinned. "You're just jealous 'cause of that ugly puss of yours."

"I guess you got me there."

The doc walked in as Hank was leaning back. "Get up off your lazy duff, boy, and walk around some."

"Really?" Tandy asked with excitement.

"I'm tired of you hanging around my office, scaring away my patients. Walk around this room a little. As soon as you're feeling strong enough, you can head down those stairs." He looked at Hank. "Though you might need some help navigating those stairs."

"Doc, I'll nursemaid him, just like I'd do one of them tiny calves."

Hank had reached for Tandy's arm, but Tandy flung his hand away. "I don't need no nursemaid. Leave me alone." He flashed a grin to soften the words.

Hank sat back and watched as his young friend swung his legs over the side of the bed, sat for a moment, then stood. Tandy's arm shot out to grab the metal bedstead. He held it until the wobbling subsided, then took his first step, and then another. He was walking around the room when Bart came in.

"Well, looky here," Bart said. "It can walk."

"Danged right I can. I'll be riding in no time."

Tandy circled the room a couple more times, then dropped on the bed. "I think I'll rest a minute."

"You do that, boy," the doc said, "but I want you up and walking every little bit. It won't be but a few more days and I'm throwing you out of here so I can treat some real sick folk." The doc turned and went back into his office.

"Hey, Doc," Hank called. "You think this young fellow could handle a steak?"

"Yes," came through the closed door, "and bring me one, too."

As Tandy stretched out on the bed, Hank stood. "How does a steak sound to you?"

"It sounds great if it includes a piece of pie, and if that pretty little girl who works in there brings it up."

Hank looked over at Bart. "I think he is feeling better."

Bart nodded and headed for the door. "Sounds like it."

The two men left the doctor's office, walked downstairs, and headed down the street toward the Drover's Hotel.

"Wonder how the boys are doing," Bart said.

"I've thought of that once or twice myself. I've known Mac and Darcy since the war. No telling if we'll ever meet up again. They're some good men. Though they needed to get back, they wouldn't leave until Doc pronounced that Tandy was going to live."

They walked into the Drover's Hotel, went into the restaurant, found a table, and sat down.

The girl Tandy was talking about pranced over to their table, pushed a lock of black hair behind an ear, and pulled out a pencil from behind the same ear. "How's Tandy?" she asked.

"Hungry," Bart said as he looked up at the raven-haired beauty, "just like us, Sissy. What'd you fix us today?"

She laughed. Her laughter attracted the attention of many of the men in the restaurant who had been on the trail for several months, not hearing a woman's laughter, nor even seeing a woman.

"Bart Porter, you know I don't cook the food. Today, it's steak, potatoes, some fresh corn that just came in on the train, beans, and apple pie."

"That's exactly what I wanted," Bart said.

"Make it four. You feel like taking one up to Tandy today?"

She looked at Hank. "Really, could I?"

"Yep, the doctor said it's time he started eating solid food."

"Honestly, is it okay for me to take it up to him?"

"One's for the doc," Hank said, "but yeah, if you can carry that much, I'm sure he'd like to see you."

The girl's face turned the color of a ripe tomato. "Well, if it's all right with the other waitress, it would be a kind act to take him a meal."

"And the doc," Hank said.

"Yes, of course, the doctor also."

She spun on her heel and escaped to the kitchen.

Bart shook his head. "Well, I'll be doggone if I ain't riding with Mr. Cupid."

Hank laughed. "I figured she would go a long way to cheering up that boy. Maybe the doc too; he needs it."

Bart grew serious. "When we headin' west?"

"As soon as Tandy's well enough to ride."

"The boy's coming with us?"

"Yep, if he wants to."

Bart nodded, buttering a big piece of cornbread from the stack of cornbread and biscuits Sissy had brought out. "I talked to the marshal today. He said some folks were killed near their claim over Denver way. Pitts and his gang are suspected."

Hank looked out the window, watching the puffy summertime clouds march across the clear blue sky. Here it was nearing the end of July. Almost half the year gone. Hopefully, Tandy'd be better soon and up for riding. They needed to be heading west.

26

Standing on the platform, waiting for the train to leave, Tandy was not the braggart Hank had met just a few months ago. He was a tall, wide-shouldered man, early in his twenties, his blond hair clipped neatly around the collar. He wore a full mustache, hiding most of the scarring around his upper lip. It would have been impossible to hide the scar from his nose to his left cheek, but it was no longer the bright red welt that it had been.

Hank looked at the young man, who over the past few months had grown out of the meanness he had learned as a boy, and now showed a wide calm face with piercing, steady blue eyes. Next to Tandy stood a girl of striking looks. Her black hair, escaping from her light blue bonnet, glistened in the afternoon sunlight, while her face was shaded from the hot sun. Her arm locked through Tandy's, in possession of the tall young man, dared anyone to draw him away.

"You're sure you want to stay?" Hank asked.

Before he could speak, Sissy spoke up. "Hank, of course he wants to stay." Her small gloved hand patted the thick forearm it was holding. She looked up at her man. "Isn't that right, Tandyman?"

She smiled at Hank and Bart. "You both are such good friends to my Tandyman. We will miss you."

Yet her eyes seemed to wish them gone.

"Ma'am," Hank said as he touched his hat brim. Then he looked at Tandy. The boy had recuperated well. It was surprising he was alive, much less looking as good as he did.

The train sounded its whistle and the conductor called, "All aboard!"

Hank extended his hand. Tandy took it in his. Both men held the grip. "Son," Hank said, "you ever need anything, you find me. I'll come a-running!"

The boy's eyes had filled. He blinked twice. "I owe you more than you'll ever know. Take care of yourself."

They broke the handshake. Bart shook Tandy's hand, and each man bent and kissed the stiff little Sissy on her cheek, turned, and jumped on the train. They made their way back to a forward-facing row of seats where they could see out one of the windows, waved once as they slowly passed the couple on the platform, and leaned back. Suddenly the trained jerked to a stop. The two men looked at each other, shrugged, and leaned back.

After no more than five minutes, the train started moving forward again. Silently, they watched first the buildings slip slowly by, then the prairie, moving faster and faster, to the rhythmic sound of the wheels over the rails.

Finally, Bart said, "That boy really surprised me, letting Sissy get her hooks into him."

From behind them a voice said, "They weren't really that deep."

Both men whipped around to see Tandy sitting behind them, a big grin on his face. "I had to think quick before the train got away. The conductor even stopped the train so I could load my horses."

Bart motioned for Tandy to move up next to them, then said, "I'm glad to see you, boy. She was a nice girl, but I could see she had her hat set for you from the first."

"She is really nice," Tandy said, "but I realized I'm just not ready to settle down." He stretched his long legs out and slid his hat to the back of his head. "Anyway, I need to be there when we catch up with Pitts."

Hank leaned forward and looked around Bart so he could see Tandy. "Just so you understand, I have a previous claim on the man."

Tandy nodded. "I just want to be there, Hank. Plus, I ain't never been to the Colorado Territory."

The three men relaxed into the cushions for the long ride. To their surprise, they had just dozed off when the train came to a stop. The conductor walked through, calling Solomon, Kansas. They were there only long enough to take on one person, water, and wood, then were on their way. No more than fifteen minutes later, they were coming to a stop in Salina. Their two-day trip continued this way, stopping at every little town along the track, and there were many.

However, it was still days faster than horseback and much more comfortable. In the late afternoon they pulled into the end of the track at Sheridan, Kansas. The three of them stood, stretched, and, with their gear, walked off the train.

Sheridan wasn't much to look at. Because of the railroad, it had been built to provide support for the workers and passengers. Though small, it was bustling. As far as Hank could see, there were at least four saloons, all lower frame tent structures, and they were filled this late in the afternoon.

"After we take care of these horses," Bart said, "I'm up for a drink."

The men removed their horses, saddles, and packs from the cattle car. Once saddled, they mounted and rode down the dusty street. What little grass there might have been originally, it had been cut to pieces by thousands of horses and wagons. Now the street was several inches deep in dust that bloomed up with every step, whether from a boot or hoof. The heavy traffic from wagons traveling between the train, town, and Fort Wallace, which was only a few miles down the road, created a cloud of choking dust that floated between the two rows of buildings.

Hank pulled his bandanna over his nose and was followed by Bart and Tandy. They located what appeared to be a permanent livery and rode their horses up to the trough. Allowing the animals to water, Hank walked over to the sliding door and banged on it. A smaller door, about the size of a man, had been cut into the large door. It opened almost immediately. A burly man, holding what had once been a white handkerchief to his nose, stepped out, closing the door behind him.

"How can I help you, fellas?"

Hank motioned toward the horses. "Need a place to leave our horses overnight, and would like 'em fed."

The man rubbed the two-day-old growth. "It'll cost you three fifty."

"Deal," Hank said.

The man stepped back inside, and moments later the door was rolled open only wide enough to lead the horses inside. He immediately closed the door. "Howdy, boys. Name's Rock Belton. I keep this door closed as much as I can to keep that infernal dust out. You think it's bad now, you should see it when it rains, almost like quicksand.

Where you stayin'?"

Hank spoke up. "Never been here before. You have any suggestions?"

"So happens I do. Mabel's Dining and Boarding. Best place in town. Course, I lean towards it a mite since I'm married to her." Rock grinned at the men. "But I ain't kiddin' you. Food's good and the beds are clean. Hard to find in this town."

"We're close to eating," Hank said, "but where would we get a drink?"

"Onliest one I ever go to, End of Track. Drinks ain't watered, at least not much, and the prices are fair. Course, that one's run by my brother-in-law, Monty. Tell him Rock sent you. You might get a free drink." This time he laughed. "That's kinda dangerous though; he might charge you double."

"How would we find these fine establishments?" Hank asked.

"Head west, just like you was going. Saloon's first and then Mabel's is a little past it. I gotta tell you about Monty, though. He don't allow no fighting, so don't start nothing." He looked over Hank and Tandy. "You two boys are mighty big, but he'd still take you on if you started somethin' in his place."

"We're peaceful folks," Hank said.

While he had been jawing with the proprietor, Tandy and Bart had been rubbing down the animals.

Rock pointed to the side of his office. "Oats is in the bin. Help yourself."

There was a bucket in the bin. Hank scooped up the oats, filling the bucket, and divided them into each trough of the seven horses, giving the big buckskin a little more. He took the bucket to the bin, dropped it in, and helped finish up the horses. Their tack and packs from the pack horse were put in the tack room, and with their saddlebags over one shoulder, they pulled their bandannas up, picked up their rifles, and headed out.

Reaching Mabel's, the three men looked over the three-story frame house, walked up the steps, and wiped their boots on the rug. Stepping inside, they pulled the bandannas back down and waited for the lady straightening the cloth on one of the dining room tables to finish.

She turned and said, "May I help you, gentlemen?"

"Yes, ma'am," Hank said. "Looking for some rooms and food."

"We don't eat for another hour, but I can get you a cup of coffee. How many rooms will you need?"

"Three, if you've got 'em."

"We are very busy, but I do happen to have three rooms on the second floor. My rooms are the most expensive in town, but we also feed you, and you don't have to worry about bedbugs or fleas." She looked them over closely after her last statement, then said, "It'll be three dollars apiece. I have a bathhouse out back, run by my son. A bath will cost you four bits, and I'd ask you to watch your language while you are in there. My son has tender ears."

None of the men hesitated. It would be good to get a bath, and good food would be worth it. They each pulled the money from their vest pockets. Bart and Hank paid three fifty, but Tandy only paid three.

Hank glanced at the younger man. "A bath would do you good."

"I'd like to, Hank," Tandy said, "but it's still hard for me to get in and out of a washtub."

Hank looked at Bart. "We'll help you."

Mabel immediately spoke up. "Have you been hurt, young man?"

"Yes, ma'am. I'm still kinda recuperating." He had to sound the last word out.

"Well, don't you worry. All of our tubs are long tubs. You won't have to scrunch up your legs."

Tandy grinned. "That sounds fine, ma'am. Thank you." He pulled out fifty cents and laid it on the desk.

"Thank you. If you will be so kind as to sign our log . . ." She slid the log across and each man signed it.

After Hank had signed, he said, "Ma'am, we're going up the street to the End of Track. Your husband recommended it."

"Yes, I'm sure he did. We eat promptly at six o'clock. After six thirty the food is taken up. Please be on time—and sober."

"Yes, ma'am," the three men said.

"Call me Mabel. The stairs are at the end of the hall." She

turned and hurried into the kitchen. Moments later they could hear her giving cooking orders.

Bart shook his head once. "She's a pistol. I bet she keeps Rock in line."

It took them only a minute to drop their gear and rifles in their rooms, and they headed out the door, pulling their bandannas up immediately on stepping outside. The three of them walked side by side along the boardwalk. Occasionally they stepped aside for a lady. Reaching the End of Track, they turned in. The sound was almost deafening.

The bar was packed. They looked around for a table, but they were all full. They were turning to try somewhere else when a man, at a table by himself, waved. The three turned and walked to his table.

"Space is scarce. Have a seat. My name's Bill Cody."

"Howdy," Hank said. "Much obliged."

They pulled out chairs and sat, offering their hands and introducing themselves on the way down. When Bart mentioned his name, a glint of recognition crossed Cody's eyes.

"You fellows look like you're from Texas."

Hank nodded. "Yes, we are. Just brought a herd up from south of San Antonio. Now we're headed to Denver."

"Not with cattle, I hope."

"No, just us and our horses. How about you, you from around here?"

"You might say, for now. I've got a contract to provide buffalo meat to the railroad while they lay track, and kinda keep an eye out for Injuns."

Tandy's eyes were big. "Are you Buffalo Bill, sir?"

The man smiled beneath the mustache and goatee. "That's what some folks call me. My friends call me Bill."

Tandy was excited. "I never thought I'd meet a real live hero. Have you killed a lot of Indians?"

Bill shook his head. "I've only killed those who needed

killing." He turned his head to lay a steady gaze on Bart. "You know about that, don't you, Bart?"

Bart, eyes steady, said, "I understand it.

A young saloon girl had taken their orders when they sat down. Bart had ordered rye, while Hank and Tandy had ordered sarsaparillas.

Bill looked at Hank. "Not a heavy drinker?"

Hank grinned. "Nope, don't touch the stuff. I'd like to give you a reason, but I have no idea why."

Bill tossed him a quizzical look. "I'm guessing there's a story behind that statement."

Hank nodded. "One too long for the telling now." He raised his glass to Bill and then clinked with the other two, taking a long sip of the elixir.

A fellow at the bar had seen the two sarsaparillas going by on the tray and had tracked them. He followed the waitress to the table, staggering a couple of times, and as Hank took a sip, he said, "That's mighty strong stuff, mister. Think you can handle it?"

Bill's face turned hard. "I'd thank you to leave us alone, please."

The drunk turned bleary eyes in Bill's direction, attempting to focus. "And who might you be, *please*?" A more sober man at the bar had been making his way to his friend. He leaned over and whispered something in the man's ear. The drunk turned pale. "Beggin' your pardon, Mr. Cody. I didn't mean no harm."

Bill waved his hand. "No harm taken." He looked at Hank. Hank also waved a hand and took another swig of the sarsaparilla.

The man turned and staggered back to the bar. Once there, he picked up and took a long drink from his glass, emptying it.

"Thanks," Hank said. "I'm too tired to fight a drunk."

"Benefits of a name, friend."

"Maybe you can help us a little more. As I said, we're heading for Denver. Should we be concerned about any Indian activity?"

Bill nodded. "In this country, you should always be concerned. The Cheyenne are restless, but last I knew, they were farther north. Just keep your eyes peeled and your ears open."

They had just finished their drinks when another man walked up, wearing a clean frock coat, with only a light layer of dust, and a bowler hat.

"Boys," Bill Cody said, "I'd like you to meet Mr. Ned Buntline, a writer from back East."

Buntline nodded to them and addressed Bill. "I believe we have a meeting, sir."

Hank took the hint, finished his drink, and stood. Bart and Tandy followed.

"Bill," Hank said, "it was a pleasure talking to you. Have a nice day." He shook the man's hand and headed for the door.

Bart and Tandy followed suit. The three of them pushed through the door and turned for Mabel's.

"I guess them Easterners don't aim to be rude," Bart said. "It just comes natural. That feller didn't even give us a howdy. If he hadn't been a friend of Cody's, I woulda had to teach him a lesson about politeness."

"Businessmen," Hank said. "All they think about is their business. You called it. They're not rude intentionally, that's just the way they are."

"That kinda unintention in this country could turn a man into a sieve."

Changing the subject, Hank said, "I don't know about you boys, but I'm taking a bath."

"Fine idea," Bart chimed in.

27

The faint blue mountains showed up on the western horizon when they were still three days east of Denver. At first, Hank thought they didn't look like much, but as they grew nearer, the mountains grew taller until they were a breathtaking sight. He had never seen anything like them. The slopes were green in the morning sun, all the way up to the tree line. Above the trees were sharp, jagged, some still snow-covered peaks, reaching up to tear the bellies out of passing clouds.

He wasn't the only one shocked. Neither of his companions had ever seen the Rockies until now. The three men found it difficult to keep watch for Indians because their eyes were constantly drawn back to the majesty of the mountains.

When they approached close enough to judge the height and massiveness of the mountains, Bart said, "My gosh, I never dreamed something like this existed. I've been used to those little hills in Texas. These mountains are almost scary."

Tandy said nothing, he just looked, and then he looked some more.

The morning they rode into Denver, they crossed Kiowa Creek and stared up at multiple peaks rising above the tree line.

"You think Pitts will be here?" Tandy asked.

"Don't know," Hank replied. "We'll just have to check around and find out."

"But look at all these people. He could be anywhere."

Hank didn't reply. They just kept riding until they came to the first saloon. Just past it was a hitching rail. He motioned toward it. The three men tied their horses and walked back to the saloon. Upon entering, Hank stopped. The almost empty room had few windows and smelled of stale beer and sweat. He waited until his eyesight adjusted, spotted the bartender, and moved down the bar near him.

"What'll it be?" the man asked.

"Two sarsaparillas and one rye," Hank said, glancing at Bart, who nodded.

When they had their drink, Hank took a long swig, set the bottle on the bar, and wiped his mouth with his sleeve. "We're looking for a man named Langston Pitts."

"Heard of him. Don't know him and don't want to," the bartender said. "You might check with the feller at the back table. He's known to deal with that kind."

Bart and Tandy leaned against the bar, sipping their drinks. Hank picked up his sarsaparilla and walked over to the man's table. Once there, the man looked up at Hank, dismissed him, and went back to nursing his glass.

"Mind if I join you?" Hank asked.

The man looked around at the empty tables. "Why?"

Hank dropped into a chair facing the man and pulled out one of his Remingtons, laying it on the table.

The man's eyes followed the weapon, then focused on Hank.

"Mister, I ain't got no idea what you want, and—"

"Relax, friend, I'm going to tell you. All I'm looking for is a little information. For instance, do you know where I can find Langston Pitts?"

"Why would I know anything about a Langston Pitts?"

"I'm not here to hurt you, friend. All I want to know is how I can find Langston Pitts."

Hank and his friends had been on the trail for over a week. Not only was he a big man, but he was unshaven, trail weary and dirty, which all added to his threatening appearance. The man looked at Hank and then at Tandy and Bart. Ripples started showing in the liquor glass he was holding. He fixed his eyes on his glass, placed it gently on the table, and spread his hands palm down next to the glass. "I ain't lookin' for no trouble, mister. I just came in here for a drink."

Hank smiled, much like a wolf might smile at a rabbit, if a wolf could smile.

The man looked down at his drink, then up at Hank, waited a bit longer, and blurted out in a rush, "I ain't seen him in over a week, and that's the gospel truth."

"I believe you, friend." He leaned forward and spoke in a whisper. "But you see the man next to the big blond fella? That's Texan Bart Porter. He'd just as soon kill a man as look at him. Right now, he's looking to find Langston Pitts. That's all that matters, not you, not me, just Langston Pitts."

Hank turned as if to say something to Bart.

"Wait, mister, wait! I'll tell you all I know, which ain't much. Pitts is in Pueblo. Yessiree, he's in Pueblo, and he ain't plannin' on coming back here."

Hank leaned back in his chair and took a sip of his drink. "You wouldn't happen to know where he's staying, would you, friend? Bart will probably want to—"

"If'n I tell you, I'm as good as dead!"

"That may be, friend." Hank turned and gave Bart a long look. He reached for his revolver and adjusted it in the holster. "But it looks like your most immediate problem isn't Langston Pitts. You've heard of Texan Bart Porter, haven't you?"

"Yes, I've heard of him. If you want Pitts, you'll find him at the

Pueblo Saloon in Pueblo. I've heard an old girlfriend is working there. That's all I know, honest."

Hank leaned forward. "Mister, I don't think you've got an honest bone in your body. You just sit nice and easy until we're out of sight. You understand me?"

Palms pressed tight against the wooden table, the man was still nodding when Hank turned and made his way back to Bart and Tandy. "Pueblo Saloon in Pueblo."

The bartender overheard him and leaned on the bar. "You fellers wanta be careful. That's the oldest saloon in Pueblo. Been several killings there."

Hank looked across at the man and tossed the money for the drinks plus a dollar on the bar. "Thanks."

The three men walked out.

"You boys need a rest?" Hank asked.

Both men shook their heads and swung up on their horses.

Tandy grinned down at Hank. "You comin' with us?"

THREE DAYS LATER, they rode into the booming town of Pueblo. Much like its sister cities, Denver and Colorado City, the discovery of gold had brought many West in hopes of striking it rich.

They rode past the newspaper office of the *Pueblo Colorado Weekly Chieftain*, the Harper and Houseman Hardware store, and the Wells Fargo Bank. They were about to dismount at the hitching rail nearest the Pueblo Saloon when Hank saw a woman enter the doctor's office.

It couldn't be, he thought. He swung down from Buck, flipped the reins over the rail, and also tied the leads for the other two horses. "Boys, don't start anything without me. I'll be right back."

"Where you going?" Tandy called to his back.

He just waved his hand and weaved between the wagons and

horses plying the street. Once across, he looked up at the sign hanging above the door, *Dr. Louis James*. He stood at the door, now undecided whether he should go in or forget about it. *I guess she did marry him, but I oughta at least say hello to the both of them. They saved my life.*

He took his hat from his head and, using it as a duster, beat his chest and chaps. Putting it back on his head, he rubbed his boots on the back of his trousers. Satisfied he was as good looking as he was ever going to be, he opened the door and stepped inside.

Immediately inside and to the left was a desk, behind which sat a middle-aged lady.

"Do you have an illness, sir?" she asked sweetly.

"No, ma'am. I was wondering if you might ask the doctor and nurse to step out here, please. I believe I know them."

Hank's deep voice had no sooner started booming in the small reception area than she stepped into the office through the back door. At first her face reflected puzzlement at the big bearded man wearing chaps and sporting two revolvers and a knife around his waist. Then recognition flooded her eyes.

"Hank? Is it you?"

He stood gazing at her. She hadn't changed a bit. If anything, the West had made her more beautiful. "Hello, Deborah," he managed to say.

In a flash she was across the room and leaping into his arms. She felt so natural as if it were only the day after he saw her last. He initially crushed her close. Then the last time he saw her flashed through his mind, and he pushed her away. An older man wearing a white coat stepped out of the back room.

He held her at arm's length. "You're looking mighty pretty, Deborah. How's Dr. James doing?"

She turned to look at the older man, then back to Hank. Hesitantly, she said, "He's doing well? How do you know him?" Then it dawned on her.

"Oh, you mean in Washington." She smiled toward the lady at the desk and turned to the man in the white coat. "These are his parents."

Seeing the puzzled look on the older couple's faces, she rushed to explain. "This man is Henry Remington. The man who had been so terribly wounded in the war. The man Louis saved."

At first there were smiles of recognition, replaced slowly by frowns.

Dr. James was the first to speak. "It is a pleasure to meet the man who represents such a success for my son. But, Mr. Remington, I must ask you, why did you leave my niece without even a goodbye? You know you broke her heart."

It was Hank's turn to be puzzled. He shook his head, trying to understand what the doctor was saying. She was brokenhearted? His mind wasn't working fast enough. Before he could stop himself, he said, "But she was embracing Dr. James. I could see there was no place for me, so I left."

Now Deborah's face lit up with realization. "You saw Louis and I hugging in his office, didn't you?"

Hank nodded his head. "I did. I felt I did not belong with you, for you had committed to him."

She threw back her head and laughed a wonderful, happy laugh of relief.

At that moment the door opened. Bart and Tandy stepped in.

Tandy looked around the room, his eyes coming to a stop at Deborah. He whipped off his hat, elbowed Bart, who removed his, and while mesmerized with Deborah, said to Hank, "We wondered why you was takin' so long."

Coolly, Bart said, "Aren't you going to introduce us to your friends, Hank?"

He gave each one a long hard look, which they both ignored. "This big blond one is Tandy Jacobs, the other one is Bart Porter. Boys, this is Deborah Coleman. I don't rightly know these other folks yet, but I'm suspecting the gentleman in the white coat is Dr. Louis James, and this pretty lady is his wife, Mrs. James."

The doctor's wife spoke up. "You boys can call me Abigail.

"Ma'am," they both said to each of the women.

"Now, go on and get out of here," Hank said. "I'll be along in a minute, and don't start anything."

The two men pushed by Hank for the door, both grinning. Bart winked at Hank as he went by. His wink got him a hard look.

He looked back at Deborah and she was smiling.

"You ninny," Deborah said. "Dr. Louis James is my uncle. The Dr. Louis James in Washington is my cousin. I should be angry at you for just assuming and saying nothing, just dashing off. However, I can see how the mistake could have been made. Oh, Hank, how are you? You look almost as thin as when you were brought to the ward."

"Your cousin? Dr. James is your cousin?"

"Yes, we grew up together. We were both going to be doctors." She shrugged.

Now his mind was working. *That explains why they were always touching and laughing and joking.*

He shook his head, embarrassed and grinning. "I guess I was pretty stupid."

"I wouldn't say stupid, but you did jump to conclusions. Hank, I was devastated when the orderly told me you were gone. I was so looking forward to our having dinner together."

Dr. James cleared his throat, stepped forward, and shook Hank's hand. "I'm glad this has been cleared up. It is very nice to meet you, Hank. My son wrote glowingly about you and your recovery."

Hank grasped the other man's hand. "Thank you, Dr. James. I'd be a dead man if it wasn't for your son and Deborah. I owe them my life."

"I don't think so. He has written that he never met a man with the will and determination to live that you demonstrated.

Now"—he turned and looked at his wife—"Abigail, why don't you give me a hand in the back."

She shook Hank's hand. "It is so nice to meet you. I'm so glad you're here. We have so—"

"Abigail?" Dr. James said.

"Coming, Louis, *dear*," she said, releasing Hank's hand, and the two disappeared into the back.

Now that they were alone, Hank felt awkward and could see that Deborah also felt a touch of discomfort, but she reached out her hand, and he took it, her small hand disappearing in his. "Come," she said, "let's sit." She led him to two chairs across from the desk.

After sitting, Hank said, "I'm really sorry I was so stupid. I've thought about you so much over the years, but I couldn't get over the picture of you and Dr. James in each other's arms."

"That was terrible timing. Louis will be devastated to think he might have caused you so much pain, but that's behind us. First, tell me, have you had any more of your memory return?"

"Not much. I've had this vague picture of a lady come to me several times, and once it was like I was sitting at a table, with others near my age around it. Unfortunately, that's all there's been."

Hank could see she was almost beside herself. "I know who you are!"

"What? How could you?"

"I'll try to make it short, but there is a family who is ranching west of here. It's several brothers and their mother. She has a family picture, and Hank, you're in it."

He couldn't believe it. All this time. He could have been searching back East, but because Tandy got beat up, he had come west. Thinking of Tandy, Hank said, "I've got to be going. There's something I need to take care of."

Puzzled, she looked up at him. "Take care of?"

"Yep. I need to get it done. Once that's done, we'll be free."

"I don't understand."

"There's too much to explain. Let me go for now. I'll be back in a while." He stood and drew her up with him. "Deborah, I'm not much of a romantic fellow, but you need to know you have been strong on my mind since we parted."

She looked up at him and came quickly into his arms. They kissed briefly, and he held her so close he could feel her heart beat. Gently pushing her away, he said, "I'll be back."

"One more thing," she said. "You have an uncle and brother in town."

"Thanks."

He turned and walked out the door. Tandy and Bart had been leaning against the wall, watching the traffic go by. Bart looked at him as he pulled the door closed.

"Something you want to tell us, pardner?"

He shook his head. "Not now, let's go to the saloon and see if we can gin up some trouble."

The three men checked their revolvers were free, and Hank also released his knife. He was a happy man. He had found the woman he hoped would be with him for the rest of his life, but right now he needed to focus. He pulled his gloves from under his gun belt and put them on. He wasn't doing any shooting. Pitts had been needing a beating for a long time, and he felt like he was the one to give it to him.

They stepped into the saloon. As soon as their eyes adjusted, they examined the clientele. The saloon was busy. All of the tables were taken. In the corner sat three old men with a younger man about Hank's age. Two Spencer and two Henry rifles lay across the table. The old men looked like mountain men past their time.

About halfway toward the back of the saloon, against the wall, Hank spotted Pitts. He sat at a table with three other men. As Hank moved toward the bar, Pitts glanced at Tandy, continued talking to one of the men at his table, then stopped, and slowly turned back. After a moment he stood.

Hank leaned over to Tandy. "Remember what I said."

The boy nodded, but held the stare of the man who had beaten him.

Glancing at neither Hank nor Bart, Pitts made his way to the bar. When he was within arm's length, a malicious grin spread across his face, and he reached for Tandy's hat. From the side, Hank's big fist slammed into his jaw, knocking him to the floor. Patrons scattered. Five men jumped to their feet, reaching for their guns.

Four rifle hammers ratcheted to full cock at the same time. Hank glanced at the mountain men, who were still seated, but with rifles aimed at the Pitts crew. Bart and Tandy had their six-guns out and pointed at the gang. Hank nodded to the strangers at the table.

One of the old ones, his voice cold as steel in the winter, said, "You boys drop those gun belts, put your hands on them tables, relax, and enjoy the show."

Hank knew that voice from somewhere, but now wasn't the time to think about it. He placed his hat on the bar. "You're welcome to try on my hat, Mr. Pitts."

The big man stood, shaking his head, and squinted at Hank. "Your voice sounds familiar, matey. Do I know you?"

The right side of Hank's head had been turned away from Pitts. Now Hank turned so the brute could get a good look. Recognition first, then shock flooded across the man's face. Then he smiled. "You take a lot of killing, Remington. It's gonna be a pleasure to finish you off." He glanced at Tandy and continued, "Like I thought I had finished your whelp here."

ank's response was another blow, straight to the man's nose and mouth, driving him back and into an already vacated table.

He came off the table with a roar, only to meet the business end of a ten-gauge shotgun, both hammers eared back. Pitts skidded to a halt. The bartender motioned toward the swinging doors with the weapon. "Take it outside. I ain't gettin' my place busted up again."

Hank took off his gun belt and laid it across the bar.

Pitts spit blood from his broken lip. As he strode past Hank, he said, "You're a dead man. Just wait till I get you outside."

Hank followed him out, and when Pitts had cleared the door, Hank put a foot on the man's rear and shoved, sending him sprawling face-first into the dirt.

He got up slowly, deliberately, and turned toward Hank, grinning again. "That's your last free one, cowgirl. By the time I'm finished with you, they won't be able to separate you from this dirt."

Hank, taller than the man, but not as wide, walked toward him. "Pitts, don't you ever stop talking?" He threw a short left.

This time Pitts wiped the blow away with his right forearm, following up with a quick left uppercut, catching Hank just below the heart. It was all Hank could do to keep from doubling over, but he knew if he bent over, he'd be at the mercy of this brawler. He stepped back, willing his lungs to work, sucking in minimal amounts of air.

Pitts followed up with a right hook, and luckily for Hank he was backing away, but the blow still had his ears ringing. He backpedaled quickly, Pitts staying with him.

"I told you, cowgirl, you're a dead man."

Hank was getting his wind back. Pitts feinted with his right, and Hank ducked directly into the oncoming left, catching it perfectly on his chin. Lights exploded in his brain. Multicolored stars cascaded all around him as the outside world faded away. He felt a blow to his cheek as he was falling, and instinctively rolled when he hit the ground.

The only thing that saved him from having his chest crushed by Pitts stomping on him was his rolling under Buck. When Pitts tried to get at him, the buckskin snapped at him, just missing the man's arm, but causing him to jump back.

The stars disappeared, and Hank felt himself coming back to consciousness. *Wake up!* his mind screamed. He continued to roll, going under Blacky. He could see again and pushed himself on all fours.

A glimpse of movement caused him to throw himself to the left. The kick Pitts had thrown just missed. He came out from under the black and threw a hard left jab into the oncoming Pitts. The man's head rocked back, but it didn't slow him down. The big man threw both arms around Hank, squeezing relentlessly and bending him back.

A flash of memory from another fight came to him. Another man wider but shorter than he had tried the same thing. It turned out to be the wrong move for that man. Hank repeated his response. Being much taller than Pitts, he lifted him completely off the ground, took a running jump, and did a belly flop right on top of him. He heard the air surge from the man's lungs, and the grip around Hank's back relaxed. He jumped to his feet. Pitts was flat on his back, his lungs soundlessly shrieking for air.

Hank backed off, shaking his head. Slowly he regained his vision and felt his strength coming back, yet he waited.

Tandy yelled, "Get him, Hank. He won't wait for you."

Hank just looked over at the boy and shook his head.

Pitts was on his knees; then he took a deep breath and lifted himself to his feet. His shirt was ripped in shreds, as was Hank's. The sailor-turned-killer grasped his shirt front in both hands and yanked it away from his body. There was a quick rip and the man's chest and back were fully exposed.

Spectators had filled the street, and, at the sight of the man's burly chest and back, the crowd took in an audible breath. *I feel the same way,* Hank thought, feeling his humor returning. With the humor he felt the confidence of knowing this was a fight he was going to win. Though his opponent was a bruiser, and he definitely would mete out more punishment, he was finished.

Pitts shuffled slowly toward Hank and saw the grin on the man's face. Hank could see the recognition in his opponent's eyes that he might lose. The two men closed, and it was brutal blow after brutal blow. The sound of fists striking flesh vibrated through the streets, yet neither man backed away.

Hank knew he was being hurt. He knew he was growing tired, but his only goal was to finish the enemy in front of him. If Mac or Darcy would have been there, they would have recognized the look. It was the same one they saw when Hank had battled the overwhelming charge.

Floyd Logan recognized it. He had seen it before in other Logans and knew this man was Will.

Hank kept working on the man's belly, because somewhere in

the past he had been told the belly was where a man lived. Pitts was heavily muscled, but he carried fat around his belly. He no longer had the muscles he needed to protect him from sustained, heavy blows.

Hank struck and dodged, dodged and struck. Though Pitts was also connecting, Hank could feel the blows weakening. He smashed another right into the man's bleeding face. It hit along a previous cut, knocking the man's head back and spraying more blood across the crowd.

Pitts now had to aim with his left eye. His right eye was closed and filled with blood. Coldly, Hank smashed another left into the right eye and watched the man wince in pain.

Now's the time, Hank thought. *He's feeling the pain. He's finished.* Hank summoned all of his strength, and from his hips up through his shoulders, he sent a sledgehammer blow to the heart of this killer. Spectators were stunned at the thud of the blow against the man's chest.

Pitts stood staring at Hank, his arms hanging to his sides, surprise on his face. Then his eyes rolled back and he crumpled to the ground. Hank looked around. Tandy was standing there, mouth open, looking down on Pitts. Bart and the men with the rifles held the gang that Pitts had led across Texas, Kansas, and the Colorado Territory.

Hank walked over to them. "You've got a choice." He motioned toward the still man lying in the dust. "You can pick him up and get out of this country, or we can find a tree that will fit all of you."

One of them spoke up. "Mister, you let us ride, and you'll never see us in this country again."

"I'd better never see you again, period. You understand?"

"Yes, sir."

"Then pick him up and go."

"Mister, we need our guns."

"No guns. Pick him up and git!"

One of them spit toward Pitts. "We don't need him. Let him take care of himself." They all turned and headed for the livery.

Hank looked at the men with the rifles. "I owe you. Don't know your reasons, but I'm much obliged. Come on in, and I'll buy you a drink." Hank turned to the crowd. "In fact, the drinks are on me."

The crowd roared and headed into the Pueblo Saloon. Hank looked at Pitts still lying on the ground in the dirt. He looked up and saw Deborah running toward him. When she reached him, he scooped her up in his arms. "You're getting blood all over your dress."

"I don't care, Hank. I'm just glad you're all right. Anyway, I'm used to it. I'm a nurse."

She pulled away, looking at his face and chest, and grabbed his hand. "You need some doctoring. Come with me."

He held onto her hand, stopping her. "You go ahead. I'll be there in just a few minutes. I need to pick up my gear and have a sarsaparilla."

She laughed and then said, "Make it quick. I'm tired of waiting."

"Yes, ma'am." He squeezed her hand and released it, turning back to the saloon. He stopped at Buck and Blacky, petting both horses. "You boys saved my bacon today. I'll get you some oats in just a bit."

Buck nodded his head as if telling him to hurry up.

Though sore and hurting, he felt better than he had felt in years. This was a good day.

"Look out!" someone shouted.

A rifle blasted in his ear, and he felt a deep, sharp pain just below his shoulder blade. He spun around to find Pitts flat on his back, a blackened bullet hole in his forehead, balanced perfectly between his eyebrows, and a bloody knife in his hand.

He looked back to see one of the old men holding a Spencer carbine. He grinned at Hank and said, "Will, boy, that feller had a knife and was tryin' to stab you. I think that's the closest shot I ever made. I just stuck the muzzle on his forehead and pulled the trigger."

He grinned back at the man, feeling like he should know him, but he was feeling faint and couldn't think straight. His shoulder was hurting and it was getting hard to breathe. The man had called him Will.

Floyd stepped forward and caught his nephew as he passed out.

THE FIRST THING he noticed was the sweet smell of pine trees. Birds were singing and there was a cool breeze drifting across his cheek. He took a deep breath and heard someone call, "I think he's awake."

He could hear running boots on the wooden floors and across the ground. He opened his eyes to see Deborah in a chair next to him, smiling. He reached for her hand, and she grasped his in both of hers, leaned forward, and kissed him on the cheek. Then she glanced up quickly and looked to the other side of the bed.

He turned his head, and there she was, clear as day, not the fuzzy vision he had in his mind. She looked older than what his mind had pictured, but she was still beautiful, in a regal fashion. Her eyes were soft like he had imagined, filled with concern, and . . . could it be love? She looked up at Deborah and smiled, then looked back down at him.

"Hello, son."

His mind started racing. *Son? Could this lady be my ma? If so, that would mean I'm home. But this is in the West, Colorado Territory, not back East.*

He smiled back at her and said, "Tandy, Bart?"

"Right here, pard," Bart said. He and Tandy were standing at the foot of his bed.

Past them he could see thick pines lifting to the sky. He was puzzled. The last thing he remembered was the blast of a rifle and the sting in his shoulder. Now he was among the pines? What was going on, and why was this lady calling him son?

He looked around to see he was surrounded by people. He was also on a bed that was outside on a wide porch. He enjoyed a deep breath.

"We've got to stop meeting like this," Deborah said. "It seems the only time I get to see you is when you've been injured."

"Injured?" Hank said. "It was just a fight."

"You're right there, boy," Floyd said, "and quite a fight. I ain't had the good fortune to see a fight like that since yore brother Callum took that land pirate apart in Arkansas. Why, I remember when he—"

"I'm sure you do, Floyd," the lady who had called him son said. She turned to Hank. "But you see, Will—"

"Will?" Hank interrupted.

"Yes, William Wallace Logan is your name," she continued. "The man you fought stabbed you with a knife, and it went quite deep. I think Deb may be able to explain it better than I."

Hank, his face a puzzle, turned to Deborah.

"He nicked your lung. Dr. James, the father James, not the son, did some fast cleaning and sewing, but you lost a lot of blood." Then she smiled at him. "As before, you owe your life to a Dr. James."

"And to Deb," the woman said. "She is quite a nurse."

Though he was feeling tired, Hank took his eyes from Deb and looked around him. His bed was surrounded with big men, and they all favored him, all except the pretty girl Tandy was standing beside. *Can that be Kate?* he thought as he laid his head back on the pillow. He wanted to open his eyes again, but the lids were so heavy. The thought drifted through his mind as sleep overcame him: *Who is Kate?*

HIS SLEEP WAS RESTLESS. Cannon blasted; screams of wounded and dying men filled his mind. His body was racked with pain. He had to get to Colonel Lewis and let him know he had given the message to General Griffin and reinforcements were on their way.

Firing was scattered throughout the timber as Blacky raced through the trees. He could feel the power of his Morgan driving forward as if it were a quiet spring day, unfazed by the gunfire. Though the firing grew heavier, he guided Blacky closer to the edge of the timber so he had a better view as the battlefield flashed by.

The Southern boys were advancing on the dug-in lines of the North. He noticed they were closing on a small pocket of Northerners. Without stopping to consider his decision, he thrust Blacky forward. The smell of burned powder, blood, and death was thick in the air. As soon as he broke out, Minié balls started whizzing past him. Guiding his horse with his knees, he pulled his Henry from the scabbard and started firing. One Reb jumped up in front of him, only to be hit and crushed by Blacky.

Reaching the men, he swung down and, with the reins in one hand, fired into the oncoming line, time and again, until the rifle snapped on an empty chamber. Dropping the Henry, he yanked his Remington .44-caliber revolver from its saddle holster just in time to shoot a charging Reb no more than ten feet away. Left and right he turned and fired. When that Remington clicked on empty, he drew the other one from the saddle.

Men were falling in front of him. Something slammed into his left leg, and he leaned on Blacky. Sorrow competed with the adrenaline coursing through his body, for he could feel his horse shudder from round after round plowing into him. But Blacky stayed on his feet.

They were close now. One man darted under Blacky's neck and thrust a long bayonet into his side. He shot the man in the face, reached down, grabbed the rifle by the barrel, and yanked it away from him, throwing it aside. He continued firing. He prayed none of his friends or brothers were in this charge.

He looked around. Men in blue uniforms were alongside him. The charge had broken. He fired the last round from his revolver and let it hang to his side. His first thought was Blacky. He reached out to comfort his horse . . .

When he woke, Deborah was wiping his brow with a cool cloth. His body was covered in sweat. He whispered to her, "I remember."

Tears leaped to her eyes. She leaned forward and held her cheek against his. She felt so warm and soft and dry.

"We thought you were better; then you developed a fever. Uncle James said if you made it through the fever, you'd be fine, but we've . . . I've been so worried. You've been rolling and thrashing for two days. Several times you called out names. Your ma *said* you were remembering. What happened? What sparked your memory?"

He thought about it. Then it came to him . . . Kate, his little sister. She had been the key that unlocked the door, and then the wagon. "It was Kate. Seeing her again must have got my memory churning. I remember the battle. I remember everything. It all came to me after the wagon bounced and hurt my leg." He looked around. "But there's no wagon."

"No, there's no wagon, but after you went back to sleep, the men moved you into the bedroom. Coming through the door, Callum tripped, and they dropped your bed. Fortunately, you didn't roll out."

"Callum." Will grinned up at Deborah. "He always was clumsy." He spread his arms and she came to him. She felt good against him.

The older woman walked into the room and smiled down at the two of them. "I see you're feeling better."

He knew her now and realized through his many battles, she had always been with him.

As tough as he was, his eyes teared up. "Thanks, Ma. It's good to be home."

AUTHOR'S NOTE

I hope you've enjoyed reading *Forgotten Season,* the fourth book in the Logan Family Series. I found doing the research on Cuba, a country I have never visited, extremely interesting.

I trust, discovering the different family members of the Logan family has been exciting for you. Each is unique in his, or her, own way. There will be more adventures of the Logans. The next book in the series will follow Floyd Logan. His character has been demanding to have his story told.

If you have any comments, what you like or what you don't, please let me know. You can email me at: Don@DonaldLRobertson.com, or you can fill in the contact form on my website.

www.DonaldLRobertson.com

I'm looking forward to hearing from you.

BOOKS
Logan Family Series

LOGAN'S WORD

THE SAVAGE VALLEY

CALLUM'S MISSION

FORGOTTEN SEASON

SOUL OF A MOUNTAIN MAN

Clay Barlow - Texas Ranger Justice Series

FORTY-FOUR CALIBER JUSTICE

LAW AND JUSTICE

LONESOME JUSTICE

NOVELLAS AND SHORT STORIES

RUSTLERS IN THE SAGE

BECAUSE OF A DOG

THE OLD RANGER

Made in the USA
Monee, IL
12 March 2022

92737051R00173